THE
GIRL
IN THE
CABIN

BOOKS BY STACY GREEN

THE
GIRL
IN THE
CABIN

STACY GREEN

bookouture

Published by Bookouture in 2023

An imprint of Storyfire Ltd.
Carmelite House
50 Victoria Embankment
London EC4Y 0DZ

www.bookouture.com

ISBN: 978-1-80314-977-6
eBook ISBN: 978-1-80314-976-9

ONE

I killed two people last month. They weren't the first. But they were different. Not because of who or what they were—they were every bit as evil as anyone else I'd killed. It's the *why* that changed everything. I took the step I swore I'd never take, catapulting right off the ledge into a black sea of soulless monsters, their scrawny arms throttling me until I couldn't draw a breath without feeling the jagged edge of guilt slicing through my lungs. I didn't kill Jake and Riley because they didn't deserve to live.

I killed them to save myself.

The person I used to be—the person I thought I was—was trapped somewhere in the abyss of guilt and anger, and I didn't know if I could escape. I thought I wanted to. At least, some days I wanted to. But deep down in the part of my stomach that twisted and turned and worried itself into a searing ulcer from the fifth ring of hell, I wasn't sure I had any choice in the matter. And it terrified me.

But it might not matter. Preacher, the pimp I'd killed last month, had been found. Snowmobilers took a wrong turn and received the surprise of their lives. The corpse in the Allegheny

National Forest was this morning's top headline, with both men rosy cheeked from the snow and excited to be on television happily describing their ordeal. Authorities had yet to identify the body, but it was only a matter of time.

Three people. I killed three people last month. My mind had a hard time counting Preacher as a person.

Chris left numerous messages of panic, all of which I ignored. Even though my guts burned like I'd swallowed turpentine, what was I supposed to do? There was nothing tying me to Preacher. My disguise at the motel had been on point; I didn't give him my real name until it didn't matter. And the man surely had plenty of enemies. No reason to suspect I had anything to do with his death.

But part of me still felt utterly alone in a world that had shifted on its axis, with me clawing at dead air for my very life, snared in the deep, black oblivion of those monsters in the pit. I'd rather crawl back into bed and let them have at me, but I'd made a promise to Justin and Todd. I wrestled my demons back into their proper place and focused on the task at hand.

My hazy gaze searched my surroundings as if I'd just set foot in the room, taking in the shining wood of the judge's chambers, which smelled faintly of wood cleaner and dusty, old paper. The ancient law books stacked neatly in the bookcases were outdated and probably for show, but their stale scent set my teeth on edge.

"You realize this is a very unusual proceeding." Philadelphia County District Judge Earl Bannam looked up from the file he'd been poring over. In his mid-fifties, Judge Bannam reminded me of the old-time gentlemen we've lost in recent years. Trimmed hair, well-cut suit with a tie that was decidedly plain. A nice watch, but not one that cost a month's mortgage. He even had a full-length dress jacket—black, of course—and a fedora hanging on the coat rack in his office, a room just as unpretentious as he. Solid wood furniture, framed law degrees, and a few family photos. Nothing flashy. Justin Beckett couldn't have gotten a better judge.

"We do." Todd spoke for his brother, who sat between us. Justin's recently cut hair and smooth face renewed his youthful innocence; he appeared buoyant—too strong for the tides of adversity to pin down. New slacks and a blue shirt I'd bought him heightened his eyes, which remained poised on the judge.

Judge Bannam pushed his reading glasses to the middle of his forehead, where they somehow balanced. "Miss Kendall, your presence here is surprising, given you were the original CPS worker on the Beckett case, and you spoke out at his parole hearing." He glanced down at the file. "Quite vehemently."

I took a deep breath. When I'd spoken out against Justin, I hadn't known about his horrific childhood or his murderous mother. I'd only seen the dead child I'd been responsible for as a social worker. "I was wrong. Mary Weston, also known as Martha Beckett, bullied and manipulated Justin into a place of impenetrable fear. As an inexperienced social worker, I was too naïve to see that." And my failure had cost countless more lives. How different would things have been if I'd been able to spot Justin's mother for what she really was? Certainly his life would have turned out differently. Maybe mine would have too. "I should have been more objective, but I couldn't get past the death of the little girl and the idea that his attacking her was the only explanation. I was there as Justin's advocate, and I failed him. I'm just as much responsible for his wrongful status as Martha Beckett."

I licked my lips. The heat of all three men's stares forced me to shift in my chair. I'd refused to discuss what I'd say to the judge, only promising to speak on Justin's behalf. Accepting my part in the mess of his life was the least I could do. Wasn't that one of the twelve steps to recovery? Accepting responsibility for one's mistakes and making amends? Somehow I didn't think the criteria applied to a murderer like me.

"And you believe Martha Beckett did these things?" Bannam's glasses still stuck to his shining forehead. "Who's to say this isn't something he's made up?"

I'd anticipated this, had spent weeks preparing for it. "You're aware there is clear evidence that Mary Weston was an active participant in the Lancaster murders of the 1980s, and law enforcement believes she's continued to torture and kill young girls in the decades since her husband was incarcerated?"

Bannam nodded.

"Are you familiar with her methods, Your Honor?" In the past few weeks, with Kelly's help, I'd learned every detail about the Weston victims. The case had been so shocking and sensationalized that a lot of the grislier aspects had leaked to the press. And there was no shortage of true crime data on the Web. But it was Todd's access to the case files that gave me the ammunition we needed.

"Only in the general sense," Bannam said.

"May I enlighten you? It pertains to Justin's case, I promise."

Justin shifted nervously, glancing at his brother, who looked remarkably calm. His faith mystified me. This man, who'd guessed at the evil inside me, still thought I had something worthy to offer the world.

"Go ahead, but be brief."

"Mary and John Weston murdered several young girls after keeping each of them at least a month." I recited the information as if the memories were my own scars, scattered over my body, deep and welted, never properly healed. "During this time, they sexually assaulted and tortured them with various objects. Horsewhips, pliers, and lighters were just some of the items found in the barn where they performed their crimes. Along with a set of wooden spoons of varying sizes." I paused, giving the information time to sink in. I should have been disgusted, but I'd read the information so many times my system had become immune. "The last victim, Jenna Richardson, had a bad case of sepsis when she was found. She was always blind-folded during her assaults, but she was able to tell officers someone used a spoon to sexually assault her. Testing revealed multiple blood types on the spoons, meaning they weren't washed from victim to victim."

"You're talking about the sort of thing that happened with childbirth in the 1800s." Bannam's upper lip curled to his nose. He spoke in a whisper, as if a normal voice made the reality worse. "Before Oliver Wendell Holmes got the bright idea of doctors washing their hands."

"Exactly," I said. "And the autopsy reports show at least one of the other victims prior to Jenna died of sepsis. I think it's safe to say the Westons enjoyed their spoons and cared little about hygiene."

Bannam's grimace once again broke his distinguished demeanor. "The vile scum that walks in our society is truly frightening. But tell me how this relates to Justin's case."

"The spoons were held back from the media, kept for law enforcement only." Those files had changed everything. Todd had barged into my apartment late one evening, completely ignoring my demands to be allowed to stay in bed and sink further into my head. "Detective Beckett secured the informa-tion two weeks ago. The Weston murders happened long before Justin was born, and, again, have been in confidential police files. Last fall, when he told me the truth about Layla's murder, he said his mother raped her with a spoon." Justin's breath hitched, but he said nothing. I knew the memory still scraped raw, and I doubted it would ever fully heal. He'd lost years of his life being blamed for a murder his mother commited.

"At the time, I believed him because of pure gut instinct that's been honed over years of CPS and private investigator work," I said. "But I knew you would need something more, so I started researching the Westons in depth. And we found out about the spoons. He didn't know about them when he first told me what really happened to Layla. He couldn't have known."

Chris had erupted with jealousy when I told him I had to help Justin before we went after their mother. I let him rage, and then I told him he'd have to wait. I had to do the right thing. For once. Their relationship was complicated and mostly nonexistent. They shared the same mother, and she'd cast a terrible shadow over their lives. In the last few months, I'd come to rely on Chris more than I liked. He knew most of my dirty secrets, and he'd helped me out of a jam or two.

Bannam stroked his chin. "You're willing to testify in court about this, knowing perjury would mean the termination of your private investigator's license?"

"Absolutely."

"And you." Bannam turned to Todd. "Same question. I realize you're in a tough situation, but your reputation and career are on the line with this."

"I accept that," Todd said.

"Your Honor." The heavy tiredness haunting me these last few weeks threatened to creep into my head. I knew what it was. Depression. That black phantom so many people refused to acknowledge. Not me. I was depressed as hell. I was a killer, and even worse, my actions hadn't made a damned bit of difference. But this one could. This one had to, because Justin deserved to have his life back. "When I forced my way into the search for Kailey Richardson, I was certain Justin had taken her. I nearly screwed up the search because I couldn't see past my own prejudices. And believe me, I know firsthand the impact sexual abuse has on a family. If I had any doubt of Justin's innocence, I wouldn't be here."

Bannam finally pushed his glasses back into their normal space. The frames left indents on his forehead. "And your research supporting the theory you've just given me, it's all in this file?"

"Every bit." I didn't need hard copies, even though Kelly insisted on having everything in triplicate. The horrors of the Westons—the crime scene photos of the abandoned girls, the torture den in the barn, and Jenna Richardson's brave testimony —were seared into my memory.

The judge seemed satisfied. He turned his attention to Justin, gazing over the top of his glasses with hawkish interest. "You're asking for your record to be expunged, even though it's a juvenile record and sealed. Why?"

Justin's cheeks hollowed as he drew a whistling breath. "Because it's the right thing. I was too scared as a kid to stand up for myself. And that cost me a lot of time." His knees bounced up and down, his slim fingers tapping a fast beat on his thighs. "But this isn't even about me, really. I've got a job. I'm taking classes. I'm working on starting over. And yet this crime is over my head, on paper, when it should be on my mother's head. How is that any kind of justice for my friend Layla? Mary Weston—Martha Beckett, whatever you want to call her—is responsible for her death, and that needs to be made right. For everyone's sake."

Pride surged over the burgeoning depression. Justin would be just fine in this life.

Me, on the other hand? I wasn't sure what I had left in the tank.

I waited for Todd and Justin outside the courtroom, feeling the ache of exhaustion in every joint of my body. The days and nights had begun to blend into one seamless blur of misery. If I wasn't curled in bed, consumed in my own bad choices, I was scouring the Weston case. My interest wasn't solely in helping Justin, although that was the driving force. I'd told Chris I needed to get inside Mother Mary's head, to figure out how she maneuvered in this life, how she was able to manipulate so many people, if we had a shot in hell of finding her. But with every new story I read, eyewitness accounts from police at the farm in Lancaster to the steadfast denial of her involvement by her imprisoned ex-husband, I sank further into the pit. I wasn't afraid of Mary. That was too simple. What jarred me were the similarities between us, even though our lives were worlds apart. The manipulation, the ability to make people around us believe we were the best thing that ever happened to them, that they were blessed by our affections—those shattered me with the force of shrapnel.

My phone rang, and I answered Chris's call, knowing what he'd say. "Todd and Justin are still in with the judge. I'm just waiting to hear what he says."

"And then what?" Chris's combative tone tweaked my already thin nerves. I'd pushed him away the past few weeks, telling him I had to do this deed first. I couldn't hold him off much longer. He frothed like an angry bull circling its competition. "Isn't it time we took action?"

I couldn't bring myself to say yes, and my indecision only made the bottomless feeling worse. Articulation failed me, but going after Mary seemed like the Spartans marching to be annihilated by the Persians in the Battle of Thermopylae. If I faced Mother Mary, I'd lose. Whether physical or psychological, facing her meant I'd lose whatever tiny bit of my humanity I had left.

"Soon."

"Right." Chris's anger didn't even sting. I understood his frustration, but I could do nothing to prevent it. All of my bravado had bled out with Riley in Jake's garage.

Todd and Justin exited the judge's chamber, giving me a blissful reprieve. "I'll talk to you soon."

"Lucy, I'm getting tired of waiting."

"I know. I've got to go." I ended the call and stood, my sluggish heart feeling a burst of excitement at the smile on Justin's face. "Well?"

"He's going to recommend the record be expunged." Justin's long strides were reminiscent of a happy toddler's drunken walk. "Thanks to you. The work you put into researching the evidence. That's what did it."

"You did it," I said. "Because you told the truth. I'm proud of you." I hugged him, feeling the recent weight gain of living a healthy and happy life.

Wearing his usual dark clothes, Todd stood next to his brother. They hung loosely off his thin frame, giving him the appearance of carrying too much weight on his shoulders. "Thank you, Lucy."

"It's the least I could do."

He scratched the back of his neck and then fiddled with his crooked tie. "Did you call the lady I mentioned?"

Todd had given me the name of a therapist who specialized in post-traumatic stress. He seemed to believe my near-assault in Jake's garage might have messed me up. As if I was fine before that. As if I could sit down with a stranger and tell her all my sins so she could cure me.

I liked that Todd wanted to help.

"Not yet, but soon. I promise."

Of course I had no intention of calling anyone. We said our goodbyes, and I went home and crawled into bed.

TWO

My windows rattled with a fresh blast of winter wind. I pulled the blanket to my chin and tried not to see the dying face of Riley. How much life had I stolen from her? Was it her destiny to die young anyway, or had I interrupted the cosmos's great plan and snuffed her out well before her time?

Or maybe there was no plan for any of us.

My happiness at Justin's chance for a new life had evaporated with each passing hour of the night, replaced by what had now become a ritual: visions of Riley's final moments haunted me with the power of demons sent straight from hell. The way her eyes widened and then flickered around the garage as she realized what would happen. The fear that painted her skin gray, and worst of all, the satisfaction I took from her death. In the days that followed, I wondered if that was the moment I purchased my ticket to hell. Riley wasn't all evil. In the right circumstances, with someone fighting for her, she could have been saved. But I couldn't trust her to keep my secret.

Self-preservation, after all.

Maybe I should have gone willingly to Mother Mary and taken my chances with whatever she'd planned. I could have killed her and then escaped to a brand new life. Or I could have allowed her to use me up and throw me out. If people knew the real truth about me, most of them would probably say my actions merited punishment.

But there's no escaping the path I'd laid out. It was all of my own choosing. My only choice was to move forward.

Then my sister took over my head the last few days. Sometimes I felt like my thoughts belonged more to her than me. I used to think she must have been crazy to end her own life, but now I realized she truly saw no other option. Victimized and accused of lying, Lily must have stood in that bathroom and looked at herself in the mirror and thought, *This is your life. It will never change. Even if you escape these circumstances, you'll always be this dirty person.*

I know that's what she thought because it was how I felt right now.

Because I could almost hear her saying those exact words to me.

What would my long-dead older sister Lily think of what I'd done? She was the one who said to take care of myself first. Surely she would understand my desire to right the wrongs committed by so many. Then again, how could I know? Lily died with the underdeveloped mind of a traumatized teenager. Just like Riley.

Because of me—both of them, really. If I'd fought for Lily, maybe she would have had the strength to live another day.

I didn't know any of the answers, but the conversation went round and round in my head until I just wanted the voices to shut up. Yesterday wasn't that day because I still had a mission to complete. But Justin no longer needed me. Today might just be that day.

Unlike my long-dead sister, I knew my options. I didn't have to limit myself to razor blades. Even though Connor the chemist got cold feet and walked out of my life months ago after my name hit the papers for saving Kailey Richardson, I still managed to get some cyanide. I still had some ketamine left over. *I bet that is a trippy way to die. Then there's the oxycodone I bought at the same time as the ketamine. I could definitely take enough to kill myself.*

Laughter swelled in my throat. How had I gone from being so afraid of the nothingness of death to being ready to embrace it?

I shoved the blanket off me and sat up. Gray morning sky now streamed beneath the drawn blinds into my dark bedroom. Sitting on the edge of the bed, my bare toes grazing the chilly wood floor, I stared at the closet. Everything I needed stashed just a few feet away. Surely it would only take a few moments. My clammy skin broke out in goose bumps. My stomach flipped the way it used to when I was kid and ready to experience something new and unknown, like the tornado rollercoaster Lily and I had gone on the summer before she died. I never knew if the feeling was fear or excitement, but I loved it.

I stared at the closet, my fingernails digging into the edge of the mattress. I extended my toes and then my entire right foot, wondering what it would feel like to make the walk across the room and open that closet door. Could I really go through with it?

Something warm and furry brushed against my dangling feet. The hollow feeling emanating from somewhere deep inside me eased just a little. I reached down to scoop the fat cat into my arms.

"Mousecop, you're the reason I'm still here," I murmured into his silky fur. "At least for tonight." And every night, really. Because this was just another one of the conversations that played in my constantly raging mind.

Should I kill myself, or should I stay?

Purring, the heavy cat settled into my lap. I stroked his fur, the silky softness and the warmth of his body the only things that made me feel any sort of life. I might have sat for hours if I hadn't noticed the blinking green light on my phone. I'd set it to vibrate sometime after dawn, knowing I'd miss a few calls or two.

The missed calls were from Chris, along with two new voicemails. I didn't really feel like listening to him rail at me again. In fact, I thought about calling and telling him to leave me alone once and for all.

I latched on to the anger and pulled up his number. It went straight to voicemail. Was he working last night? Chris worked as a paramedic, and his schedule often changed. I ran through my fuzzy memories, trying to remember what Chris told me yesterday. No, he'd had the night off.

I called again. Same result.

So he'd decided to ignore me. At last, some sort of peace. At least I'd have a break from the questions about his mother. Kelly had hoped to get information from the email addresses I'd stolen off Jake's computer, but so far, she'd found nothing that led us back to Mother Mary's physical whereabouts. But Chris carried on daily about making a plan because surely the information would present itself soon, and we needed to find her before the police did. For Lucy Kendall justice. He embraced that term so lovingly, as if it were some sort of rare gem instead of poison.

With the worst of my personal darkness shoved into its proper cage for the moment, a shower sounded good. I left Mousecop on his side of the bed and headed for the bathroom. The hot water soothed my tense muscles, and the steam seemed to clear my head of a few shadows. I even brushed my teeth. *Tomorrow I might change my sheets.*

But the blinking message light tormented me—a dangling carrot of confrontation I could only avoid for so long. Finally I decided that listening to it would give me more reason to be irritated and feel sorry for myself. Hearing Chris's voice was just a bonus. Bargain made, I called my voicemail.

"It's me." The tiny note of something different in Chris's voice set my nerves on edge. He took his time, breathing into the phone, evidently thinking about what he wanted to say. "So I know you're all messed up in the head. And I'm not helping the situation. I get that." He sighed, and I imagined him scratching his cheek or the back of his head the way he did when he concentrated. "But you keep doing all this research and coming up with all these excuses why we can't just do something, and I can't keep waiting. That's not on you, it's on me. Kelly hasn't been able to find anything, and I don't think she likes dealing with me anyway. So I did something you're not going to like."

I paced beside my bed. At his words, I stopped short, my movements matching the uptick in my anxiety level. "What did you do?" I whispered to the empty room.

Mousecop yawned and stretched, going back to sleep.

"The email Mother Mary used to contact Jake, it bounces off a foreign server." Chris had bestowed the nickname on his biological mother after finding out about Justin and how she'd ruined his life. He spoke faster, obviously amped up from the courage of calling. "Kelly's stuck, like I said. So, I figured why not email Mary back? Worst thing she can do is not answer. Or answer, depending on how this all turns out."

Another pause. Shifting. Had he been pacing too?

"But she did answer. I thought about lying and pretending to be Jake, but he's all over the news. So, I told Mother Mary that I was her older son, and that I wanted to see her. I promised I just wanted answers. And that's not a lie. I don't know anything about her side of the family. Why is she like this? What made her this way? I don't know if she'll tell me anything, and maybe I'm just kidding myself. But I can't stop thinking about it. I want to talk to her, face to face."

"Are you nuts?" My shocked voice woke up the dozing cat, who laid his ears back in disgust. Now I felt out of breath. Surely he couldn't be that stupid, could he?

"So it's five a.m., and I'm leaving for Harford County, Maryland. Jarrettsville is the name of the town. I'm supposed to email her when I get there, and she will tell me where to meet."

He didn't go alone. He wouldn't be that damned dumb. He'd called the state police, told them everything. He must have.

"I don't know if I'm going to talk to her." He stumbled over the last word but then cleared his throat. "If it's even her. Maybe she's working with someone. Maybe she'll send someone to deal with me. I know this sounds nuts, and I'm an idiot, but I've got to do this."

"Call the police!" I screamed this time. Mousecop jumped in the twisted way that only cats can do and then leapt off the bed, disappearing under it.

"I'll call you when I get there."

For a brief moment, I debated calling the police, but inviting them into our twisted web of vigilante justice didn't seem like a great idea. And Chris could take care of himself.

The call ended, and the pleasant computer voice asked me if I wanted to save or delete my message. I saved and went on to the next. Three hours later.

"Lucy." Chris's voice hissed into my ear. "Why haven't you checked your voicemail all day? I guess some part of me thought I'd hear from you, and you'd tell me to get back home where I belonged. But I said I was going, and I couldn't chicken out." He huffed, and I pictured him slogging through the cold and snow, cheeks pink, his impenetrable blue eyes shining with fury. "She sent me to some empty lot for sale, out in the sticks. Prime hunting land, according to the 'For Sale' sign. Nothing but woods and snow and fucking misery. She didn't show. I should have known she wouldn't."

Part of me was glad I couldn't see his face. The pain in his voice made me feel lousy enough.

"I guess there's something wrong with me," Chris continued, still sounding as if he were walking. "Even after all this time, all the terrible things she's done, I don't understand how she can completely reject the person she gave birth to. Doesn't she have some kind of maternal flickering?"

"No." I hadn't realized how much the child in Chris still longed for his mother's affection and approval, and I understood that need. But I'd also learned it would never be fulfilled and that sometimes all we can do is cut our losses and move on. I spoke out loud as if he could really hear me. "She doesn't. Just because she could physically create a child doesn't mean the connection was there. She's a psychopath, period."

"So I'm headed back to my car." He sighed again, the restlessness from earlier in the morning now sounding like despair. "I know it's dumb, but part of me still feels like the abandoned five-year-old she dumped on her brother-in-law."

My heart jammed into my throat, half relieved, half broken. I felt for his pain, but he wasn't equipped to handle this alone, especially if his mother stuck to her usual mode of operation and had a partner. I didn't know what to say to make the empty ache in his heart go away, and I wasn't sure if that was even possible. Some wounds don't heal. They just keep festering, and a person has to put up with the scab.

But why had his phone gone straight to voicemail when I'd called back? If he were driving back, he would have had the phone connected to the Bluetooth in the car. He'd have known it was me calling.

Maybe it died.

Maybe he'd caught his mother and had done something terrible and didn't want to talk.

"Lucy, I wish you'd answered the phone." Chris's snappy tone listed toward impatience. "I know that's shitty, but I really do. Anyway, I'm going to call the police. That's what I should have done in the first place."

I prayed that's exactly what he'd done, but the pit forming

inside me said otherwise. Had he brought any kind of weapon, thinking he'd have the courage to attack her? Or was he defenseless? Why didn't he answer his phone?

"Hang on," Chris's recorded voice said. "I see... oh shit. Someone's coming. I can't tell if it's a man or a woman, but they're in a hurry."

I pressed the phone to my ear as if that would somehow give me a vision of what had happened over two hours ago.

Shuffling, quick breaths, and a faraway shout.

Followed by an ear-splitting gunshot.

THREE

One hundred and thirty-seven minutes ago, Chris's message ended with a gunshot. My call still went straight to his voicemail. Standing motionless in the center of my dark bedroom, I stared at my phone. The back of my neck felt as if I'd been doused with a spray bottle, my face warm and my heart racing until it seemed ready to burst from exhaustion.

What do I do?

My brain slogged to catch up.

Call the police.

They'll think you're crazy. You could make up a story. But then if something did happen, that's one more lie to deal with.

What happened to Chris?

Call Todd.

My fingers searched for the number in my phone before I registered the relief the idea brought me. And before I could stop and think about what I wanted to say or how to protect myself.

"Lucy." Todd's steady voice gave me hope. "I'm so glad to hear from you."

"I need help." I cut him off before he had a chance to ask

about my fragile psyche. "Chris went after his mother, and I think something happened to him."

"What? What do you mean he went after his mother? No one knows where she is."

"It's a long story, and I promise I'll tell you, but I need your help first." My head pounded, tiny nails of fear inching their way into my brain. "He's in Maryland, in Harford County, in Jarrettsville. She sent him to some hunting ground that was for sale. He was supposed to meet her there." I fired the words like shots from an automatic weapon. They sounded scrambled to my ears, and I hoped Todd could understand me. "He left me a message almost two hours ago that he didn't know if she was there, and he was going to call the police. But then he thought he saw something, and there was a gunshot. And now he's not answering his phone."

"You've got to be kidding me."

"I'm not," I said. "I swear I'll tell you everything, but right now we need the police to go out there and see what happened. Something's wrong. He wouldn't have ignored my calls." I dug my toes into the floor in the hopes of finding some kind of anchor before I fell over.

"I've got a friend with the state police," Todd said. "Let me call him and see what he can do, but those are pretty ambiguous directions."

I dropped the phone on the bed. Sitting tight wasn't exactly my strong suit, even if I'd gotten rusty over the past month. I switched on my lamp and immediately swore at the intrusive bright light. Whatever had happened to Chris happened in another state, and somehow I knew I needed to be there.

My suitcase was in the closet. I allowed a second to appreciate the irony that just a couple of hours ago, that closet represented the end of everything for me, and then got busy packing. I'd be driving to Maryland. No need to worry about airport security. I stashed my drug kit in the suitcase's bottom compartment. I wished I'd taken the time to get my weapons license. Since I'd been wearing nothing but pajamas the last several days, most of my clothes were clean. Jeans, sweaters, and other necessities were shoved into the suitcase, followed by an extra pair of shoes. Snow still covered the tri-state area. I'd need to wear my boots.

What about the cat?

Mousecop sat in the bedroom doorway, flicking his tail, eyes narrowed as if he knew I'd nearly forgotten about his ever-demanding tummy and his litter box.

I'd call Justin. He'd want to help with Chris, but he'd take care of Mousecop for me. And the cat abandoned me every time Justin came over, so the little traitor would be just fine.

My phone rang, Todd's number flashing on the screen.

I snatched it off the bed. "Did they find him?"

"No."

I knew it then, the frigid truth infecting my system. I liked to think I could handle a crisis—I've certainly created enough of them and come out physically unscathed. But the lack of control and being miles away, completely powerless, made me feel like jumping out the window. "They found something."

Todd cleared his throat. "No, they haven't found anything yet. It sounds like there are a few different acreages for sale, and they've got to search them all. I'm sure you realize that's manpower the state police won't use without more information."

"Are you telling me they just blew you off?" No matter. I'd find Chris myself.

"No," Todd said. "But it's limited. My friend called the county sheriff, and they've sent a couple of deputies out to look. But it's going to take a while."

The part of me that had been feeling sorry for herself and doing nothing for far too long wanted to crawl back into bed. Fortunately, the real Lucy Kendall was a lot more stubborn than that, and she hadn't evaporated completely. Not yet, anyway. "I'm heading there now."

"I knew you'd say that."

Todd didn't trust Chris's motivations given his hatred for his mother, and I understood his position, but now wasn't the time. My apartment suddenly became a prison I had to escape. "Please don't argue. If the police are stretched too thin, I'll help search. And I've got to call Justin to see if he'll feed the cat."

"You can do that while you wait for me."

That took me off guard. I stopped in the middle of my bedroom, hairbrush in hand. "What?"

"You're not going into this by yourself. Not after everything else. I'll be there in half an hour."

Todd's four-door sedan was more immaculate than I'd expected. The dash gleamed as if it had been freshly shined, and the slightly overpowering scent of vanilla made my already queasy stomach churn. As we rushed down I-95 toward Maryland, I tried to distract myself by debating whether or not the poison tucked away in my bag, in the backseat of a cop's car, would be considered irony.

"Thanks for taking me. I hope you didn't have to take vacation days."

"I did," Todd said. "Unpaid since we're short-staffed and it's not exactly family emergency."

"That's not right," I said. "I'll reimburse you."

"Stop. I don't want you going through this alone, especially with your state of mind the last few weeks," he said. "If I had my way, you wouldn't be going at all. You need to take care of yourself first, for once."

I dragged my teeth over my lip, momentarily stunned by the wave of gratitude. It was more emotion than I'd felt since killing Riley and Jake. My peripheral gaze shifted to Todd's tense form.

His mustache hadn't returned, and his face looked slightly fuller. The wrinkles around his eyes suited him, as if each were a testament to the good he'd done in the world. Including being a good friend to me when he believed I'd done despicable things.

"The National Center for Missing and Exploited Children called a couple of days ago." I needed to combat the war inside my head, and talking about something other than whatever tragedy we were racing towards sounded like a good way to pass the time. "They'd like to talk to me about a position in their Washington, D.C. office."

"Really?" Todd bounced in his seat a little, a hint of excitement in his usually calm voice.

"Apparently word travels," I said. "The supervisor who left the message said they'd heard of my work on the Kailey Richardson case and the recent sex trafficking ring, and that I'd be a good fit for a support specialist in the Child Victim Identification Program." I'd almost laughed when she'd first asked. Me, with unlimited access to the nation's best program for catching child predators. Like handing a match to a pyromaniac.

"Big stuff," Todd said. "We've got information from them before. You'd be working directly with law enforcement, right? Helping to ID the kids and get the various jurisdictions what they need?"

"I suppose so," I said. "I haven't followed up."

"You should." His enthusiasm didn't make the situation any less comical. "It might be just the change you need."

I didn't respond, because I didn't know what to say. Change scared me, as it did so many people, but the idea of working for a national organization that helped law enforcement—playing by the rules—after all the things I'd done was impossible. Not after all this time. Hadn't I decided long ago that I'd accept my chosen path no matter where it took me, consequences and all? What right did I have to try to turn back now?

"So tell me the full story." Todd finally said the words I'd been dreading. My brain still felt like it was working at partial speed, his words sounding as if he were speaking through some kind of muzzle. "How could Chris possibly be in communication with his mother? I double checked with ADA Hale on the way to your place, and he insists there's no way Chris has been talking with her."

I hadn't even thought about Chris's aunt and uncle, the assistant district attorney. I should have called them, but my primary concern had been Chris and getting to Maryland. I needed to be there, even if police forced me to stalk the sidelines. Typical one-track-mind Lucy. "Are they coming to Maryland too?"

"The ADA is, most likely," Todd said. "Answer my question."

"Email."

"And he just found that via a Google search? Man, I bet the FBI is going to wish they thought of that." Todd gripped the wheel, glaring at the road as if he expected it to rise up and block our way. "Come on, Lucy."

"I'm serious." I couldn't think of a way to explain without giving too much of myself away. And then I decided I didn't care if I did. Beyond that, I trusted Todd. Too many days of feeling sorry for myself might have clouded my judgment, but I took the chance. "That day in the garage, Jake told me he reached out to his contacts and had a buyer for me named Mary. I knew it was her."

Jake's sex trafficking ring stretched across at least three states, and while he primarily sold kids, he'd been willing to make an exception for me. I examined my dry hands and wondered if I'd make the same choices in the garage today if I'd known I'd be as twisted up about my life as I was now. Most people would still be reeling from the trauma of being kidnapped and nearly sold like a slave, but I had bigger problems.

Todd's eyes remained steadfastly forward, his jaw locked tightly enough to look painful.

I figured I might as well keep going. "I assumed she wanted revenge since I helped Justin tell the truth. She'd purchased from Jake before, and I guess dumb luck brought us all together. Anyway—" I almost said, *after I killed Jake and Riley*, but I caught myself—"before you got there, I checked Jake's computer and made a copy of the hard drive and sent it to my computer expert. She found the email address Mary used."

"So what?" Todd said. "I mean, I know it's typical, spoiled Chris. Raised with a silver spoon and all that, thinking he could do better. But the police and the FBI have all of that as well. Every single account taken from Jake's computer bounces off foreign servers. The task force is taking them down the old-fashioned way—sting operations. There's no way your hacker is better than the FBI's people, sorry." His chin jerked up and down to emphasize his point.

I wasn't sure I agreed, but I didn't argue. "You're right. We hit a dead end. And I've been... out of commission. Chris got impatient."

"I don't understand where you're going with this," Todd said. "And I'd love to know exactly what you planned to do with information you stole." His sideways glare told me he was afraid he knew exactly what I planned to do with it.

"Let me play you his voicemail," I said. Chris hadn't said anything about killing his mother on the message. Playing it for Todd saved me precious energy.

Chris's husky voice filled the small car. A wave of emotion I hadn't expected threatened to drown me. I might not see him again, and I'd have a brand new death on my conscience. Our relationship was platonic—we were too much alike to ever work as anything more than friends—but he was also the only person who truly understood me. Losing him would be the end for me. The only question would be the final lines I chose to write on this life's pathetic page.

The second message brought fresh fear. We both jumped as the recorded shot reverberated through the car's confined space.

Todd's face reddened. "What the hell was he thinking? More importantly, what were you two planning?"

"Nothing." At least that much was true. "My focus has been helping Justin, and you know that."

"Chris expected your help. To do what, exactly?"

I shrugged. "Moral support? Talk him out of it? I don't know."

"I'm not sure I believe that."

I waited for more accusations, but he let it drop. "You need to prepare yourself. If this was his mother, he's a threat to her. And that was clearly a gunshot."

"She didn't kill him," I said. "Not yet. She took him." I couldn't explain where that thought came from, but I didn't doubt myself. I'd snag the answer from my subconscious eventually.

"How is a fifty-something-year-old woman going to haul away a guy Chris's size?" Todd asked. "Especially if he's wounded and can't walk?"

"We don't know that he couldn't walk. Maybe he was shot in the arm or the shoulder. And she doesn't work alone. She never has. When we thought we'd found Kailey in the farmhouse, who else was there? A dead man. It's her pattern."

"I suppose she's only learned how to manipulate better as the years have gone by," Todd said. "And she certainly knows how to pick the right partner."

"Just like a pimp," I said.

"Even so," he said. "What makes you think she took him? What's the point?"

I looked at him in disbelief. "Seriously? She's proven she

likes to torture people. Chris is the one who accidentally messed up her original operation when he was a kid, and now he's involved in screwing her over a second time. You don't think she'd want to torture him?"

"You're assuming this is really his mother he's been talking to and not just some jerk yanking his chain. And how do you know that's how she'd see it?"

Because that's how I'd see it. "I just do. Common sense." I changed gears. "What about the gunshot? Why isn't he answering his phone?"

"I'm not saying something hasn't happened to him," Todd said. "But right now, I'd put my bet on a hunting accident before his mother. I'd guess he wasn't wearing an orange vest, was he?"

I didn't respond, but I knew damned well Chris wouldn't be caught dead wearing some bright orange vest that made him look as hick as everyone else. He was too much of a snob for that.

"And you haven't even mentioned the fact he communicated with his mother without telling anyone, including you." Todd dribbled some salt into my open wounds. "It doesn't bother you that he basically decided to risk lives to go after her himself?"

"I don't know." More like I didn't want to think about it right now. Thinking about it meant taking on more guilt, and my shoulders nearly scraped the ground as it was.

"Then again, it's no different from what you've done. Had you two talked about killing her?" Todd tried sound firm, but a smattering of empathy leaked into his tone. He'd understand wanting to kill her. She destroyed countless children's lives. He probably wanted to do it himself. But while the line of right and wrong was a faint gray for me, Todd saw it as a pristine white mark.

I closed my eyes. "I'm not even going to dignify that ridiculous question with a response."

"You don't need to," Todd said. "Let's just hope I'm right about the hunting accident. Because if his mother has him, we're talking about a whole other level of crazy."

FOUR

On another day, under different circumstances, I might have considered rural Harford County quaint. Just twenty-five miles from Baltimore, Harford County's proximity to Chesapeake Bay made it a tourist destination. Or rather, made the southern part of the county a tourist destination. Instead of being directly off I-95, Jarrettsville was much farther north, off the beaten path, the route taking too many detours for my impatient taste. The northern end of the county seemed to be nothing more than the usual small rural town with struggling mom and pop shops, a couple of department store giants, and lots of gun shops. The recent snow no longer appeared fluffy and white but instead had become muddy river sand, courtesy of the highway department.

I wanted to get straight to the search, but Todd insisted we meet up with the county sheriff deputy.

"Here it is." Todd pulled into the parking lot of a newer-looking sheriff's office. A perfect brick rectangle, it could have fit inside half the restaurants in Philadelphia.

"They don't have city police?" I asked.

"Nope. The Harford County Sheriff has a few different

precincts. This is the North Precinct, and we're meeting with Deputy Gerry Frost."

My impatience swelled. "This building's small enough we'll have no trouble finding Barney Fife."

"It would be Barnette Fife in this case, and drop the attitude," Todd said. "They're helping us out. Don't try to take control. Not everyone is as patient as I am."

"I just want to find Chris."

Todd ducked his head, his shoulders hunched against the wind, and headed into the small building. I followed, anxiety flooding my system. Without the protection of the city's tall buildings, the wind screamed through the town's muddy streets, blowing wisps of dirty snow. The cold settled into my throat, making me feel as if I could choke at any moment.

Chris is out in this misery.

A tall, athletic-looking brunette in an asexual uniform greeted us before we made it past the administration desk. "Chief Deputy Gerry Frost. Trooper Evans said you've got a friend who might be in some sort of trouble."

I wanted to tell her that he was definitely in trouble, but I let Todd answer. "He was supposed to meet someone at a property for sale, and she didn't show up." Todd turned to me, a warning in his eyes. "This is Lucy Kendall. The missing man, Chris Hale, was in the process of leaving her a message when a shot was fired and the call disconnected. He hasn't answered his phone since. Before that happened, he said he was going to call the police and let them know about the woman he was looking for."

Deputy Frost nodded. "I checked with dispatch. There's been no matching call. We're a small staff, but I've got a deputy out looking. Problem is, we've got a few acreages that are for sale." She turned her dark eyes to me. Her square jaw and sloping nose set like a mask. "Why would he call us about this woman?"

I stared back at her. Women who tried to intimidate me instantly pissed me off. "Because she's a wanted criminal." Already prepared, I played the voicemail for her. Frost listened with interest, her eyes darting between Todd and me as Chris lamented about his mother. I expected to feel a fresh dose of fear at the sound of the gunshot, but my body had gone numb.

"So," Frost said when the message ended. As Chris's message played, the deputy's stance had subtly shifted from wary to glittering anticipation. "We're going to have to search each acreage one by one. Good news is the snow will help us out with footprints. And blood." She looked at me as she spoke, as if expecting me to wilt at the word. I met her gaze until she looked away. "What's his mother wanted for?"

Todd glanced at me. I shrugged. He could deal with the exchange of information. I wanted to get out and do something. "I asked Trooper Evans to keep the details quiet because I don't want it going out over the radio and causing an uproar. Are you familiar with the Mary Weston/Martha Beckett case?"

Frost's eyebrows knitted together. "The names sound familiar. Is this out of Lancaster?"

"Yes." Todd's carefully controlled, monotone voice disguised his personal hatred of his stepmother. "Mary Weston and her husband John Weston kidnapped and killed several girls in the eighties. Their streak ended when their five-year-old son, Chris, accidentally found one of the girls in the barn. At the time, it was believed Mary was a victim of her husband's abuse, and he was found guilty and incarcerated. Mary gave the boy to his aunt and uncle to raise and moved on with her life." Todd's jaw worked in circles. "It's recently been discovered that after she married Josh Beckett, she again began killing girls. By the time the connection was made, she was on the run again."

"I've heard of the case." Deputy Frost's face practically sparkled with eagerness. She probably spent her days dealing with domestic violence and drug users. A criminal like Mary came along once in a cop's lifetime—if that. Apprehending her would change Frost's career, assuming she had dreams beyond Harford County. "She let her boy take the rap for something, didn't she?"

"The younger boy, Justin Beckett," Todd said. "He spent years in juvenile detention and was labeled as a sex offender because of her actions." The left corner of his mouth twitched, but only someone who already knew the anger he carried for Mary would have caught it. Todd's stalwart control amazed me.

"Chris Hale, the missing man, is her older son," I said. "He found the girl in the barn in Lancaster in 1987. The discovery of his mother's involvement in those murders and her new life have messed up his head."

"A small positive is that he's also a paramedic," Todd said. "If he has been shot and isn't mortally wounded, he's capable of helping himself."

The reminder should have given me hope, but I felt nothing but mounting fear that my world and everything I knew to be true and real was spinning rapidly out of control. Dizziness crashed over me. I gritted my teeth and stood motionless.

"All right." Deputy Frost rocked back on her heels, as though she needed to get moving. "And you're assuming Martha is still in good enough health to be dangerous? How old is she?"

"We believe she's in her mid-fifties, early sixties," Todd said. "And as of her most recent known killings in Lancaster, she had an accomplice."

"Is he with her?"

"She killed him," I said. "So she could escape. That's what she does. But she might have another."

Frost nodded. "Self-preservation—every killer's hidden talent."

The words slapped me in the face and knocked me off

balance, making me spin as though I'd just stuttered off the merry-go-round. I grabbed Todd's arm.

He steadied me. "We don't know exactly what Chris encountered, but it's unlike him to continue to ignore phone calls. We have to assume something has happened."

Frost pulled on her heavy jacket. "He said in the message he was heading back to his car, so that might help us narrow things down. I'll have my deputy check for it before going on foot. What is he driving?"

For some reason, my throat closed up. Todd answered for me. "A 2013 black Audi A4. Sticks out."

Frost raised her eyebrows. "Nice car for a paramedic." At least she was astute enough to question that.

"His aunt and uncle have money. They set up a trust fund," I said lamely, feeling the need to defend Chris's more extravagant choices. "His uncle is Frank Hale, assistant district attorney for Pennsylvania. Frank is also primed to be the next district attorney when the incumbent retires this fall."

To her credit, Frost didn't call me on the power play. She zipped her jacket and pulled on a knit cap. "We've only got a couple of hours of daylight left. Let's get out there and find him."

FIVE

Todd and I followed Chief Deputy Frost's cruiser to the western edge of town, where the blacktop road cut through acres of timber. Still covered with snow, the trees stood like white giants, their gnarled limbs stretching overhead and blocking out the already gray sky. I folded my arms over my chest, digging my fingers into my heavy winter coat. Beneath the wool, my skin heated and prickled. An army marched through my stomach and into my legs until my knees bounced high enough to smack the dash.

Frost's comment about self-preservation had my head ringing, but I tried to focus on Chris. "We're not going to find him."

"We might." Todd's flat voice held little hope.

"More than likely, we're going to find a crime scene," I said. "Hours after the crime occurred. Without a sign of Chris."

"That's if he's alive." Todd kept his gaze forward as he spoke. "If you were anyone else, I'd try to be gentle. But I think we're past that."

His act of kindness by speaking the truth made my throat swell. All I managed was a jerk of my head.

"Maybe you're right and she took him." He spoke quietly

but without the same gentleness he'd use on a less experienced person. As though I were an equal. "She's sadistic enough I won't be entirely surprised. But she's also on the run and desperate. It's very likely that she—or an accomplice—shot Chris and left him to die."

"You said yourself, he's a paramedic."

"I did," Todd said. "But he's not God. And it's damned cold. Being exposed to the elements might slow the bleeding, but he's also facing hypothermia. I want you to be prepared."

"I know you do, and I appreciate that." I struggled to speak over the heavy band of affection wrapping itself around my throat. "But if all she planned to do was kill him, why even respond to the email? He wasn't a threat. He couldn't find her. Even the FBI couldn't find her."

"I don't know," Todd said. "Maybe she didn't want to take any chances. I've no doubt she resents Chris for her recent predicament. After all, if she planned to buy you from Jake, is it that much of a stretch she'd sucker Chris into meeting her?"

It wasn't. Todd's reasoning made more sense than mine, and yet I clung to the brewing instinct that Chris had been carted off by Mother Mary. Because if I were her, I'd want to torture him first. I'd want him to know how much he'd screwed up my plans and my life. He would know real, pants-filling fear before I finished with him.

If I were Mary.

But you're not. Are you?

I'm going crazy.

"Is that why you went silent?"

His question caught me off guard and yanked me back from whatever insane edge I'd ventured over to. After a second of confusion, I managed to ask, "What?"

"After everything that happened with Jake and Riley, you find out Mary Weston is after you too. Is that what dragged you down?" Todd glanced at me, evidently sensing the crack in my mental capacity. I needed to sew it up before he permanently cut me out of the case.

The easiest answer was yes, so I nodded. "Part of it. But what I had to do in the garage has been on a loop in my head. I couldn't face anything else."

Todd didn't answer right away. He watched the road, his index finger tapping the wheel. "I'd have thought that part came easier to you."

I leaned my head against the window, watching the trees become bigger and denser. "That's your mistake."

He didn't challenge me, and I didn't have time to worry about whether or not he really believed I'd killed other people. The deputy turned right onto a trodden path covered with snow, and we followed. She drove until she came to a red, metal gate. Although it was padlocked and "no trespassing" signs were clearly posted, anyone could have scaled the gate and ventured into the woods. She waved us around, and we parked beside her. All the nervous energy that had been brewing once again numbed. Like a robot, I pulled on my gloves and hat, wrapped my scarf tightly around my face to protect my sensitive skin from the cold wind, and exited the car.

"This is 189 acres of hunting land for sale." Frost had to raise her voice over the gusting wind. She pointed to the sign, barely visible beneath snow. "I'd assume he stayed on the perimeter. We don't know how far away he's parked." She pointed to the east. "Why don't you two walk this fence row and search for any sign he's been here? This road goes a couple miles farther south, and then it forks. There's a couple of ways he could have gotten here, and there's a lot better parking there. I'm going to drive down and check."

"This isn't the place," I said.

Both Todd and Frost stared at me, but the deputy spoke first. "How do you know that?"

"Because the Audi would be right here. There's no way

Chris would park it a mile down the road, out of his sight, in a strange place. He loves that car." I looked at Todd, knowing he'd back me up.

"This isn't exactly easy territory for a car like that." Frost shook her head, speaking as if I were no more than a dumb city girl who didn't know jack about the country. She glanced at Todd. "How'd yours handle coming down the side road?"

"Not great," Todd said. "Lucy, she has a point."

I gritted my teeth. "She's wrong."

Chief Deputy Foster didn't rise to my disrespect. She simply ignored me. "Go ahead and walk the fence line. I'll be back in a few minutes."

I waited until her vehicle disappeared behind the tree line. "This is a waste of time."

Todd had already started following the barbed wire fence. With meticulous steps, his head tucked down against the bristling wind, he walked east. "Go the other way. Look for footsteps. Blood. You know the drill."

A disgusting feeling of powerlessness surged through me. This was a waste of time. Why didn't the deputy want to listen to what I had to say? Was it a female power thing? I hoped not, because I didn't have the time or the patience for that juvenile crap. My days of playing that game were over. My boots sank through the snow as I plowed down the fence line, looking for things I knew weren't there. A thicket of brambles snagged on my jeans, a needle piercing the denim and snagging my skin. I cursed and jerked away.

How could Chris do this? I'd been out of touch for the past couple of weeks, but had he felt so abandoned that he'd gone completely stupid? If he'd only waited...

But then what would I have done? The day Jake and Riley kidnapped me, I'd sworn my allegiance to him and to killing his mother. The day I killed Riley and Jake, on the way to the station, with Todd fussing over me, my mind had already jumped ahead thinking about how we'd find Mary and what I planned to do. How dare she think she could buy me and subject me to those horrible things? I even pictured the look on her face as she realized who really had the upper hand.

But the adrenaline-injected fury faded as the hours passed, replaced by Riley's face and words. I crashed hard. And I had no plans of getting up.

Chris was left on his own.

Again.

I stepped on an icy patch of snow and nearly lost my footing.

You didn't abandon him. She did. You are not her.

The satisfaction I took from killing Preacher and Jake and even Riley didn't amount to what she'd done.

Did it?

Frost's dirty patrol car came back into view. Driving faster than she should have been, she skidded to a stop on the sliver of gravel masquerading as the side of the road.

I couldn't move.

She jumped out of the car, bracing herself on the open door. She glanced at me, almost as if she couldn't control it and then looked at Todd.

"My deputy found his car off Quail Road."

SIX

The sight of the Audi smacked me in the chest like the blow of an errant baseball bat. Dirt covered its shiny, black exterior and dulled the wheels. Chunks of the thick sand used to make snow-covered roads drivable hung behind the tires like mutated coconuts. Straddling the side of the road, it looked small and lost, the dog waiting on the owner who would never return.

I forced myself out of Todd's car, my body moving on autopilot. Another deputy stood beside the Audi, peering inside. Beneath his hat, the gray hair at his temples made him look older than Chief Deputy Frost. My wicked mind wondered how she'd earned the title as a female at such a young age.

"The car's locked." The deputy spoke as Frost approached him. "Appears to be an overnight bag in the backseat. Other than that, it looks clean."

"I know the keyless entry." My voice sounded frail against the increasing wind. I cleared my throat. "Anyone have a pair of latex gloves, or are my wool ones all right?"

Frost raised her eyebrow. "Crime shows?"

"Private investigator." I didn't even try to keep the snap out of my voice.

Todd gently pushed his way past me, a glove already on. "Give me the code, Lucy."

It seemed a gross miscarriage of trust. Chris said I was the only person he'd ever given the code to. He'd be furious I'd given it to Todd, of all people.

"Lucy."

I rattled off the code.

Todd opened the door and then stepped back. "Deputy Frost, this is your jurisdiction. If there's a crime scene here, let's do it right."

She nodded, donning gloves.

My insides soured as she and deputy nameless began to sift through the Audi. Todd circled like a hungry dog.

I turned away and looked at the vast expanse of woods and open pasture. This time, the "for sale" sign could be seen clearly from the road. At least a hundred feet of cold, snowy pasture separated the tree line from the gate I could barely make out near the trees.

Closing my eyes, the north icy wind feeling colder than it had just minutes ago, I pictured Chris standing in this very spot. He wouldn't have been able to stay in the car. He'd have started out leaning against it, watching. Shifting from foot to foot, kinetic and restless as always. Impatience would have moved him forward and away from the safety of the Audi.

He'd have worn his wool pea coat and probably a hat. If he'd worn boots, they wouldn't be appropriate for slogging through inches of snow. They would be narrow at the toe, heavy in the sole. My eyes open, my gaze dropped to the ground. Careful to stay in the ditch, I walked down the road. If he'd left footprints, the wind had already blanketed them with snow.

Not wanting to get snow in his too-short boots, he'd have

hovered on the side of the road, debating about heading toward the trees.

But why go to the trees?

Because she would have chosen cover, just as I would have.

Chris wouldn't have been able to wait. His mind would trip and fumble until he couldn't resist. He'd come too far to not try everything possible. He'd wonder if there wasn't another way into the woods, if she wasn't standing just on the other side of that gate, waiting to see what he'd do.

He wouldn't be able to leave without checking.

I searched the ditch, looking for some set of footprints in the mounds of ugly snow, but the blowing and drifting had done its job. I'd reached the dirt drive that cut through the pasture and toward the gate at the woods. Were those footprints?

Another gust of wind blew a fresh wave of snow over the very tracks I observed and sent flakes into my eyes. I smeared them off my face and started down the path. I no longer felt the cold or the relentless wind. Even with Todd and the deputies fifty feet away, I felt like the last person on earth, walking to my doom.

No drumming of my heart in my ears. No ominous silence, either. Just the sound of the wind and my boots and the numbness that seemed to accompany me these days. One foot in front of the other, day by day, until it ended and I could sleep. That's what I'd told myself the first few days after the garage. And gradually I took fewer steps and slept more. I'd have preferred to do that today.

Instead I stood near the edge of a forlorn patch of woods, the tree limbs bare and twisted, some of them stark white and others still smattered with snow. The wind whistled in the trees, hitting me in the face as though Mother Nature wanted me to drop to my knees and pray for my sins. But I didn't move. My stomach clenched and twisted itself into a knot. The sound of the wind roared in my ears, making my brain feel as if it had been scrambled. I blinked, hoping the thing I'd seen would disappear into my imagination, but when I opened my eyes, it remained as brilliant as ever.

A crimson pool in the snow.

SEVEN

I called Todd over, my voice sucked away by the harsh wind.

Breathing hard, Todd suddenly appeared next to me, along with Frost and no-name deputy.

"Shit." She knelt in front of the blood. "It's dark and drying already and partially covered from the blowing snow. I'd say it's at least a couple of hours old."

"It happened at 10:07 a.m.," I said. "I played you the voicemail."

Todd's hand gripped my elbow. "You should go back to the car."

"Are you serious? You've got to care more about me than that."

He winced but drew his shoulders back out of his usual slouch. "I do. It's cold, and you're not yourself. This is police business."

"And I'm not damaging the scene any more than anyone else," I said. "I haven't touched anything." I didn't want to be alone in the car with nothing but my own head to keep me company.

"These impressions"—the deputy pointed to the area

surrounding the bloody snow—"indicate he might have fallen, but the wind's blown enough I can't tell if he lay there or not. But there's no blood trail. So what happened to him?"

"She bandaged him up—or he did it himself—and she made him leave with her," I said. "Isn't it obvious?" I turned to Frost, fear doing what it always did to me: morphing into anger. Anger was easier to weaponize. "You don't know what you're dealing with here. Did you look up Mary Weston or Martha Beckett? Have you seen the things she's done?"

"Why would she take him?" Frost's rational question made me want to smack her.

"Because she's a psychopath. And she's obviously not here." I spread my arms wide, anxiety shelling my system. I felt unsteady, out of control. Irrational. If I could have hit something —Deputy Frost would do—and gotten away with it, I'd have beaten her until I felt better. "So what are you going to do about it?"

"Search," she said. "Right now, we call in the auxiliary volunteers and the state police. Crime scene techs too. Your friend didn't just vanish, so however he got away, the blowing snow has destroyed the path. Which means we form a grid and start looking." She pointed to the other deputy, her voice controlled but still ringing with excitement. "The landowner lives out of state. See if you can contact the realtor and get their information. If they gave anyone permission to hunt, we might have a lead."

"There's no time for your grid." I wanted to scream at her. I stepped closer, into her face, feeling my own harden into the mask I used when people needed to get their stupidity and agenda out of my way. When I wanted to make them afraid of me. "She's taken him somewhere else. You're killing him."

"Lucy." The sound of Todd saying my name like that grated on my nerves, but it also pulled me a foot back off the edge. "You have to step aside."

"Let me ask you this." Frost hadn't backed down. Instead, she glared at me, her squared jaw taut, her body leaning forward just enough to remind me who was in charge. "Do you have any idea where she might have taken him? Where she came from? What device she used to communicate with him? Did she email him from our library? Does she have a phone that might have GPS?"

"I don't know." I hated saying the words because Frost was out of her league and wasting time. "But Mary Weston is true evil. She convinced her first husband to lie for her. In nearly thirty years, he's never implicated her in the Lancaster crimes— not even when the recent evidence came up. She's a chameleon, constantly reinventing herself. As Martha Beckett, she raped a little girl with wooden spoons and then beat her to death. She forced her young son to take part and then let that child go to prison while she skipped off to start over yet again." My voice rose as I spoke, taking on the shrill tone of someone on the verge of panic. "You cannot comprehend the kind of person you're dealing with. She's too smart and experienced to be anywhere nearby. She's got a plan, and you need to notify your superiors and the state police immediately."

"The FBI has tried numerous ways to track her." Todd's hand rested on my shoulder—stable, but warning. "She's gone off the grid. No cell, no credit cards. Unless she's suckered someone else into letting her use his. Which is very possible."

"So I'll have another deputy check the local Wi-Fi hotspots and the library, see if she's been inside. I'm betting on no, but we've got to try. In the meantime, this"—Frost gestured to the acreage—"is our best lead. We're not only looking for him, we're looking for any kind of evidence we can use. You understand?"

A month ago, I'd have been thinking of ways to humiliate this woman, even imagining dousing her with poison. But arguing with her had exhausted me, and the numbness crept back in. The situation was hopeless, anyway. Mary had won.

"Yes. But you're making a mistake, and it's going to come back to haunt you."

She ignored me and looked up at Todd. "I'm assuming his cell is off, so we can't track it via GPS," Frost said. "But I'll take the number in case. Meanwhile, I'd like you to return to Detective Beckett's car and wait. You're a civilian, and this is a crime scene." She tilted her chin up and narrowed her eyes, ice cold and fringed with thick lashes. I wanted to yank them out one by one.

Frost raised her voice against the miserable wind. "Detective *Beckett*. Are you related to Justin Beckett and this whole mess?"

She should have made that connection in the first ten minutes. Mary probably chose this area because of its inexperienced police force. It's what I would have done.

I turned and walked away.

Night fell before the search grid was fully set up. A crime scene van arrived, and technicians began picking through the snow as if they might actually find something useful. Trooper Evans, Todd's friend from the Maryland State Police, showed up. Todd introduced me to him, but I only noticed he was short with a deep voice. Sitting in Todd's car, my legs curled beneath me, I watched the scene as though I weren't a part of it, pretending every second ticking by didn't sound like a clock in my head.

Then they found Chris's phone. Tossed aside in the snow a few feet away from the blood and near the trees. Frost concentrated her grid around that, and the group continued to search.

Frost loved being in charge. She paraded around the edge of the scene, pointing and constantly talking, either to another deputy or to one of the crime scene techs. Instead of looking miserable like the rest of the group forced to suffer the inclement weather, Frost strutted as if the frozen tundra of acreage was her personal catwalk. When Trooper Evans arrived, Frost drew herself up tall, her blunt chin leading the charge. I waited for her to lift her leg over the crime scene tape and decorate the snow, but Evans seemed smart enough to let her think she was in charge. He joined the search, along with Todd. Knowing he was out with the rest of the group gave me a shred of hope.

"Are they checking hospitals?" Kelly's voice drifted through my speaker, providing a small sense of comfort.

"Yes. So far, he hasn't shown up at any within a seventy-five-mile radius. But they've got an APB out on him. As if that is going to help."

"Do you think he's alive?" Kelly sounded as if she had to choke out the question.

"I think he left here with her, alive. But that was hours ago." If he hadn't been severely injured and was somewhere inside away from the elements, I didn't think Mary would have killed him. Not yet.

"I can't believe the wind blew hard enough to cover the tracks."

"Because you've never been out in the open country. Changes everything." I stared out the window, looking at the bright lights the CSIs had set up. Wind sent shimmering streams of snow over the scene, into the techs' faces and equipment, and into the empty fields. The snow drifted away to the next place, white and silent, the only witness to Chris's fate.

"I shouldn't have blown him off yesterday." Guilt thickened Kelly's voice. "He said you weren't answering his calls, and he was going to go over to your place again. I talked him out of it and told him to leave you alone until you were ready. If I hadn't, maybe he would have come over and somehow this would have turned out differently."

"It wouldn't have." Flashlights floated in the dark woods—searchers finding nothing. "I'd have ignored him."

"I don't understand her. Why go to all this trouble?"

"Because she's no longer in control, and she's desperate." A thought clawed at my subconscious. I couldn't allow myself to acknowledge it. "Chris represents things going wrong for her, and he practically asked her to do this. He handed himself over." I turned the heat down a notch.

"How could he think she'd just let him walk away?"

"I don't know," I said. "Maybe he didn't. Maybe he planned to kill her himself and just couldn't do it. If I find them, I'll be sure to ask."

"All right." Kelly's voice remained calm. "So you're stuck waiting until the cops allow you to move on to the next step. So let's do what we do."

"I'm not sure I know what I do anymore, Kel." The woman who had moved fearlessly throughout the bowels of Philadelphia chasing monsters seemed like a fantasy. Had she ever been real, or just a figment of my imagination? I longed to be fearless and invincible just one more time. To finish this mess. But I couldn't find anything to ignite the flame.

"We find people who do bad things," Kelly said. "This is no different. So first things first. Why Harford County?"

"I don't know." I'd been asking the same question all day and still couldn't come up with anything other than its remoteness. And possibly inept police force, but I supposed I might have been biased. "Can you get into his email by chance?"

"Do you know the account and the password?"

"No. But he doesn't have his laptop." An idea flickered, but I couldn't voice it. Asking Kelly to go clear to Chris's neighborhood in her mental condition was out of the question.

"If I thought I could get in and get it, I would," she said, reading my mind. "But chatter is that ADA Hale already has the police at Chris's. I'm sure they'll take the laptop. And I honestly don't think they'll find anything useful. She's too smart for that."

"So I'm back here, with no place to start." The flashlights bounced again, glowing orbs shooting in and out of the trees. A fresh blast of wind pelted the car.

"That's not true," Kelly said. "You know Chris, and we know how this woman works. If she takes him out of control, what's her end game? Punishment? What's she going to do in the meantime? Tell him family stories that have been handed down from generation to generation?"

I jerked up from my slouch. Pain shot through my cramped back. "Chris said something about that a while ago. He said he didn't know anything about her side of the family, and I got the impression he wished he did."

"Okay," Kelly said. "Keep going."

"So if she took him, and he's alive and able to talk, then he's going to ask her about her life, her past. He's going to try to get as many answers as he can in the time he's got left. He's smart enough to read her and stall her any way he can." I didn't give the implication of the words time to sink in.

"Maybe that's why he's still alive, even now," she said. "She —or someone with her—shoots him, he's down. They move in for the final shot, and he appeals to her. So she decides to tell him. But why? She cut him out of her life years ago. If she wants revenge for messing things up now, just kill him."

"Because she doesn't just kill." I felt scummy, almost as if I'd snuck into someone's house and hid in the closet while they were having sex. "She doesn't get her kicks from that. She gets them from hurting people, from controlling them. Chris would be no different."

"And she gave birth to him."

"She was nothing more than a vessel," I said. "But we'll never find him if we don't find a starting point. So far Chief Deputy Frost is just circling the obvious."

"Todd's there," Kelly said. "ADA Hale is probably on his way. This won't be dropped. They'll find something."

I hoped she was right, but the sight of Todd coming toward me with a grim expression brought a sickening sense of déjà vu. "I'll call you back, Kel."

"Text me if anything comes up."

Feeling suffocated in the warm car, I opened the door and stepped into the bitter night. The wind had blown the clouds out, leaving the black sky and its millions of shining stars. "What is it?"

Todd carried a plastic bag. Food, I realized. He went around to the driver's side and got into the car. I took a few cold breaths to wake up my system and then returned to the heat.

"Here." Todd handed me a gas station sandwich. "Turkey and cheese. Figured everybody likes that, right?"

I wasn't hungry, but since my last meal had been some time yesterday evening, I took the sandwich. "Sure." I bit into the thick hoagie bun, the bread immediately sticking to my teeth. "The searchers haven't found anything?"

"Even the dogs are coming up empty," Todd said. "The wind and snow are screwing their senses up, and it's so cold they can't stay out too long."

"They didn't just fly away."

He shot me a look. "I realize that. Obviously they walked to a vehicle and left. Trooper Evans thinks it's time to give up on the grid, but Frost insists on searching the acreage in case he was dumped somewhere. Which isn't outside the realm of possibility."

I thought of Chris and me dumping Preacher's body. The idea the same thing might have happened to Chris reeked of cruel karma. "What about the owner of the property or the realtor?"

"Can't reach them." Todd took a large bite, barely chewed, and then took a drink of water. "ADA Hale's on his way."

"Good." I'd only met the assistant district attorney once, but I got the impression he knew how to get things done. He wouldn't appreciate Frost's star-seeking. "What about the sher-iff? Who does Frost answer to? Don't they have an investigative branch?"

"She claimed she called their Major Case detective." Todd's derisive tone didn't help my confidence in the deputy. "Trooper Evans is going to call the sheriff himself just to make sure." He cleared his throat. "But it's probably not going to matter. ADA Hale's bringing the FBI."

"What?" I shouldn't have been surprised. Mary had become the FBI's case even before Chris's disappearance. But I didn't want them snooping around me.

"ADA Hale had a police tech go with him to Chris's apart-ment," Todd said. "They found his computer and got into the email." Kelly had been right. Thank God I hadn't asked her to go over there. "ADA Hale believes it was definitely Mary communicating, because she mentioned things only she would know, like dates and certain events."

"Did they get a location?"

"The local FBI office is working on it, but so far nothing."

I tried to tell myself my reaction was based on surprise, but I recognized the stirrings of jealousy. Chris hadn't shared any of this with me. "What things did she say? They actually had a real conversation?"

"Apparently. I didn't ask. But ADA Hale said he would tell you and me everything he knew when he got here."

"Thank God he's not shutting me out." Whatever thread of sanity I possessed would have snapped if that happened.

Todd finished his sandwich. "Why would he do that?"

"Because Chris's life has gone to shit since he met me."

"Depends on how you look at it," Todd said. "And no one forced him to make this decision. This is his bad choice."

His tone reminded me how much he didn't care for Chris. "Thank you for being here. For staying out in this weather. I know you're doing it for me, and I really appreciate it."

He turned to face me, his eyes bright. His plain face seemed sharper somehow, his almond-shaped eyes more unique, the crooked slope of his nose endearing. "I am doing this for you. And only you."

The back of my neck heated up. Uncomfortable silence settled between us, and I twisted to stare back at the woods, the ghostlike flashlights still dancing.

"You know," Todd said. "When my father introduced me to Mary, I was just a kid. Still using training wheels. I was scared of her because she was tall and imposing. But I had no idea what kind of evil had walked into our lives."

He rarely talked about his memories of her. Our conversations were centered on her specific actions and their impact on Justin. Todd always pretended Mary's presence in his life never affected him personally, and I never pushed.

"Most people never do," I said. "A few can sense it. They can tell something's off about a person, but they rarely allow their minds to jump to the worst conclusions."

"I suppose," Todd said. "When everything happened with Justin, I knew she'd been involved. I just couldn't prove it, and I didn't know how." He balled up the wrapper from the sandwich and shoved it back into the container. "If I'd had the courage to speak my mind, how differently would this have turned out?"

"You can't think that way," I said, the ultimate hypocrite. "It will eat you alive, and it serves no purpose here. The only thing you can do is focus on what's happening right now."

"Is that how you get through the days?" He spoke in a hushed whisper, as if we were sharing the deepest secrets of our souls, as if maybe the tone of his voice would lull me into making a mistake.

I changed the subject. "So Kelly is right."

"How so?" He smiled warily, admitting defeat—at least for now.

"Remember in the message, Chris talked about how he

didn't know anything about her side of the family, or her? That's why he's still alive. Or was. She's telling him what he wants to know before she kills him."

Just like I did with Riley.

The teenager's terror-stricken face flashed in front of me, as vivid as if she'd just walked in front of the car. I gasped and nearly choked on the sandwich.

"Jesus, you all right?" Todd reached to pat my back, but I blocked his arm. I couldn't stand his touch right now.

"Fine. Wrong pipe."

Through stinging eyes, I saw no-name deputy looming toward us. He walked with purpose, his steps wide and his gait fast. "They have something," I whispered.

Todd and I both exited the car as the deputy came within earshot. The grim set of his mouth and the creases around his eyes sent shivers of fear down my spine. This time I read the name on his uniform: Roberts.

Deputy Roberts stopped in front of me, so close I could smell the coffee he'd been drinking. "We found a hunting cabin."

EIGHT

I waited for Roberts to spit out the rest of the information he was obviously chewing on.

"It's a female," he said. "Probably under twenty. We haven't touched her yet. The medical examiner's on her way."

Todd cursed and kicked a chunk of snow. I ducked my head into my zipped collar, warming my face. The shivers attacking my body had nothing to do with the temperature. I spoke through the layer of clothing. "Is there any sign of Chris?"

"There's no one on the property," Deputy Roberts said. "We're still processing the scene." He looked past me, into the bleak winter night. I thought about sidling up to him, letting my body heat mingle with his, allowing him to catch a whiff of my perfume. Appeal to the appreciation I saw in his eyes every time he looked at me. But Todd stood a foot away, talking on the phone to someone. I didn't want him to see me stoop that low.

"Will you please keep us updated?" I said. "I'm not sure how much you've been told about Mary Weston, but torturing and killing young girls is her specialty. I'd guess she's at it again."

Roberts glanced back into the woods, his shoulders taut as if pulled up by imaginary strings. When he faced me again, the lines between his eyes were a little deeper, his face somehow stretched longer. "I've been on the job for a long time. Seen my fair share of killing. But nothing like this. Nothing." He spit the last word out as though it would cleanse his memory.

"She's brutal. And she's been doing this a long time."

Roberts's pinched face made me wonder who he was thinking about. Daughter? Niece? "Once the medical examiner gets here, we'll know more. I'll talk to Deputy Frost about how much I can share with you." He headed back towards the black woods, his strides long and steps deep.

"I think they found something about Chris too," I said to Todd as soon as he ended his call. "Roberts looked like he wanted to say more. He's probably been told not to."

Todd's grim face gave me no optimism. "ADA Hale and the FBI agent should be here in about an hour. If this is another victim of Mary's, there's going to be a jurisdictional pissing contest."

"Chief Deputy Frost isn't going to like that," I said. "But Mary's out of their league and beyond their resources. And the FBI has the right to take the case, don't they?" My petty side hoped I had a front row seat to the conflict. Frost wouldn't go down without a fight, but she needed to swallow her pride and let the FBI take over.

"Since she's crossed state lines, yes," Todd said. "But the issue is proving it was Mary. Chris's emails will probably help us with that."

"How much did he talk to her?"

"Multiple conversations." The sharp wind did nothing to soften Todd's harsh voice. "I told you he's not right."

Another stab of betrayal sliced my frozen skin. "That's unfair. Why *would* he be right?"

Todd looked away, toward the woods. He clearly didn't know how to answer, and I had no interest in winning an argument. A deep ache, one that pervaded past the muscle and into the very fibers of the bone, settled over me. And the ache had nothing to do with the cold.

"Get back in where it's warm," Todd said. "I'm going to talk to Frost and see what I can find out."

The warmth did nothing for the pain or the weariness in my head. The only other time I'd felt like this had been after my sister's death. It lingered until her abuser showed up and tried to turn me into his next victim. Cracking his skull with a base-ball bat had been wonderful shock therapy.

I wondered what that said about me. My ability to stop that line of thinking and redirect to something more productive seemed to have vanished with killing Riley. Shame and confusion and bitter negativity dragged me into a bottomless pit with no way out I could see.

But I had to find a way back because Chris needed my help.

As had become my custom these past days, I closed my eyes and drifted off.

Todd's rap on the glass yanked me out of my dazed nap. I rolled down the window.

"They want you on the scene."

With my gloved hands jammed into my pockets, I walked beside Todd as we followed Deputy Roberts into the woods. The darkness felt thicker, as if it had physical mass and might wrap itself around my throat at any moment. The bobbing flash-lights and white snow did nothing to ease the sensation of walking into a black void.

The sleeping, bare trees provided a minimal windbreak, but my system was too desensitized to feel much of anything. According to Roberts, the hunting cabin was a two room, sparse shelter for the serious deer hunters who wanted to be out from sunup to sundown.

"With the land for sale and the owner out of state, the cabin hadn't been checked on in a while." The wind carried Roberts's voice back to me, making it sound like a recorded version of itself. "I suppose she saw the listing and figured it was the perfect place."

"She did more than that," I said. "She knew the owner wasn't around. She probably knew the realtor didn't check up on the place. And I guarantee she knows everything about the area."

"How do you know that?" Roberts asked.

Because it's what I would do.

"Intuition."

"Has the girl's body been removed?" Todd asked.

"No." Roberts's windswept voice took on a chilled edge. "The FBI agent called and asked the medical examiner to wait to move it until he arrived."

Todd grunted, glancing at me. So the fight had already begun.

A parting in the trees diverted my attention. Crime scene lights shined like some kind of bizarre beacon, turning the snow almost iridescent. The yellow tape surrounding the cabin looked woefully out of place, as if the artist's color palette had been tampered with. The cabin itself looked as I'd assumed any hunting cabin did. Heavy logs mucked together, with a single window facing east. I wondered if that was intentional, to make sure the hunters didn't sleep in.

"How did the medical examiner get here?" I pointed to the black SUV with its rear door open to reveal the waiting gurney. "Did she come in while I fell asleep?"

"There's another access road," Todd said. "To the south, and it's less than a quarter mile off the main highway."

"Doesn't that mean this place isn't very well hidden?" That couldn't be right. Mary wouldn't make that kind of mistake.

"Not if no one is checking the place," Roberts said. "It's got a generator, so there's electricity. Looks like she used a space heater."

Chief Deputy Frost exited the narrow, crudely hewn doorway. The last time I saw her, her cheeks were still bright with the prospect of the hunt. She'd been in control of the search and believed she'd find Chris in the woods.

She looked like a pale shell of that woman now. I stamped out the smile that begged at my lips.

"Detective Beckett," she said. "Miss Kendall—"

"Lucy. Please."

A jerk of her chin was the only acknowledgment. "Here's what we have: the medical examiner puts the girl at around sixteen. She doesn't have any identification on her, but Trooper Evans recognized her. She's been missing from the southern part of the state for more than two weeks."

I tried to hide my surprise at her sharing the information with me. I guess Todd's presence and my private investigator's license counted for something. "And Chris?"

"The girl is in the bedroom. She's been..." Frost faltered for the first time, no longer the big woman in charge but realizing how blessed she'd been to work in a small town with normal problems. I could have taunted her, asked her what she thought of her shot at the big time now, and I almost did. Todd's presence by my side stopped me.

Frost kept shaking her head like the images would somehow disappear. Eventually she'd realized that whatever she'd seen in that cabin was tattooed in her memory. She'd probably still remember the girl's mutilated body when she was ninety and on her own deathbed. "Sexually tortured and subjected to various physical attacks. Bruises show signs of healing, so we're assuming she's been here a while. As for your friend, we found something in the bathroom."

She held out an evidence bag. For a moment, my stinging and tired eyes couldn't see past the plastic. And then I saw the gray fabric, the intricately woven pattern of black and white. "That's Chris's scarf."

"It's stained with blood," Frost said. "And the bathroom has several areas that glowed with the luminol. Since this is a hunting cabin, some of it may well be animal blood. But I think your friend made it this far. I think he—or someone—staunched his bleeding with the scarf. And then he left."

Just like I'd told her hours ago. If only she'd listened. But so what? What exactly would have turned out differently? I didn't know, but that didn't stop me from blaming her.

"He didn't leave," I said. "She took him. Or they took him."

"I agree," Todd said. "If he's shot and left to die, he's not walking into the woods. He's going back to his car to call for help. I checked with OnStar. No calls made, and no sign of blood anywhere on or near the Audi."

"I'm not arguing that fact," Frost said. "I'm telling you what I know. I needed you to identify the evidence."

"Why didn't you bring it to the car?" I asked. I looked at the cabin, knowing the slain girl was still inside. "Do you think Chris was here when Mary killed her?"

"We don't know." Trooper Evans appeared behind Frost, stepping around her. What he lacked in height he made up for in girth, and I guessed the majority of his mass was solid muscle. His bald head shined almost as bright as the snow, and the bulletproof vest added extra bulge beneath this jacket. "The ME's preliminary exam puts death sometime in the last twenty-four hours. The cold slowed down the decomposition process, and she's going to have to run tests to get us more answers. I spoke with the sheriff's Major Case detective"—he shot a cold glance at Frost, who seemed to shrink into her jacket—"and he's on his way."

His glittering, sharp eyes honed in on me. "As for why you're here, the FBI requested you view the scene, if you're willing."

I could do nothing but stare dumbly back at him. "Why?"

"Ask Beckett."

I turned to the man standing beside me. Todd sighed, his breath wisping out in cold crystals. His composure remained, but the edge in his voice told me he'd been dreading this moment. "When I called ADA Hale earlier, he put me on with Agent Lennox of the Pennsylvania office. He knows who you are and what you did for Kailey Richardson as well as the recent trafficking ring. He also knows you and Chris are close. I told him"—he glanced at me, a shadow in his eyes—"that you were as familiar with Mary as anyone else at this point."

"Why would you say that?" My voice pitched high, a child caught in the act of lying. Did Todd hear it too? Did he see the big black shadow creeping up on me? The horrendous similarities between Mary and me I could barely deny?

"You already told me you were looking for her." The words practically sang with deeper implications. "And I know you."

We stared at one another, the unspoken accusation feeling like a shouting match. I had to say something before my nerves got the better of me.

"So what does the FBI agent want me to do?"

"He wants you to walk the scene," Trooper Evans said. "He'd like your opinion on whether this is really Mary Weston or someone else altogether."

"Like a copycat who suckered Chris?"

Evans shrugged. "I'm just relaying the information. Normally, the state police handle murders. But this is apparently... different."

I realized I was supposed to feel discomfort at the jurisdictional jockeying, that I should do an internal curtsey and soothe Evans's feelings.

But soothing required precious energy, and I wasn't sure I had enough to make it through the night as it was. "Show me the scene."

NINE

The cabin should have smelled musty. I expected something similar to my grandparents' basement—a foreign, dark place I'd feared as a child—closed up, with droplets of moisture seeping through the rudimentary caulking and around the window. The nights I stayed with them, I'd walk by the basement doorway—always open for the cat—and catch a whiff of that sad, moldy smell and see the bulging darkness. Then I'd race to my bedroom and lock the door.

Instead, a faded, but still cloying odor of incense remained.

Mary's house in Philadelphia flashed before me, Justin's voice in my head whispering about how much his mother loved to burn the stinking things.

"Mary is known to use incense." I glanced at Todd, who jerked a single nod.

Beyond the smell, the tiny building was nothing special. A roughly twelve-by-fifteen box served as the main room and kitchen, with a sink that drained into a bucket underneath. A cobbled-together antique cook stove vented into a small pipe I'd noticed sticking out of the roof. Pushed up against the wall, a table and chairs looked like they'd been dug out of

Grandma's basement. Lying innocently on a ceramic plate were the remains of the incense sticks, charred to their pointed tips.

A bag of paper plates and other throwaway kitchenware sat on the table. A small couch flush against the other wall, its worn edge butting up against an interior doorframe.

"Bedroom?"

"Bathroom." Evans pointed to the closed door on the other side of the tiny room, just past the kitchen table. "That's the bedroom." He cleared his throat and looked at Todd.

"Lucy." Todd's cold fingers closed around my wrist. "You can handle this, right? It's pretty brutal."

The retort "I thought you knew me" brewed on my lips, but Todd's quick look at the trooper told me the question was more for his benefit.

"I can."

I didn't know if my steady voice or something about the hardness of my gaze did the trick, but Evans took four short steps and opened the bedroom door.

Without moving, I saw her bare, dirty feet dangling off a cot with frayed edges. I followed Evans, waiting to feel a rush of some sort of emotion. Praying for it.

If I feel nothing at the sight of this girl, then I am truly a monster.

"Bedroom" was a generous term. Barely big enough to fit the cot and the woman I assumed was the medical examiner, the room steamed from the bright lights aimed at the dead girl.

"What's her name?" I asked, uncertain of why I cared.

"Amy." Trooper Evans's simple answer smacked me hard in the chest, as if he'd taken electric paddles to my heart. In the span of a second, my pulse pounded in my ears until I thought it would burst, my palms broke out in a sweat, my stomach roiled. My hand instinctively reached for the weapon I didn't have.

My eyes welled up. My vision clouded. I smelled the girl's

blood and decay, and the urge to scream, to punch the wall, to hurt someone, ripped through me like a wild beast.

I blinked. The room and the people and the circumstances suddenly came into sharp focus, as if I'd switched from analog television to high definition. My ears unclogged.

I'd breached the surface of the black hole I'd been living in.

"You all right?" The presumed medical examiner looked at me with concern.

"Fine." Even my voice sounded stronger.

I looked at the girl.

At Amy.

Anger tasted metallic on my tongue. Energy flowed through me, my system suddenly plugged in to whatever electric current it craved in order to operate at full capacity. And I vowed I'd kill Mary Weston by whatever means necessary.

Amy lay flat on her back, her bound hands over her head and zip-tied to the metal edge of the cot. Her slack mouth looked stuck in a silent wail. Her vacant eyes followed me like the eyes of a painting. Bruises of various sizes and color dotted her face. Hand marks around her neck.

"Strangled?" I asked.

"Yes," the medical examiner said. She was a tall African American woman with skin like silk and solemn eyes. Her cropped hair suited her sculpted face, her soft voice coloring the room like an emotional aura. "It's impossible to tell for certain, but judging by the different stages of bruising, I think she was strangled more than once over the past week."

"Sick." Frost's voice came from somewhere behind me, the chief deputy stuck in line behind people now deemed more essential to the case than she was. I felt no pity.

"It's one of her favorite things," I said. "All of her known victims had different stages of bruising in the same spots." I studied Amy's emaciated, naked body. Random cuts, probably from a dulled knife, covered her small breasts. More than one appeared to be in the early stages of infection. "Will the infected cuts help with time of death or figuring out how long she's been here?"

"Probably not," the medical examiner said. "Depending on how dirty the knife was, infection can set in quickly. But this one"—her gloved hand touched a particularly dark slash across Amy's left breast—"is fairly healed. Once I get her into better lighting, I might be able to get a more exact timeframe. Going by the time of her disappearance, I think it's safe to say she was brought here early on."

"Mary sat on her when she strangled her," I said.

The doctor's keen eyes met mine. Todd shifted behind me. "How do you know that?"

"Because Jenna Richardson remembers someone sitting on her when she was strangled, and because this girl is bruised on both sides of her hips. Probably from Mary's knees."

"She's got at least two broken ribs." The medical examiner looked down at the sad body. "And possibly a fractured pelvis. I figured that was from the repeated sexual assaults, but is Mary a heavy woman?"

"Sturdy," Todd said. "Built like a Mack truck. Damn near twice the size of this girl."

My eyes drifted to Amy's genitals. Dried blood pooled beneath her and painted her muscular thighs. "Foreign object was probably used. If she has a partner, then he might have joined in too, but Mary likes to physically get in on the action. Look for wooden spoons."

Somewhere behind me, a woman gagged. I turned to see Frost, her face a sickly green. "I saw a wooden one in the trash. It had something red on it—I figured it was food."

"Go bag it," Trooper Evans snapped. Frost slunk away, and I felt a tiny moment of pity for her. It wasn't her fault she lived in a peaceful area and didn't have the experience needed to deal with Mary.

The medical examiner returned her focus to the body. "I'll keep an eye out for any slivers of wood in her genital area."

Oval-shaped burn marks covered the girl's left thigh. "She used a heated tablespoon on one of the Lancaster victims. Or John Weston did. No one knows for sure, but detectives back then matched the shape up to a blackened spoon found in the barn. I'd say that's the same thing that's happened here."

"You mentioned an accomplice." The doctor again leaned over the body. This time, she touched Amy's pubis. "Judging by the blood in this area, she was assaulted shortly before death. I can't say by looking if it was by an object or a man, but the discarded condom wrapper found near her body makes me think it may have been a man."

"That adds up," Todd said. "Mary might be strong, but she couldn't have handled Chris—especially since he was likely injured—without help."

My head roared like a swollen river. A muscle in my leg twitched and throbbed, urging me to take action. My brain raced. So many things to do. *Find Chris. Save Chris. Kill Mary. After I make her suffer for a while.* "Broken toes."

The medical examiner smiled grimly. "I wondered if you'd notice that."

"All of the Lancaster victims had broken big toes, including Jenna Richardson. She had to have surgery to have hers reset." I turned around. Todd leaned against the door, close enough to touch. Behind the entry stood Evans and then Frost. "Like I said several hours ago, this is Mary Weston's work."

"I'll call Agent Lennox," Todd said.

"I want to see the bathroom." I expected an argument from one of the officers, but Evans nodded.

"Stay in the doorway and don't touch anything."

I did as directed, crossing the living area with the adrenaline rush usually reserved for finding a new target. The back of my neck felt clammy. I dabbed the moisture off my forehead with the sleeve of my now heavy coat. The bathroom door creaked when I opened it. As described, fresh blood stained the sink. A bunched-up, dirty towel sat on the back of the toilet. Older droplets of blood stained the peel-and-stick vinyl, but my eyes trained on the red in the sink.

Chris.

How badly was he injured? Had he walked out of this place, or had Mary and her partner taken him somewhere and dumped him?

What would I do if he were dead?

I didn't have time to craft an answer. Trooper Evans appeared at my shoulder. "We're setting up roadblocks and checking all vehicles. The snow makes it impossible to match tire tracks, so we're checking everyone. We're circulating Mary and Chris's pictures on every TV station and at every gas station and grocery store in the state. The ME's best guess right now is that the girl died sometime after noon today, and we found the cabin around six p.m. So Mary's got at least a six-hour head start."

"What about bordering states?" I asked. "She could easily be in Pennsylvania by now. And why weren't roadblocks set up earlier?" I turned to glare at Frost, who still looked ghostlike. My pity had quickly evaporated. "I told you they'd get farther than you thought. You should have listened to me and notified the sheriff and the Major Case detective immediately. The only reason Trooper Evans showed up is because Todd called him. If he hadn't been here and made the call to Major Case for you, how long would it have taken you to hand over the case to someone with more experience?"

She jerked and then straightened. Color flashed into her cheeks, but I didn't flinch. As far as I was concerned, she was another obstacle that needed to be moved. My usual methods had failed earlier—my heart hadn't caught up to the task yet. But it pumped ferociously now, shooting an intoxicating medley of adrenaline and anger into my veins. From the way Frost's eyes widened and she took a step back, I knew she'd seen exactly what I wanted her to. *She should fear me.*

"I'm coordinating with other state police as well," Evans said. "And the FBI is mobilizing, according to Detective Beckett."

I looked again at the bathroom. For some foolish reason, I'd hoped to see some sort of sign from Chris, a message left for me to let me know he was still alive. A clue as to where that bitch had taken him.

But there was only his blood.

I left the bathroom and walked back to Todd. He nodded, dropping his phone in his pocket. "ADA Hale and Agent Lennox are here. They'll be at the cabin in a few minutes."

Lucy Kendall working with the FBI.

I'd be lucky to stay out of jail this time.

TEN

I chose to wait outside for ADA Hale and Agent Lennox. Cold pierced my layers of clothes, but my insides had overheated. Standing around, waiting to be told the next move, made me feel about as useless as a slug. If I could only get out there and do my thing, then I could... what? Find her? I laughed out loud, catching the surprised eye of a crime scene technician as he carried an evidence bag out of the cabin. Too tired and too jacked up to worry about looking crazy, I ignored him.

I couldn't find her on my own.

The FBI couldn't find her.

Chances of us working together in harmony for a positive outcome were probably nil.

Mary was going to win this game, and Chris was going to die.

An imposing African American man in a long, wool coat and hiking boots approached. He didn't hunch against the wind but walked straight into it, tenacious and bold, the regal leader come to save the day. Broad shoulders, leather-gloved hands and just the hint of a swagger—probably a former athlete. A few feet away, and his eyes latched on to mine and riveted me to the spot. I tried to play it off, act like I wasn't intimidated, but the man's attention felt like a weight dropped onto my shoulders.

"Lucy Kendall." His baritone waved over me so that I barely noticed his extended gloved hand. "Agent André Lennox, FBI."

Whatever bravado I'd gleaned from looking at Amy's body evaporated at the agent's dogged gaze. "Thanks for letting me help."

"I'm well aware of your history," Lennox said. "I decided making an ally of you would be better than worrying about your running your own investigation."

I wanted to march back into the cabin and demand to know how much Todd had told Lennox, but I didn't dare show that much weakness. "I'm counting on you to find Chris."

"So am I." ADA Hale appeared beside Lennox, looking far removed from the courtroom. Dressed in jeans and snow boots, with a thick parka and winter hat, he could have passed for any local. "Detective Beckett says you're both sure his mother is behind this."

"There's no doubt in my mind," I said. "I didn't need to see the crime scene to tell me that."

"Do you think he's alive?" Hale's voice didn't waver.

"For now, I'm still hoping," I said.

"I want to see this for myself." Lennox went inside and Hale followed. I had no choice but to do the same.

The main area of the cabin was filled to bursting, with each section of law enforcement officers in their own huddles. Evans and Frost stood at the bedroom door, as if they were considering blocking Lennox's access. Todd stood against the sink, out of place and unsure. In the center of the room, Lennox's imposing form commanded attention, but unlike Frost, he didn't appear to be a hyper puppy in need of potty training. Lennox was the old dog who knew the tricks of the game, his relentless gaze showing no surprise at the violence that had occurred here.

He introduced himself to Evans and Frost. "Thank you for allowing me to join the investigation." His height easily allowed him to peer over Evans's shoulder. "Poor girl."

Evans cleared his throat. "I assume Detective Beckett informed you of the medical examiner's preliminary findings, as well as Ms. Kendall's thoughts?"

"He did, and I agree, this is Mary Weston. You've set up roadblocks and contacted other agencies, but they've got several hours on us," Lennox said. "I've got my people trying to figure out where she used the Internet, but we're not having much luck. What about any sightings in the community?"

"So far, not many, but we're just starting that end of the search." Frost cut in, standing tall and rigid. "She's a woman who stands out, and this is a small town, so I'm hopeful."

"She didn't go into town," Lennox said. "She's too smart for that. We need to find out if there's any strange men out there, ages mid-forties and up, who are new in the community. I wish the roadblocks had been set up immediately, but we'll have to move forward as best we can."

Frost's face reddened, but she nodded. "Someone who came in and bought a lot of supplies at once. Maybe some of them for a woman. Someone who didn't want to talk or share anything about himself. Probably paid in cash."

"Good," Lennox said. "Get your people on that, if you don't mind. I'd like to take a closer look at the body. Your medical examiner can run through it with me."

"Sure thing," Trooper Evans said before Frost could respond. I rolled my eyes. Had these people never seen an FBI agent? They weren't actually godlike creatures, despite what half of them wanted the public to believe.

"Frank," Lennox said as he headed into the bedroom. "Why don't you go back to the station with Lucy and Detective Beckett and show them the emails? Might as well let them know what we're dealing with. I'll follow shortly."

Hale nodded, his gaze drifting toward the bathroom. I thought he'd ask to see it, but instead he turned and walked out of the cabin.

A warning pinged in my head. I caught Todd's eye and felt a flash of relief that his expression mirrored my own questions. What exactly were we dealing with?

The ride back to the police station was spent in silence, partially because the blowing snow had turned the roads into a wicked sheet of ice. Todd gripped the wheel hard, hunched forward so his chin hovered over the steering wheel. Hale seemed unbothered by the danger, sitting quiet and still. I wondered why he'd driven out with Lennox in the first place. I supposed he needed to see the place Chris had been taken.

Treacherously steep ditches gradually gave way to smoother embankments, and soon we eased into Jarrettsville. This time of night, most shops were closed, their dark windows like spying eyes in the winter night. Only the bright signs of the fast-food joints, an all-night department store, and a couple of gas stations offered a chance at sustenance. I realized Todd and I had no place to stay and hoped this town had a motel.

Inside the police station, we were taken past the entrance by a yawning deputy. "Sorry, I've got a newborn at home. I've set you up in the administrative conference room." He yawned again. "It's actually our only conference room, and it's also the break room, so there's coffee and a few donuts from this morning. I can order a pizza if you guys are hungry."

"No thanks," Todd said. "We just need a table and chairs."

And warmth. My fingers were still stiff from the cold, my toes barely moving. My face burned from the wind. I wished I'd packed lotion.

Hale set down his bag and shrugged out of his green parka, draping it over the chair. He took off his hat and ran his fingers through his silver hair. He braced his hands on the back of the chair and sighed. "I think I always knew this day would come."

I wanted to ask why, but suddenly felt too tired to speak. And now that I was inside, sheltered from the scene, Chris's foolishness sparked new anger. He was the calm one, always urging me to think things through. Of course he was emotionally attached this time, but still, how could he be so naïve? I regretted shutting him out more than ever, because I just could not get into his headspace right now, almost as if I were dealing with a stranger. We had to be missing information. The pinging returned, this time in the form of a whine deep inside my ears. I wasn't sure I wanted to hear what Hale had to say.

Todd pulled out a chair and motioned for me to sit. I didn't want to even though my legs felt like jelly, my muscles weak from laziness. But sitting implied I wasn't doing anything, and I needed to do something.

Todd waited, and I sat. He did the same and then Hale reached into his leather bag and produced several printed pages. He looked at me. "Last month, you and Chris discovered Jake planned to sell you to Mary Weston. Correct?"

His cool demeanor surprised me, but then again, he was a prosecutor. And he'd experienced the aftermath of the Lancaster killings as a shamed family member. His skin had to be thick as a dragon's. "Yes. I have a computer specialist who helps me with business. She searched in depth to find a physical location to the email address but couldn't. I... took a vacation."

"I don't blame you," Hale said. "Chris apparently didn't have the patience. He emailed the account three days after you discovered it."

The pinging turned into a loud crash. My head throbbed. "What?"

"She didn't respond immediately, and he continued to contact her." Hale placed two printed sheets in front of me. Todd leaned closer to read over my shoulder.

The first message, sent three days after I'd killed Jake and Riley, just as ADA Hale said.

My name is Christopher Alan Hale, born Christopher Alan Weston. You contacted the Candy Market specifically wanting them to locate and deliver Lucy Kendall to you. I know you are Mary Weston, and I know you are my mother. Let's talk.

The second email, sent two days later, reeked of Chris's trademark impatience. I bit my lip, overwhelmed with the stark realization that he was out there somewhere, hurt and terrified, while I sat here trying to unravel the puzzle he'd screwed up.

Mom. Can I still call you that? Mommy certainly doesn't fit. I know what you're doing. I have questions. If you don't respond, I'm going to the police.

More messages in the same vein—threatening, nagging, cajoling. It wasn't until the fourth, when Chris said he just wanted to know about his family and her background, about why she'd done the things she had, that he received a response.

Why do you care?

"'Because I need to know.'" I read the words out loud in the hopes they might make sense. "'Not just why you did the terrible things you did, but why my father took the blame for you. Why you allowed that to happen to your son. Why you ruined Justin's life. Why are you such a monster?'"

More messages like that, with Chris taking a pleading tone. Desperate. He unraveled in words as vividly as if I'd been sitting beside him and watching it all happen.

"Why in the hell didn't he contact the police as soon as she responded?" Todd's indignant voice added to the general off-balance feeling of the room. "Someone might have been able to track her down."

"I doubt it." My eyes remained glued to the paper. "She knows how to go deep on the Internet and hide. Impressive, actually. Some of her generation still fumbles with technology."

"He should have called the police." Todd looked at Hale,

who'd sat with his head down, listening to the exchange. "Why do you think he didn't tell someone?"

The assistant district attorney finally looked up, weary. "He wants answers she can't give. Or won't give. He always has." He rubbed his temples. "I thought maybe, after all this time, he'd made some kind of peace with it, but finding out about Justin just brought everything back."

"He was only five when he found Jenna Richardson. He had the chance to start over." Todd either couldn't or wouldn't hide the bitterness. "Did you get him therapy?"

"Of course," Hale said. "He spent two years with a counselor, and then, after... an unfortunate event at school, we were forced to move to another part of the city. Give him another fresh start."

"What happened at school?" Todd asked.

"Some kid found out about Chris's parents, and Chris beat the kid up pretty badly." I answered without looking up. The tone of Chris's emails still mesmerized me. His desperation made me feel strange, like I was standing outside myself, watching.

Hale's silence caught my attention, and I finally raised my eyes to meet his. A chill shuddered through my already cold hands. The assistant district attorney's eyes bored into mine, and I struggled to maintain eye contact.

"He told you about that?"

I managed to nod. "After a bad shift a few months ago. It reminded him of what he'd done."

"I see." Hale continued to stare, and irritation prickled through me. Why did he care that Chris had told me?

"What happened to the kid?"

Hale finally shifted his attention back to Todd. "He moved on as well."

"Were you guys sued?" Todd asked.

"We settled."

I listened to the verbal volley with nagging interest, as if I knew I'd forgotten something but whatever it was clung stubbornly to the dark areas of my brain. My attention was still diverted by Mary's words, the simplicity of the web she spun, sucking Chris in bit by bit.

You don't need to know these things. They'll do you no good.

I'm no one in your life, I've got nothing to say. And if I did, you wouldn't believe me anyway.

Why upset your perfect world now? Aren't you happy with the life you were given?

What could I possibly offer you?

"After we moved," Hale continued, "we enrolled him in a summer camp for kids who've experienced traumatic experiences and needed help channeling their feelings, namely anger. It worked quite well."

My once cold skin suddenly felt flushed and clammy beneath my sweater, and the nagging feeling became a full-fledged rash of panic. "What was the name of the camp?"

"Camp Hopeful, on Blackwood Lake." Hale tried to smile. "He spent three summers there. I think he was twelve when he last attended. The place did wonders for him. He donates to them every year, and he even volunteered as a counselor during college."

I pretended to listen, but my thoughts were scrambled. This simply could not be.

But it very clearly was. And Chris's original interest in me made a lot more sense.

I'd gone to Camp Hopeful the summer I was fifteen. Chris would have been around the same age. I didn't remember him, but that meant nothing. I was an angry teenager just waiting for the hot summer days to fade into fall so I could go back to school and hide.

I tried to grab on to some kind of logical explanation, but all I could think of was the way Chris had popped into my life last year. His eventual explanation—that he'd heard my name from his uncle and followed the Justin Beckett trial and subsequent parole—seemed plausible enough, especially after he'd admitted who his parents were. He'd been afraid of where he'd come from, and believed he might have some sort of genetic blueprint to turn into his parents. He'd thought it was his destiny, and so he'd reached out.

But Camp Hopeful? Was it really possible that our paths had crossed all those years before and neither one of us knew it? I certainly hadn't, but what if Chris had known all along?

Todd jabbed at the paper containing the emails. "I think it's safe to say Chris isn't over his mother's decision to leave him. He's begging her to tell him why she did those things. Not just why she killed but why she chose killing over him."

"He feels abandoned," Hale said. "My wife and I brought him up as though he were our own, but he's never let it go. Now knowing his father is in prison, choosing to remain silent, when he could have had some kind of a life with Chris, for this Mary? Chris can't get past it." His chin sank to his chest, and he stared at the table.

"He wants to meet her as an adult," I said. "Because he doesn't understand how she could have fooled so many people and manipulated them." I looked back at the emails with a sickening feeling. "But he's being manipulated during these communications. Her responses are deliberately making him more agitated. She wanted him to beg."

"Of course she did," Hale said. "That bitch is a sadist."

"How well did you know her?" Todd asked. "I don't remember her every being pleasant, but until I got older, I didn't realize how bad she was. Did the rest of your family ever like her?"

Hale sighed. "By then, there wasn't a rest of the family. My parents were killed in a car accident when my brother John—Chris's father—was fifteen. I was twenty and in school. John lived with our grandparents, and I was too selfish to watch over him. I think his finding out the truth after our parents' death is what really shook his confidence. That and living with my grandmother, who resented him."

I tried to focus on what ADA Hale was saying, but I couldn't stop thinking about Camp Hopeful and everything its connection implied.

What else did Chris keep from me?

"What truth?" Todd asked.

"John was adopted," Hale said. "My parents couldn't have any more kids after me, and so they adopted him when he was just a year old. I'm sure they planned to tell us, but they never got around to it. He already felt like the black sheep. Finding this out after their death just solidified it."

That caught my attention. "So John's real parents are named Weston? I thought your wife's maiden name was Hale and you took it to protect Chris's identity."

"That's what we told Chris," Hale said. "John never found his real parents that I know of. But when he married Mary, he took her name. He wanted nothing to do with the Hales."

"Chris doesn't know this." I alternated between anger and pity for Chris. He'd been lied to his entire life. How should he know any better?

"I didn't see the point," Hale said. "He was young and troubled, and we just wanted him to get better. I thought a clean break from all of those people was the best thing."

"Do you think he found out about it?" Todd asked. "There's nothing in the emails that mentions it."

"Not directly." I pointed to one of the final lines of communication from Mary and read it out loud, Mary's grand finale after an effective buildup. "'There is so much about your father and me you were never told. I am not the only person who has wronged you. If I tell you what you want to know, will you allow me to remain free?'"

"And he promised her he would." Todd looked disgusted. "Damn him."

"I don't think he meant it," I said. Truthfully, I didn't know what I believed at this point. Would Chris have killed her if he had the chance? Called the police? Or would he have been pulled into her lies? I needed to find out more about Chris's time at Camp Hopeful. I needed to know if it was all a freakish coincidence. Or something much, much worse.

"Agent Lennox took Chris's computer," Hale said. "His people are working on it, but so far, they aren't finding anything more than these emails. It's clear he tried to find his mother by doing his own search, but nothing beyond that."

"What does Agent Lennox want me to do?" I looked at Todd. "You told him I knew Mary. Like I'm some kind of expert on her."

"You are as much as anyone," Todd said. "We both know it. You're a resource. Lennox hasn't given me specifics, but he agreed he wanted to keep you close."

Hale nodded. "I'd like you to help as well. You care for Chris—I know the two of you are close. And you get things done. You can help."

I didn't know how I was supposed to do that, especially with my head spinning out of control. I stood up, my legs wobbling so that I had to grab Todd's shoulder for support. "I need to go to the bathroom."

I hadn't done that in hours, I realized as I found my way to the women's restroom. I hadn't drunk much either, giving me a pounding headache. I splashed water on my face and tried to think through the mass of shock. None of this made any sense. If Chris had lied to me all this time, what else had he lied about? Or was he still really just a victim? I thought of the pool of blood in the snow and in the cabin's pitiful sink.

Chris had been shot. And kidnapped. He'd been a fool, led by desperation and emotion.

His uncle said Chris felt abandoned. What if he'd found out the truth about his father? How would he react if he knew his aunt and uncle—the people he believed in—had lied to him as well?

He'd do something really stupid, like contact his mother.

I dropped my forehead against the mirror. Somehow, I needed to find out if Chris and I had been at camp at the same time. Until then, I wouldn't be able to focus.

ELEVEN

When I returned to the conference room, Lennox had arrived, bringing with him the vague scent of cold and snow. He'd shed his coat to reveal a well-fitted, basic black suit, matched with a purple shirt and lilac tie that somehow made him look even more masculine. Just as he'd done at the cabin, he captivated everyone's attention simply by walking into the room. He nodded at me, a knowing expression in his dark eyes. "Have a seat. I'm going to brief everyone, and then I'll let you get some rest."

"I'm not sure where we'll do that." Todd's embarrassment stood out in stark contrast to Lennox sweltering aura of confidence. "We didn't look for rooms."

"We took care of it," Hale said. "I booked us all four rooms at the motel down the street."

"Thank you." I appreciated the chance to lock myself away from everyone, but I wouldn't be able to sleep until I had answers.

Still standing, Lennox cleared his throat. "The state police have put as much manpower as possible working roadblocks and patrolling the major highways. The deputies are going door to door in Jarrettsville and the outlying homes. We're in contact with the state police of the surrounding states. We have no idea what kind of vehicle Mary is in, but I've sent out photos of her and Chris to every law enforcement agency in a two-hundred-mile radius."

"They could be anywhere at this point," Todd said. "Did you find anything in the cabin that gives us a starting point?"

Still standing, Lennox shook his head. "Chris is injured. The medical examiner took a look at the original blood found. She thinks he's lost enough to slow him down, but at the time he left the cabin, not enough to be fatal." He glanced at me, and I forced myself not to flinch under his observation. He continued, "We didn't find any more blood using the luminol, which means there wasn't a big puddle cleaned up. We're checking hospitals and clinics. We're still searching the cabin for anything she might have left behind that gives us a lead as to where she'd go next."

"She wouldn't do that," I said. "She's too smart."

"But she left in a hurry," Lennox said. "There were dishes in the sink, fresh food in the fridge. She'd very recently burned incense—it was still burning when Deputy Frost found the cabin. So we're hopeful she's not too far ahead."

"Why did she leave in a hurry?" I asked. I really wanted to point out that Deputy Frost had given Mary plenty of time to get her act together, and if the stubborn officer had involved the state police right away, the roadblocks might have had a chance to work. But it didn't matter at this point.

"Because of you," both Todd and Lennox said. Lennox nodded to Todd. "Go ahead."

"Chris probably told her that you knew where he'd gone, thinking he'd rattle her," Todd said. "He knows you've been analyzing the Lancaster cases, trying to get Justin's record expunged. He uses whatever he can to shake her, but she's not easily rattled. She knows she's got to pack up and leave quickly."

"She didn't pack everything," Lennox said. "A few clothes were left in the bottom dresser. We'll check them for DNA. Since Justin Beckett's is in the system, we can get a matriarchal match. That'll take a while, though."

"In the meantime, we wait." Waiting made me feel like tiny creatures were crawling on my skin, making it itch and ripple.

Lennox's sharp eyes trained on me. "I know that's not your forte. And I'd like to hear your thoughts on Mary's state of mind. You've seen the emails?"

"Yes." How the hell was I supposed to know her state of mind? The itching turned to agitation, as if the rash had spread to my insides. How much had Todd told Lennox? I didn't think he'd betray me and share his theories with someone like Lennox, but what did I know? Lennox's demeanor, his watching me, as though waiting for me to do something crazy or dangerous, made me want to get up and do exactly that.

"What do you think?" He leaned against the wall, crossing his arms and then his ankles, smiling as if we were talking about the weather instead of a killer. But more than that, he looked through me, straight into my well of secrets. I swore I could see all the bad things I'd done reflected in his eyes.

Maybe I'd gone mad after all.

"She's getting off on his desperation to know the truth." I tried to keep my voice steady. "She's a control freak who's feasted on creating pain and havoc for most of her life. What did your brother see in her?" I threw the spotlight back to the assistant district attorney, who'd been watching the exchange in silence.

Hale shrugged. "You know, she wasn't an unattractive woman when they met. Her features were... fine. Extreme, maybe, but she stood out. I could understand his noticing her, but beyond that..." Hale shook his head. "Talking to her was a different story. It felt like shouting into a void that only sent back your echoes."

"What do you mean?" Lennox asked. "She didn't talk? Wasn't interested in being friendly?"

"Not so much that," Hale said. "She just seemed sponge-ish. A mirror. That's better. She reflected back whatever she thought you wanted to see, but never had any depth. It was all a careful act. Does that make sense?"

Lennox's head bobbed up and down; Todd murmured his agreement. I tried not to get sick. I'd thought the same thing of myself when I'd gone undercover in various cases, especially with Preacher. And I'd been proud of it.

"Anyway," Hale continued. "John met her at a time when he was vulnerable—March of 1978. He was nineteen and still bitter about finding out he was adopted. He was practically a transient, working for the Maryland State Highway Associa-tion. They met somewhere on the road and got married six months later."

"How old was she?" I asked.

"Twenty-four, I think." Hale's face twisted as if he'd bit into something sour. "He was enamored with her because she was older and had all this experience. And I've always believed she played a part in dropping his surname and taking hers. It's control."

More than control. Manipulation at its finest. I shuddered, crossing my arms over my chest as though it would make a difference. Understanding Mary made me feel like I'd just put on a pair of dirty underwear.

"Did she drive a truck too?" Lennox asked.

Hale raised his shoulders. "He said she worked for her father. That's all I knew."

"She obviously lied to them about her surname being West-on," Lennox said. "We checked back through the seventies.

There's a handful of Mary Westons in the tri-state area, and they're all decent people living their lives."

"John and I didn't speak much by then." Hale's eyes clouded with regret. "I was too busy with my own life, and he was so bitter. I never found out anything about her family. I don't even know if she shared it with him."

"I assume since ADA Hale notified you of Chris's disappearance that you've been working Mary's case since we found out the truth about her last fall?" I asked Lennox. "You've found nothing beyond the Weston alias? She didn't just spring up out of nowhere."

"You assume correctly," Lennox said. "I'd hoped she had a Social Security number, but it wasn't required for kids to be listed on a tax return until the late eighties. Before that, most people were around fourteen when they applied for the number. There's no record of Mary Weston doing so. Martha Beckett did, however, shortly after she married your father." Lennox glanced at Todd, whose jaw looked tight enough to break. "Because of her age, no one questioned why she didn't have one. And until then, she'd never filed for taxes."

"Another dead end," I said.

"Checking every Mary Weston who matches her rough age takes a while, even with the FBI's resources, and none of them have panned out," Lennox continued. "As far as we know, only two people know anything about her: Mary and John Weston. And he absolutely refuses to talk."

That much I knew. Chris's uncle had told him a few months ago his father had been visited by the FBI several times since we'd uncovered the truth about Mary, and he hadn't said a word. His loyalty was admirable, but bothersome. Most people didn't keep their mouths shut unless they were afraid or they were getting something out of it. Since I didn't see how spending his life in a supermax prison was much of a gift, I'd bet on the former.

"What about now?" I said. "His son is in danger. Couldn't you appeal to him?"

Hale scoffed. "I called the prison on the way down here. He refused to take my call. I had the warden pass on the message, but so far we haven't heard a damn thing. He's loyal to her. So damned brainwashed. He chose Mary over his son a long time ago."

Everyone else at the table looked shocked and confused at the idea, but it made sense to me, and my skin started to quiver all over again. My own mother had essentially done the same thing to my sister. Some people were so wrapped up in their own needs they didn't care. And I didn't believe everyone had some kind of natural parental instinct.

I looked at the picture of Mary that Lennox had laid on the table. It was taken years ago, likely when the Lancaster killings were first discovered. Despite her height and sturdy girth, she managed to look equal parts shocked and vulnerable. And she looked very different than she had when I met her. By then the softness in her face was gone, replaced by rigidity that only heightened her coldness.

Cold to the core, a psychopath at her very best. Able to manipulate whomever she wanted at whim.

Just like you. All those dirty men you killed. The Harrison brothers. Preacher. You got them exactly where you wanted them, and then you struck.

"What about your father?" I directed my question to Todd. "What has he told you about Mary when they were married? What do you remember?"

Todd scowled. "I haven't talked to him in years. He's a drunk in and out of jail. At the time, I never knew what he saw in her, because she had zero feminine qualities." He looked down at the table. "My dad said she'd been in some kind of car accident, which affected the nerves in her face and her arms. He said that's why she was so... robotic looking. But maybe it was like you said." He looked at Hale. "Because she was pretending."

"I'd forgotten about the car accident," I said. "Maybe that's why she didn't kill when they were married. She wasn't able to."

"She went through physical therapy," Todd said. "I remember that, and by the time I was older, she seemed pretty much recovered. There were certain things she stumbled over, like cooking, but I always figured that's because she hated to do it."

"Sounds familiar," ADA Hale said. "Although, I wouldn't go so far as to say she didn't have any femininity when she was younger. It was just more restrained. Everything about her was wound quite tightly."

Todd nodded. "After my brother went into the system, my father and Mary divorced. She basically abandoned Justin, and within a couple of years, my father did as well. I was the only person the kid had. And to answer your question, my father never told me what he saw in her. For all I know she had him doing despicable things too. Maybe that's what started his drinking. He barely touched the stuff before her."

"Your father's name is Josh Beckett, right? He married Mary when you were about six?" Agent Lennox scribbled in his notebook.

"Yeah, but I wasn't around all that much, thank God. I lived with my mother, so I didn't really spend much time with them until Justin was a toddler, and that's because I wanted to look out for him. Even then I could tell she was off. I just thought she hated him." He clenched his jaw, his voice shaky.

So many people screwed up in Mary's wake. Todd harbored the same sort of guilt over his brother as I did over Lily. Compassion thickened my throat, and I suddenly wanted to reach out and take his hand, to somehow tell him that I understood and it wasn't his fault. But I couldn't make myself move.

"Do you remember her last name—the one she used when she met your father?" Lennox asked.

"No clue. He only referred to her as Mary, and then next thing I knew, they were married. Like I said, I didn't see them a lot, and my mother hated her. Him too, for that matter." Todd glared at the table, caught in his memories.

"Makes sense," Lennox said. "Your father still living in Philly?"

"As far as I know."

"I'll have the office do some digging, see if we can find him and get some information. Maybe she told him something we can use."

"Good luck," Todd said. "We tried that as soon as we made the connection between Mary Weston and Martha Beckett. I stayed away, but my superiors got nothing out of him. Mary's got a way of rendering her men mute. Somehow, she wins their loyalty despite the terrible things she does." His gaze listed to me.

I looked away. "She's going to mess with Chris's head. She'll probably tell him everything he wants to know, maybe even let him think they're bonding. Before I read those emails, I would have said she wouldn't fool him. But now, I don't know. ADA Hale, do you know anything more about Chris's emotional state? What do you think he'll do?"

Hale's shoulders drooped in the chair, his chin sagging. His body no longer looked robust and healthy but utterly worn out. "The hardest part for Chris, I think, is that not all of his memories of his mother are bad. She was strict with him, but kids see things differently. He remembers her making cookies and letting him lick the spoon. Or reading a story. These things stick out to him every bit as much as the things he saw in the barn, and he has trouble meshing the two into one person."

"And she'll sense that," I said. All eyes in the room turned to me—my turn in the spotlight of this very lousy play. "We know she's extremely smart, and she's got to be good at reading people. If she weren't, she would have been caught a long time ago. She'll figure this out about Chris—if she hasn't already—and then she'll kill him." I hated saying the words because I couldn't take them back and because I knew I was right. My vacillating anger for Chris ebbed once more and was again replaced by fear. How badly would she make him suffer?

"Not if we find him first." Lennox's hard voice made it clear he took my words as a personal insult and challenge. Good. Maybe he'd do a better job finding her than he had in the past few months.

"I'm sorry I don't have a lot of hope for that."

He shrugged, still relaxed, but his eyes smoldered. "Tell me what you would do."

"I'm not a cop. Or an FBI agent. Why do you keep asking me?"

"I know about the things you've done," Lennox said. "Your tenacity and capabilities. I'd like your opinion."

The underlying layer of accusation in his quiet, almost melodic voice sent a fresh wave of apprehension through me. Exactly to what things was he referring?

"Go back to the past," I said. "Find out who she is. I think that's our best shot at figuring out where she's taken him."

"Why?" Todd said.

"Because that's what he wants," I said. "He wants to know where he came from and why she did those things. And she enjoys manipulating and mind games. What better way to make him feel like he's winning than to take him back to her beginnings?"

"The house in Lancaster burned down," Todd said. "You saw it."

"I'm not talking about Lancaster. I don't think those were her first kills. Not with the way she framed John Weston. Her backup plan was too good to be from an amateur. She's done this before, and not in Pennsylvania."

"Agreed." Lennox looked impressed. "I've got techs coming in from the Maryland field office in the morning. ViCAP only goes back to 1985, so it's not going to be much help. I'll have them search the various police records back to 1972, which puts Mary at eighteen if ADA Hale's right about her age. But it's going to be tough, because we don't know if she limited her movement to Maryland and Pennsylvania."

"Crimes going that far back can be hit or miss too," Todd said. "Although if it were as violent as the one we saw tonight, I'd think it would stand out."

"John and Mary met in Maryland?" I asked ADA Hale. "Do you know where?"

"He never told me. I'm assuming it was Maryland because he worked for the highway department at the time."

Lennox scribbled it down. "I've got my people checking with the department, trying to find his address at the time of employment with them, but Maryland's state records before everything was digitized are sketchy." He turned to me. "I'd like you to work with my techs tomorrow going through the information. They're damned good at what they do, spotting patterns and whatnot, but some of this is going to be old school. And you're familiar with Mary. You might see something they don't." He glanced at Todd. "You're welcome to stay as well."

"I can take a couple of days," Todd said. "I'd like to help."

I watched Lennox, waiting for the other shoe to drop. He had something more to say to me. Finally, he smiled, revealing a row of white teeth. "Give your hacker a call as well. She might be able to find something my people can't."

TWELVE

While Lennox left to join the door-to-door canvass, the rest of our exhausted group went to the motel. My body felt like I'd gone a few rounds with an MMA fighter. My muscles groaned in agony, and I suspected dehydration was the culprit. I needed to drink some water and try to clear my head. Figure out what to do about this new information on Chris.

The small standard motel lobby smelled like incense, sending my stomach into knots. Todd wiped his nose, and ADA Hale coughed. It didn't matter the scent was a warm vanilla and drastically different from the stick left burning in the cabin. It still had the same smoky thickness that clung to my throat, and it still induced the same shivering sense of dread.

"Thank you for paying for my room," I said to the attorney as we followed him down the narrow, dimly lit hallway on the first floor. "Please let me reimburse you."

"Nonsense," Hale said. "I covered tonight, and you can take care of the rest. How's that?"

Todd and I agreed, although I wasn't sure how much longer I'd remain in Maryland.

Hale stopped in front of room 109 and then turned to us

with bloodshot eyes. His hunched shoulders betrayed his exhaustion and worry. "Thank you both for everything. I'll see you in the morning."

I nodded, unsure of what to say. If I'd answered my phone, none of this would be happening.

Todd and I reached my room first. He hovered at my shoulder, making me feel claustrophobic in the already small space. "What?"

"Something about all of this isn't sitting right with me," he said.

"Just one thing?" I tried to laugh, but it sounded more like choking.

"Chris lied to you about how much he'd communicated with his mother."

It hadn't taken him very long to jump on that bandwagon. "Technically, he didn't. He's not required to give me any information. I never asked him, did I?"

Todd hesitated, his teeth digging into his bottom chapped lip. "You planned to go after her, didn't you? Take care of her yourself?"

My last thread of patience snapped. "I don't know why you'd think that, and I'm getting tired of hearing it."

"Because that's what you do."

"We've had this discussion. I'm too tired to have it again." I couldn't continue to look Todd in the eyes and lie, either. Each time made me feel like I'd sunk a little lower into the grime of the earth.

"Chris was going to help you?" Todd didn't seem to care about my frustration. He had to be worn thin too. Sometimes it was easier to harp on the thing you couldn't control than the few things you could. He'd probably latched on to my involvement with Chris in order to keep his thoughts away from his former stepmother and all the trouble she'd caused in his life.

"Has he helped you before? Is that why he'd think he could handle her himself?"

"Again, you're creating scenarios in your head." I just wanted to be left alone and sink into my own head, dark as it was. I needed to figure out my next move before tomorrow morning. "You read the emails. It's pretty obvious Chris was in a bad place and got sucked in by her."

"He came to kill her, didn't he?"

"Stop." I didn't try to be nice this time. "I've told you everything I know. I shared the voicemails with you. If my computer specialist actually found anything that pointed to Mary's location, I would have shared it with you. In case you haven't noticed, I've spent the last month holed up in my apartment feeling sorry for myself."

"Why? So you killed a man." He said it without any doubt in his tone, baiting me. "It's nothing you haven't done before."

I turned and jammed my keycard into the metal slot. "I'm done with this conversation. Thanks for driving me here and for your help today." I opened the door and then faced Todd again. He hadn't moved, his tall frame taut with tension. "And for letting Lennox in on your wild theory of me. That's really something I need."

"That's not just me, Lucy. You don't think rumors have gone around since Kailey's case and Brian Harrison's body?"

"Rumors you started." I clung to the door handle, dizzy. How far had these rumors gone?

"They took on a life of their own real quick," Todd said. "And then you're after this sex trafficking ring and wind up killing the big dog. And Preacher's still missing, although I've got a feeling the body in the Allegheny Forest is going to be his. The description matches." He let that sit, and I wanted to lunge at him, claw his throat. But I didn't dare let go of the door. My legs weren't strong enough to hold me.

Todd kept going, his voice starting to remind me of the fly

that gets trapped in the house in the fall and just won't freaking die. "The FBI is all over the trafficking ring. You don't think the rumors about you are going to travel?"

"No thanks to you."

Todd bristled, pointing his finger at me. His hand was chapped from the wind. "Thanks to me, Lennox is trusting you. I told him you could handle yourself in this case, that you would be an asset to figuring out Mary's mindset. And I promised him you'd do what he told you to do and not take off and start your own investigation. I stood up for you, despite everything my gut tells me."

He moved forward as he spoke, closing the space between us. An aura of anger surrounded him, his intense eyes loaded with emotion I didn't want to process.

"Thanks for sticking up for me." I stepped into the dark hotel room and turned on the light. Standard double bed, nightstand, and dresser. Flatscreen television I wouldn't use. Bathroom to the right. "I'm exhausted. So are you. Let's just get some sleep and start fresh in the morning. I don't want to fight with you."

"Yeah, whatever." He stepped back, the red in his cheeks fading. "Justin texted me earlier. The cat ate, and he stayed to pet him for a while. He'll stop back in the morning."

"I'll check in with him and see if he can stop by the next few days," I said. "Sounds like we won't be home soon."

Todd shrugged and headed down the hall, resigned to leave me be—at least until he couldn't stand it any longer and had to dig in yet again. I closed the door, the click of the deadbolt sounding like bliss. I tossed my bag on the bed and debated doing the same with my worn-out self, but I had things to take care of. A bottle of lukewarm water sat on the dresser next to the complimentary plastic cups. I unscrewed the cap and chugged the liquid until my stomach hurt.

Camp Hopeful.

How the hell could I find out if Chris and I crossed paths when I couldn't ask him?

That summer at the camp had been one of the most irritating of my life. I didn't want the anger classes, didn't want to talk about my grief or my mother or my choice to act out by having sex with boys and drinking. I wanted to rankle the counselors, get them mad enough to throw me out. So every activity, every group meeting, I acted like a jerk.

They never lost their patience, and I hated them for it. It wasn't until several years later in college, when I finally admitted my anger and actions were tied up with my guilt over being angry with my sister, that I appreciated the lessons the camp tried to teach.

But that summer, I didn't want to make friends. I couldn't remember bonding with anyone.

I'd remember Chris Hale.

But what if he'd known me? Watched me from afar? It was definitely possible.

So what? He could have forgotten all about it and then put two and two together when he heard about my connection to Justin Beckett's parole hearing. His story could still be true.

But then why wouldn't he have told me?

I refilled the water bottle at the bathroom sink. My reflection was dreadful. Face white enough the freckles over my nose looked more like small moles. Smudges under my eyes, limp hair, chapped lips. Chapped cheeks.

My eyes were cloudy and still, like my reflection wasn't real. Or off, somehow. The person in the mirror wasn't really me, just what my mind thought I should see.

I swayed at the thought and then grabbed the sample of hand lotion off the sink, tore open the packet, and smeared some onto my cheeks. The tender skin stung, but it was better than nothing.

Still sucking down water, I paced the small room. I needed

to find out if Chris had remembered me from camp. Every bit of instinct I possessed demanded it, and I would be useless to the investigation until I had my answer.

On impulse, I grabbed the receiver, ignoring the thin film of other people's germs on it, and dialed ADA Hale's room.

He answered quickly. "Yes?"

"Mr. Hale, it's Lucy."

"Have you heard from Chris?" His words quickened. "Did something happen?"

Guilt swept over me. "No, I'm sorry. I just had a question."

"Go ahead."

"This is going to sound strange, but Camp Hopeful. I've... heard of it. So I'm familiar with what they do." I twisted the cord around my finger, trying to sound as nonchalant as possible. "And I was thinking, even if it's a long shot, does Chris still talk to anyone from the camp? Is there someone he might confide in that we could reach out to? Someone who might know something we don't?"

"I'm honestly not sure," Hale said. "But the FBI has his computer and now his phone, so I'm sure they'll find out if that's true."

"Good point." I hadn't thought of that. "Still, I just wish I could do something now. I thought you might have a name, someone we could talk to."

"As far as I know, he hasn't visited the camp in a while. He's so busy with work he doesn't have as much time to volunteer like he used to. But he donates because the place is so important to him." Pride reverberated in his voice.

"It helped him."

"Oh yes," Hale said. "He came home changed that summer, really able to process things so much better. And he still goes back to the techniques he learned there. I think that's why he keeps the memory box."

I sat up straight. Finally, something that might help. "Memory box?"

"That's what he calls it. It's all the literature he got that summer, plus journals he kept. We haven't discussed this in a long time, but I know he used to revisit those things when he was having a down spell."

"Down spell. Like depression?" Chris had never mentioned this to me, but I wasn't surprised. He was so intense and internalized so much, combined with all the guilt he carried over the girls in the barn and the abandonment by his mother, he had to have trouble coping at times.

"I suppose. He used to take medication for that and anxiety, but he's worked hard to come to terms with everything that happened and what he did. I thought he had but now…"

"What he did," I repeated. "You mean the fight with the kid at school?"

"Yes." Hale's answer was short. "Of course."

I suddenly felt guilty. Frank Hale was worried about the nephew he'd raised as a son, and I was asking questions for my sole benefit. "I'm sorry about all of this, sir. If Chris hadn't met me, none of this would have happened."

"Don't be sorry. You still would have found Kailey, and we'd still know the truth about Mary. She'd be in the news. We'd have found out about Justin and what she did." He cleared his throat. "I think that's what he can't get past. That she went on and had another child, but she left Chris."

"She treated Justin much worse." At least Chris had a second chance at a normal life. He didn't spend his childhood in a juvenile facility, serving time for a murder he hadn't committed. Compared to Justin, the anger Chris carried about life seemed a little ridiculous. But everyone processed differently, and I certainly had no room to judge.

"But she still gave birth to him," ADA Hale said. "Chris feels abandoned. And guilty because he's always thought he should have remembered more about what happened in Lancaster. That he should have known his mother was involved all along."

"He was a kid," I said. "She was the authority figure. It probably wouldn't have made any difference."

"That's what I've told him. But as I'm sure you know, he doesn't always listen."

I tried to laugh, but it caught in my throat. My mind kept going back to the memory box.

"I've got to check in with my wife," Hale said. "Is there anything else?"

Chris's aunt. A prominent pediatrician. Is that why she wasn't here? He never spoke about her as much as he did his uncle.

"Of course. Goodnight."

I hung up the phone, a second wave of guilt rising. Todd was going to be awfully disappointed in me tomorrow morning.

THIRTEEN

The next morning, after a few measly hours of sleep, sheer luck helped me sneak out of the hotel and into the waiting cab without Todd or Hale seeing me. The rental car place didn't open until seven, and I spent thirty long, freezing minutes outside its doors, waiting in fear Todd would show up at any moment. I hadn't left any sort of message, and I'd booked my room for one more night. I hoped if he discovered I wasn't in the motel, he'd assume I'd gone for a walk or to breakfast.

By the time I was well out of town in my rental, my phone had started to ring, with Todd's number popping up on the screen. I couldn't put him off any longer.

"Where are you?" His harsh tone left little hope of smoothing things over.

"I needed to head back to the city," I said. "I'll be back in Jarrettsville by this evening."

"What for?"

I slipped into the left lane to pass a meandering wind-up car. "Personal reasons."

"Personal like what? Something you shouldn't be doing?"

"Personal like none of your business," I snapped. "Tell

Lennox and ADA Hale I had a family emergency, but I'll be back."

"Lennox is going to love that. He specifically told you—"

"Not to do my own investigation," I said. "I'm not. This has nothing to do with Chris's disappearance." At least it wasn't a lie.

Todd's silence lasted long enough I thought he'd hung up on me. "Lucy, I swear to God, if you're screwing me over on this, I'm done."

"I'm not." I ended the call and focused on the drive.

Not soon enough, the city's skyline emerged. Tall and foreboding in the gray light of winter, the Comcast Center and the Liberty Place buildings gave the skyline a more modern feel, while Three Logan Square reminded travelers of Philadelphia's rich history. That building had changed names more than once, and I much preferred the name Bell Atlantic Tower—its historical ring fit the city a lot better and made me think of a time when we still used phone books and the cordless phone was an astounding modern convenience—as if the steel-and-girders skyline warned me to turn back and let the past remain hidden. *I've never been very good at that.* Besides, every person on this earth is a product of a past. They might tell themselves it's a forgotten thing, but that's not really true. Even if their previous experiences don't drive their everyday existence, those moments shape the people they have become. So the past never disappears.

Some of us are better at acknowledging it than others.

The outskirts of the city gradually metamorphosed from small neighborhoods with struggling local businesses to middleclass suburbs protected from the highway noise by great brown sound barriers, to the grittier part of the city along the Schuylkill River. Instead of staying on the interstate, I took Grays Ferry Avenue into the deeper part of the city, skirting the Devil's Pocket area. I liked the name and the old row houses intermixed with the industrialized landscape of the river. My grandfather had grown up there, and he used to talk about the Pocket as if it really were Satan's backyard. The name allegedly came from a local priest who said the neighborhood kids were such hoods they'd steal a chain out of the devil's pocket. I didn't know if the story was true or not, but I loved the analogy. Stealing from the devil took a lot of guts.

By the time I squeezed my small rental into a parking spot in Center City, my stomach felt like I'd eaten a pound of greasy bacon. The tall buildings blocked much of the wind that had given my car the wicked shimmies for most of the ride, but I still tucked my head to my chin and braced myself as if I'd walked into the heart of the weather.

Inside Chris's modern and clean building, I punched in the code he'd given me and then entered the elevator without anyone giving me a second glance. Too soon, the bell dinged, and I crossed the threshold to his floor. Sturdy carpet muted my footsteps as I made my way to his corner apartment. The roots of my hair itched; my skin felt damp against my scarf. My spare key shook in my hand as I unlocked the door.

It swung open, and I realized I'd stopped breathing. What had I expected? To find Chris asleep on the couch with a bandaged flesh wound on his arm and a guilty smile?

Silence pressed against me as I shut the door. His pristine, minimal decor seemed even colder than it had when I'd visited before. His counters gleamed as dark as a wet blacktop on a hot summer's day, his stainless-steel kitchen clean enough to eat off any surface. Nothing in the garbage can, no lingering scent of cooking or cleaning or takeout food. Just vacant.

I wound my way through the living room and into the bath-room to find the same results. The guest bathroom was clean and cold, the toilet paper stocked and the modern, raised circular sink dry.

The bedroom waited, and I hesitated near the door, my feet shuffling against the dark wood floors. I didn't doubt my decision to search for the memory box. But the dread of the answers I might find made me feel like lead weight sinking to the bottom of the river.

I yanked the edges of my scarf, unwinding the warm material from around my neck, and stuffed it into my pocket. Then I threaded my hair into a quick ponytail. Unbuttoned my warm coat, folded it over my arm. I slung my bag over my shoulder, gripping the leather strap so tightly my hand stung.

Finally I pushed the door open. My throat swelled up at the faint whisper of Chris's cologne. I ignored it and took stock of the room. Plush, beige carpet offset the masculine black and silver comforter, and the espresso furniture was a nice, if not impersonal, touch.

I deposited my stuff on the edge of the bed and forced myself to check the master bathroom. For what, I still wasn't sure.

It hadn't been used recently, either.

His shower essentials still sat in their places; I assumed he'd taken travel-sized items. His toothbrush wasn't in the holder on the sink.

Impulsively, and uncertain of what I was looking for, I checked the medicine cabinet.

Antipsychotics? Antidepressants? A medication that treats pathological liars?

I found nothing but some basic over-the-counter cold medicine, vitamins, and men's grooming items that looked far more complicated than anything I'd ever owned.

I couldn't put off the inevitable any longer. Chris's large, walk-in closet loomed before me. The doors softly popped when I pulled them open, revealing the sort of organization I'd come to expect from him. Dress clothes on the right, dress shoes lined up beneath. Work and casual on the left, shoes lined up beneath. The back of the closet held several storage shelves, and I focused on them. Chris owned several watches. Most of them probably cost half a month's rent for me. Another compartment for what looked like financial papers. Those should have been in a safe, but whatever. Hats and gloves and scarves compulsively arranged on a single shelf.

A narrow drawer held something that sent a wave of confusion and then pulsating anger through me. I stared at the generic plastic bag, trying to reconcile what I saw with what I knew.

These were the sort of bags issued by prisons and used to house an inmate's personal effects. Inmates didn't get them back until they'd been released.

I didn't need to open these to see they belonged to John Weston. His driver's license mocked me beneath the plastic, along with a gold ring, a tarnished chain, and a picture of a woman who had to be Mary.

With cold fingers, I slipped the Polaroid out of the bag. It was curved and wrinkled, as if it had been carried around in a butt pocket for too long.

Mary.

She was much younger than in any picture I'd seen of her. Tall and domineering, yes, but also attractive. Black hair down past her shoulders, hips cocked in a way that suggested both command and awareness of her power. Her smile wasn't as much of a smile as an acknowledgment, as if her allowing the picture to be taken was pleasant enough.

Blocky handwriting on the bottom read " 1980."

This had been taken before Chris was born. A quick search of the bag revealed nothing else. At the time of his arrest, John Weston had no pictures of his son. Only one of Mary, the woman who'd been his doom.

How had Chris felt about all of this?

And when had he seen his father? John Weston would have been required to sign a form allowing Chris to take these. He didn't have a chance at parole, so it wasn't unusual. Unless the person who'd been given the items maintained he hadn't seen his father since he was a child.

Just another lie.

But a truth that wasn't owed to me.

One I might be able to forgive if I didn't find anything else. I sensed that wasn't going to be the case.

The memory box was tucked so far back into the closet I almost didn't see it. On hands and knees, I pulled it out from beneath a shelf of sweaters and stared at it. Nothing special. One of those cardboard photo boxes with pretty designs and a high price tag. I traced the scrolls, all sorts of nefarious images racing through my head. The greasy bacon sensation reared its head, and I almost raced for the bathroom.

Instead, I opened the lid.

And then I ran for the toilet.

FOURTEEN

Dry-heaving left my throat raw and my head aching. Sitting back on my heels, I slashed the spittle off my mouth. He'd lied. He'd lied to cover up the lie. How long had he been watching me?

I flushed the toilet and then rinsed out my mouth, making sure to dry up the sink. My body seemed hollow as I went back to the closet, as if I'd become nothing but a worn-out shell.

The box lay open as I'd left it. A picture of me, taken from a distance, in the warm weather—a season I hadn't yet experienced with Chris—gazed up at me. I sank back down onto the thick, cushy carpet and reached inside the box, half-expecting an electric shock to attack me.

Instead I found more pictures of me, all taken during a warmer season. Last summer. I recognized the white sundress I'd purchased in May. Each picture was taken from subterfuge, and usually while I'd been walking down the street. One showed me getting into my car, the next texting on my phone. As if to distract myself from what I was seeing, I thought about how Chris was the only person I knew who still used a digital camera and had the pictures printed out. Most people just used their phones and stored their memories in the cloud.

A particularly grainy shot stood out. Taken at night, as I'd come out of a restaurant on the south side. I'd been tracking Mark Smith, the pedophile with the cocker spaniel. The one Chris told me he first noticed me going after. But that was in August. I'd bought the white dress in May.

But Chris said he came looking for you after Justin made the news, after hearing his uncle talk about your fight to keep Justin in prison. That he'd been worried about his own mental state.

He'd admitted he'd followed me, but I'd never asked when. I'd assumed it had been around the time he'd checked up on Justin, like he'd once said. So that wasn't true.

I could deal with that lie.

The pictures were another story.

The one with the white dress was the oldest I could find. Then I came to the stuff about Camp Hopeful. Brochures from recent years with quotes from Chris about how the camp had helped his anger issues. Copies of letters from kids writing to him during his years as a counselor, thanking him for his help and understanding.

He'd done good things for these kids. That should have softened my ire, but the feeling of waiting for the last shoe to drop, of getting ready to jump off a cliff, kept me from feeling anything other than fear.

Near the bottom of the box were dog-eared printouts. I recognized them as the sort of handouts I'd received during my summer at Camp Hopeful. Printed from a dot matrix printer and loaded with guidelines on how to process your emotions. I hadn't read any of them at the time.

There were four group photos with kids of varying ages in attire that clearly suggested early nineties. My heart rate again accelerated as I thumbed through the 5x7s.

And there it was. I stood in the back row, my shaggy hair

blowing in the wind and my teenaged face blank in defiance. I couldn't pick Chris out of the group until I compared the picture with the others. I found him in the front row, kneeling, a sort-of smile on his face. His round haircut framed his chubby face, and he wore glasses. His hiked-up socks looked too small for his thick calves.

We'd been there together.

But that wasn't the worst part. What really made my head swim and my heart drop to my numb legs was the thing safety-pinned to the picture. An old notebook page, yellow and stiff like some of the other papers, had been ripped out at some point and attached to this picture. As I read the slanted scrawl, each word a thunderclap, I realized why.

Today in my group we talked about bad decisions. Counselor Mackie asked for volunteers to talk about something stupid they'd done, but no one wanted to. I thought about raising my hand, but I didn't want to share either. They might think of me as really bad once they found out the truth, and people liked me here.

So Mackie started asking questions, making everybody tell something. When it got to be my turn, I got all sweaty and stupid and blurted out about lying to my uncle. Like I hadn't done much worse things. But Mackie seemed satisfied.

He asked me why I'd lied. I said I didn't want to get in trouble. Then he started asking about the consequences of getting caught lying. I told him about how I got grounded from the Nintendo for a week and couldn't go to the school bake sale. As if I gave a crap about that. Counselor Mackie wanted to know if the lie had been worth the punishment. Of course it wasn't! I still got in trouble and had to deal with the BS that came with it. Dumb question, if you ask me, but I went along with it.

Then it was her turn. The redhead. Lucy. She never says much, and she looks at all the adults like she wants to kill them. I want to know what's going on inside her head because it's got to be a lot more interesting than most of the other kids' problems. None of them have seen anything like what happened at my house. But when I look at this girl, I think she might have.

She rolled her eyes when Mackie asked the question. Then she told him that everyone lies—even him. Mackie looked pissed, but I wanted to laugh because it was true. He asked her why she thought that, and she said because of self-preservation. I had to think about what that meant because she wouldn't say anything more.

It took me a while, but I think she meant we lie because we care more about what we want to do than what people think we should do. That's what self-preservation means to me. Putting myself first.

I want to ask her, but she ignores everyone. Maybe I'll try again tomorrow.

Crouched down, knees popping, I rocked back and forth. I might throw up again. Or cry. Maybe both.

Counselor Mackie—the hippie with the comb-over and the soft voice. He'd meant well, and he'd irritated me to no end that year. I'd loved messing with his head, which was exactly what I was doing the day Chris wrote about. The day he must have taken notice of me.

And he'd found me all those years later.

Had he been looking? Or had he told the truth about recognizing my name during Justin's parole hearing? Even if he had done so, he started stalking me after that.

I attempted to make an excuse—God knows I wanted to—but my mind flailed.

And the sound of the apartment door opening and then closing proved to be a bit of a distraction.

FIFTEEN

Out of practice.

I couldn't think of anything else as I hunkered on the closet floor, my head whipping back and forth like a broken doll's. The doors were wide open, exposing me to whomever had entered the apartment.

But what if Chris had somehow come home?

Or Mary forced him here?

My bag with the hidden weapons sat on the bed, completely exposed and useless.

A woman coughed. My throat knotted; my fingernails dug into the carpet until I could feel the netting beneath the plush fibers. I listened for more voices, for an injured Chris to speak. But instead I heard only sniffling and footsteps. Then she blew her nose.

Mary certainly wouldn't cry over her son.

Slowly, my clothes feeling as if I'd worn them for a dip in the pool, I slipped out of the closet to position myself between it and the partially open bedroom door. My hair fell into my face as I peered into the living area.

At first I saw only the empty apartment, but footsteps

reminded me she was still there. And then a small woman with stylishly cropped gray hair and hands that looked stricken with arthritis sat down in Chris's favorite chair. Elbows on her knees, she put her head in her hands. A soft mewl escaped her.

Chris's aunt. I'd never met her, but I recognized her from one of the few pictures sitting around his apartment.

At least it wasn't Mary. But I'd snuck into the apartment. Although not really, since I had a key.

I breathed deeply, trying to be quiet, and gathered my thoughts. Working this situation was no problem. My specialty, in fact. Surely I still had it.

I cleared my throat. "Mrs. Hale, I don't want to scare you."

"Good Lord." She jumped up, putting the chair and then the kitchen counter between us. I heard her draw a knife from the block.

"It's Lucy Kendall. Chris's friend." Hands raised, I exited the bedroom.

Mrs. Hale stood in the kitchen, a gleaming and most likely very sharp knife poised to strike. "What are you doing here? Frank said you were in Maryland."

"I was, but I..." What? The thought dried up, and again I felt completely out of my element. What lie could I tell? What possible reason did I have for being here that would pacify her?

"You what?" She lowered the knife, but still kept a tight grip on it.

I wet my lips; our eyes locked. And suddenly I decided I really didn't care about keeping Chris's possible crazy a secret. "Because Frank mentioned Chris had attended Camp Hopeful. I did too, and I was there at the same time. I needed to find out if Chris knew that."

She slid the knife back into its place in the block, the scraping sound pricking my nerves. "I'm sure Christopher knew that. He never does anything by accident."

"He followed me for a while, over the summer," I said. "I found pictures."

She shrugged. "I'm not surprised. He'd heard his uncle talk about your involvement in the Justin Beckett case." Her words sounded hollow, careless. She obviously had more important things to worry about.

"Why would he follow me?"

Walking as if she could barely take another step, she returned to the chair. "You'd have to ask him."

Still wary, I moved to sit on the edge of the couch, my back facing the windows with the view of the city. "Mrs. Hale."

"Elizabeth," she said. "Please." Her head dropped to her hand again, her mouth screwing up like a baby's ready to wail. "I can't believe this is happening."

I hadn't thought about her suffering. She'd raised Chris as her own, knowing he'd likely come with problems. From everything I'd heard, she'd been as good to him as his uncle, never once making him feel unwanted. "You sacrificed so much for him."

"No," she said. "We couldn't have children of our own, and having the chance to raise Chris was a blessing, no matter the baggage that came with it." A shadow crossed her eyes. "That woman. The day I met her, I told Frank I prayed she would never have children. He told me the psychology course I was taking affected my judgment."

"You were still in medical school?"

"First year," she said. "I waited until Frank got a decent job before applying."

"So you've been together for a long time."

"Since we were teenagers," she said. A smile ghosted across her lips. "Poor John. He couldn't take the truth about his adoption, although I never understood why. He wasn't mistreated at all by their parents. But some people are just born with a chip on their shoulder."

"Mary knew he was an easy mark."

Her head jerked up, her eyes meeting mine. "Chris said you were good at reading people. And yes, she did."

"What was she like, in those days?" I wasn't sure I wanted to know.

"Cold. Blank, but yet... present." Elizabeth's hands wrung. "I only met her twice. Her height and stature weren't as intimidating as she liked to think. I could tell she enjoyed being taller and bigger, that it made her feel more in control. At first I thought it was because she was insecure. But then I watched her for a while. Everything was just an act. Like she'd put on some kind of mask that didn't quite fit. I know that doesn't make sense." She echoed her husband's words from last night. She picked at her fingernails, her eyebrows knitted into a thick line. I tasted the guilt in the air. The Hales both thought they should have seen Mary coming, just as Todd did. But no one ever wanted to believe that sort of evil can waltz into their world.

"It makes perfect sense," I said. "She had no interest in you or Frank, and her interest in John came from his vulnerability and her ability to control him."

Elizabeth shifted, her stare uneasy. "Yes, that's it. And for some reason, he was smitten with her. I guess because she played the part well. She relished being the center of his attention, and she didn't like it when he acknowledged me in any way. She barely tolerated his having a conversation with Frank."

"Which is why you prayed she'd never have kids," I said.

"More than that," Elizabeth said. "Can you imagine her with an infant, of her bonding with something that couldn't do anything but love in return? She couldn't do it."

"Is that how it was with Chris?"

Elizabeth again looked down at her ruined hands. "He was three when we first met him. So serious. And so quiet. He didn't climb on her lap or seek attention. Once, I thought he might try. He'd fallen and scraped his knee. I remember him standing there with his chubby leg bleeding and her doing nothing but handing him a towel. She told him to go to the bathroom and clean it." She punched her thighs. "A three-year-old! He wanted to cry, but I could see him fighting it off. Like he knew the tears would make his situation worse. I couldn't stand it. I took him to the bathroom and cleaned him myself." Elizabeth wiped her eyes. "And when I hugged him, he acted as if he didn't know what to do."

Working with CPS, I'd encountered other children like this, mostly due to their parents' drug habits. The little ones were left unattended and half wild. Any sort of mental or physical interaction confused and frightened them. "What did Mary do?"

"Oh, she was furious," Elizabeth said. "I expected her to yell at me over involving myself with matters that didn't concern me, but she said nothing. She just glared at me the rest of the afternoon." Elizabeth shuddered. "That was much worse than her yelling. I've never met a person who could accomplish what she can in just a look."

You have now. I shoved the thought away. "So when Chris came to you, did you have to teach him how to be affectionate? To be normal?"

Elizabeth nodded, wiping her eyes again. "It was as if his emotional growth was stunted, but he didn't throw tantrums. He didn't have trouble processing things when he was told no. He just accepted it and moved on, as if he dared not challenge. But he didn't know how to be happy or how to be a child."

"But you were able to change that?"

She smiled through her tears. "To an extent, yes. But he was always too serious, too reflective. He worried. And his night-mares didn't help."

"He talks about those sometimes," I said. "He thinks he saw more than what he realized, and he feels responsible for what happened to those girls." I thought he'd told me everything, but he'd only scratched the surface. I couldn't decide if I was more hurt or angry.

"For not realizing it sooner, I know," Elizabeth said. "His nightmares were awful. He'd wake up screaming about women being beaten and crying. Frank kept saying he was just drawing it from what he saw and heard about Jenna Richardson, but I knew. I knew he'd seen more. And I never believed Mary wasn't involved."

I struggled to choose the right words, not wanting to sound accusatory. The Hales certainly weren't the first people to be shocked by the cruelty of someone in their family. "From what I've read, some of the detectives working the case wondered too, but after seeing those videotapes of John abusing her sexually, they seem to have dropped the issue. Of course, we know now those were staged by her."

"She's brilliant," Elizabeth said. "And she wanted to take Chris with her. We fought like hell for him."

Dread spread over me, entwining itself with my already burning nerves. "What? I thought she asked you to take him."

Elizabeth looked ashamed. "No, that's what we told him. I didn't want her to have him. She didn't deserve him. She certainly couldn't take care of him, and he was so unloved, so broken. I convinced Frank to petition the court, and she lost custody."

"I can't imagine a woman like Mary Weston took that very well," I said. Mary would have seen that as a defeat—a loss of control.

"She didn't," Elizabeth said. "After the verdict, she caught up with me in the ladies' room." A shudder racked her small body. "She never touched me. She just blocked the way and glared at me with those deep, hateful eyes. And then she left. It wasn't until very recently I realized how lucky I was to be alive."

She truly was, but a bigger problem had taken over my

thoughts. "Chris doesn't know any of this, does he? He thinks she chose to abandon him."

"Not anymore." Elizabeth tore her tissue in half and fell back in the recliner. "I didn't know he was emailing her until Frank filled me in on everything late last night. If I'd known that was happening, I wouldn't have kept Chris's confronting me a secret."

"Confronting you?" Yet another thing he hadn't told me about, but I had been out of commission recently. Still, at this point I wasn't feeling especially forgiving.

"Three days ago," she said. "He came into my office and waited until I'd finished with my last patient. He didn't tell me he'd spoken with her, but he claimed he'd been doing some research and discovered the information about the court hearing. I didn't know how because it was closed. But he pressed, and I caved." She clasped her hands together, bringing them to her flattened lips. She shook her head as if trying to vanquish the memory. "I've always felt so guilty for lying to him, and it was time he knew the truth. So I told him."

"You did it to protect him." I knew Chris wouldn't feel the same way. Not at first. He would have heard nothing but the realization his beloved aunt and uncle had lied to him. With Mary already in his head from the emails, his actions from the last two days finally began to make sense.

Elizabeth wiped her tears. "I expected a blowout. Instead, he just looked at me with a coldness in his eyes I'd never seen. He reminded me of her, that day in the courthouse." She shuddered. "When Frank told me about the emails, I put two and two together. She'd told him. Found his weak spot just like she did his father's."

"It makes sense now," I said. "I saw the emails and knew what she was doing, but part of me couldn't figure out why Chris allowed her into his head. But he's angry and feeling betrayed. He's right where she wants him."

"Exactly," Elizabeth said. "All these years, we've done everything we could to protect him, to shield him from the truth. But our choices are going to get him killed."

"You can't think that way." I didn't sound like I believed it any more than she did. "Agent Lennox is very good, and I'm going to help. I'll do everything I can to make sure he's brought home safely."

"Even though he followed you?"

Because he followed me. I wanted answers. I needed them. "I'll worry about that later."

"He doesn't understand women, you know." Elizabeth dug a fresh tissue out of her bag. "He's never had a real relationship, and he's afraid of rejection. So whatever interest he had in you, whether it was about Justin or something more, he didn't know how to take it. So he watched until he'd gained the confidence."

That much I could understand. I could even accept the journal entry—he'd kept the thing when he was a kid, in a tumultuous time. The stalking was the issue. But I'd have to find Chris if I wanted answers.

Now that I finally understood his mindset, I might just be able to pull it off.

SIXTEEN

I called Todd on the way to Kelly's apartment. "I just talked to Chris's aunt. She told me Chris found out about the custody battle a few days ago."

"ADA Hale told us this morning," Todd said. "Which you would have known had you been here. Did you get your personal matter taken care of?"

"Almost." I didn't respond to the challenge in his voice. "I've got another stop to make, and then I'm stopping at home for clothes. I'll be back by tonight. Are there any leads?"

"Lennox is furious with you," Todd said. "His tech could have really used your assistance today."

"They'll get it tomorrow. I'm not convinced going through a bunch of files from years ago is the best way to find Mary now." I agreed with the theory—that we needed to understand Mary's past—but I could read people well enough to know Lennox had decided to give me busywork in the hopes I'd stay out of the way. "No leads?"

"Actually, there is. The local grocery store reports the same man coming in once a week for the last couple of months to buy supplies. He's older, probably in his eighties, and walks with a cane. He's got bad arthritis in his right hand—I guess it's pretty gnarled up—so he stands out. No one else in town knows who he is."

"That doesn't exactly sound like an able-bodied accomplice," I said.

"It's the best we've got right now. No sightings anywhere, no hits on Chris's credit cards. Lennox has a sketch artist working on a composite of the elderly man."

Good for him. Mary had more than some old geezer doing her grunt work. "Call me if anything else happens," I said. "I'll let you know when I'm back."

He didn't say goodbye.

Kelly's relieved smile sent a shiver of warmth over me. Barefoot as usual, with her toenails painted a bright green, she ushered me inside. The purple highlights in her hair had grown out to just the tips, and her usual spikey look had given away to a softer, wispy shape around her face that made her look like a sweet woodland fairy from one of the popular children's movies.

We didn't speak as I hung my coat near the door or while she poured me a cup of coffee. Finally, when I took my customary seat at her tiny counter, she broke the silence.

"No leads?"

"Not exactly." I told her about the old man sighted in Jarrettsville. "I'm not convinced it will pan out to anything."

"But there's something else," Kelly said. "You look like you're coming down from an all-nighter and need another hit. What is it?"

I took my time, staring first at the coffee and then at the various magnets on her fridge. Most of them were snarky phrases and the result of online shopping. Same with her coffee cups. The one in my hand offered a middle finger as a design, and it was my usual cup. "Chris stalked me."

"We knew that already." This was one of the things I loved most about Kelly: her practical approach. She didn't see the need to sugarcoat anything. In fact, she was one of the few people I knew who realized how valuable the raw truth really was.

"Not so much." I told her about Camp Hopeful and the memory box. "I don't even know how to feel, and I really don't know how to process it because he's missing, and I have to help find him."

Kelly pushed her empty cup to the side, her elfin, pale cheeks bright. "But do you really? He's the one who inserted himself into your life, not the other way around. He's an adult and made this choice. The FBI is already involved. What do you owe him? Especially after finding out all of this?"

"I shut him out this last month."

"So what? You shut us all out. It happens."

I smiled. Someday, I'd have to make sure Kelly realized she was the strongest person I'd ever known. "But Chris needed me. I'm one of the few people he trusts. And we all let him down."

"We?"

"His aunt and uncle lied to him about his parents." I understood their motives, but at the same time, I wanted to yell at them both. They knew Chris felt abandoned. Why hadn't they told him the truth when he was a child? Wouldn't it have been better to know his mother wanted him on some level, but the courts decided against it? Why allow him to continue to feel orphaned?

"What could they have kept from him that was so bad?"

I ticked off the lies on my fingers. "His father was adopted, so he's not blood relation to Frank Hale." As I spoke, understanding flashed in my weary head. "Frank Hale is good. He's normal. He was the biological link Chris clung to. His parents might be monsters, but Frank Hale wasn't. So Chris didn't have to be. But now, he knows that's not true, and he knows very little about his family. His head's a wreck, and he starts talking to his mother." I held up a second finger. "Who tells him about big, fat lie number two: she didn't give him up, she lost custody. His aunt confirmed this to him just a few days ago."

"And just like that, Mother Mary's in his head." Some of the anger melted off Kelly's face.

"Exactly. He's feeling totally lost, and now she's in his ear. His aunt said Mary never showed him any affection, but I think Chris longs for something from her, even if it's just information. And between my shutting him out and his aunt and uncle's lies, his foundation crumbles. Mary leeches in."

"The mother of all bad timing." Kelly winced at the bad joke. "But that doesn't mean you need to feel guilty. You didn't lie. You were a mess. Sometimes you have to take care of yourself and say to hell with everyone else for a while."

"I shouldn't have shut him out." I couldn't get past that part, even with the discovery about Camp Hopeful.

"You didn't know," Kelly said. "And let's put Chris aside for a minute. How are you? Because less than forty-eight hours ago, you weren't doing so hot."

Several words tumbled through my brain. Manic, angry, confused, betrayed, exhausted. "I think I'm better," I said. "I feel something. Something other than pity for myself. Something other than nothing."

"It's called depression," Kelly said. "They have medicine for it."

"I know, but you have to see a doctor first. What am I going to tell him?" The image almost made me laugh. I'd either have to make up some elaborate lie, which came naturally but would make me feel even worse about myself, or tell him the truth, which would put the doctor in a legal conundrum. At least I'd have some entertainment.

Kelly looked me straight in the eye, no longer delicate but fiercely protective. "You tell him you've never gotten over the death of your sister, and it led you to becoming a private investigator obsessed with pedophiles. Recent events led you to kill a person in self-defense, and you don't know how to deal with it. You can skip the illegal parts and still get help."

My hackles were up. "I got over Lily's death."

"Stop." Kelly held up her hand, the kitchen light catching an old, jagged scar on her palm, courtesy of her cruel stepfather. "Saying it out loud just makes it worse. You know her death and your guilt drive everything you do, even if you don't want to admit it yet."

I drank my coffee, feeling the heat steam my insides. "Back to Chris. I get his headspace now. And I certainly get hers."

She raised her eyebrow, and then nodded. I'd earned a pass —for now. "What's her end game, though?" Kelly asked.

"He's hurt and needs her. Everyone he knows lied. Who knows what she can convince him of?" If he was in the right headspace, manipulating him would be so easy, anyone with a small amount of skill could do it. And Mary certainly had the skill.

"You don't think he'd do something awful for her?" Kelly asked.

"He's thought about doing it on his own, even thought about killing her," I said. "And he helped me get rid of Preacher's body. He's angry and hurt, and now she's in control. Who knows?" I pushed my coffee aside, my stomach burning. "The FBI seems to think I can help with their search into Mary's background. Apparently they believe I have inside knowledge of the case. I think Lennox just wants to keep an eye on me."

"You can't blame him." Kelly bit her lip, looking around her apartment. "You're supposed to work with the tech, going through records?"

"A lot of them aren't even online," I said. "It's going to take a lot of phone calls and begging for cooperation."

"With Lennox over your shoulder," Kelly said. "And I doubt Todd will be able to stay much longer."

"He probably doesn't want to." The thought of Todd leaving bothered me more than it should have. "But I don't want to talk about him."

Something sparkled in Kelly's eyes, as if she knew exactly what sort of torment flowed through me. "That's fine. You can tell me more in the car."

"What?" I stared at her, the fine hairs on my neck suddenly standing up.

"I'm going back to Maryland with you."

SEVENTEEN

We drove south in darkness. Yesterday's wind had died down, but fresh snow, just enough to be dangerous, fell and made traffic slow. Kelly sat rigidly in the passenger seat, her tiny fingers clutching the seatbelt and her wide eyes taking everything in as though she'd never seen a busy interstate.

"How long has it been?" I asked.

"Four years since I left my neighborhood, and that was only for therapy. I can't remember the last time I was in something like this."

She didn't know how to drive. Her stepfather had been too busy using her as a sex slave to teach her. "This snow isn't bad. There's enough traffic to keep the pavement warm. As long as we take it easy, we'll be fine."

"I trust you."

Those words should never apply to me, but hearing her say it gave me the slightest hope that something would turn out right. At least for one of us. "I am so proud of you. This is such a big step. And I can't tell you how much it means that you're making it for me."

Kelly finally tore her eyes from the traffic. "You're the only person I'd do it for. You're the reason I'm still alive."

My eyes welled. I couldn't speak.

"You didn't know that?" Kelly's soft, steady voice bolstered my urge to cry. "You're the one who got me out of that house, and you didn't give up on me when the PTSD was so bad I couldn't stand to be touched. You're the closest thing I have to family, and I want to help you."

Several seconds passed before I trusted myself to speak. "I don't know what to say."

"You don't have to say anything," Kelly said. "I just want you to be happy, and finding Chris will make you happy. And maybe, with the FBI breathing down your neck and keeping you in line, you'll realize you can still be the person you want to be. Without killing."

Kelly had no qualms about my killing pedophiles. Her issue was always my well-being. "I think that ship has sailed, Kel."

"It hasn't. But it will if you keep thinking that way."

"I'll try to remember that," I said as I took our exit. "But most days it feels like I've royally screwed up and I've got no choice but to keep walking the path to my own personal hell."

"There's always a choice," she said. "One day you'll see it."

I swallowed, telling myself to focus on the slippery exit ramp. When we finally made it safely to the stop sign, I turned to face her. "You're my family too. Never forget that."

Snow rained down like hail by the time we arrived at the motel. My fingers numbed as I fumbled with Kelly's bags and the additional items I'd grabbed at my apartment while a disapproving Mousecop looked on. My face burned from the cold and wet, and I wanted to run for the hotel. But Kelly stood rooted like an ancient tree, looking trapped in her heavy parka. With the hood pulled over her head and the dark, fur-like lining against her pale face, she could have passed for a child.

"I won't let anyone cross your boundaries." I offered her my hand, uncertain if she would take it.

Her gaze swept over the motel and the parking lot, down the small-town street with its flickering lights and vacant shops, and then finally to my outstretched hand. "I trust you."

She took my hand, and I was again struck with a feeling I couldn't quite name. It wasn't really pride, although that was certainly in the mix. Love? Yes. I cared for Kelly more than anyone else in my life. But there was more, a realization that I'd been such an impact on her life. And no one had gotten hurt in the process.

I guided her into the motel and through the small lobby. Its few tables and chairs were empty, and the television droned with a rerun of a generic sitcom. A lone woman with a pile of blond hair fiddled with the coffee pot, waiting as it doled out its contents. She glanced at us, and I realized she wasn't a hotel worker but another guest. Before she had the opportunity to make small talk, I hustled Kelly down the hall to my room.

Once inside, she dropped my hand and sat on the end of the bed, breathing hard. I wanted to take off her coat, smooth back her hair, make sure she wasn't having a panic attack. But she needed space. I put the bags on the other bed and then filled a newly placed plastic cup from the tap in the bathroom.

"Here," I said. "This might help."

She took it gladly, sucking down the water. It was nothing more than a distraction from her fear, but I hoped it gave her some kind of relief.

"I'm going to get a cot brought in," I said, shaking off my coat. "And I'll sleep on that. You can have the bed."

Kelly finally pulled her hood down. Her hair had been flattened by the weight of the material. She held up her sleeping bag. "No way. I'll sleep on the cot."

"We can flip for it, how's that?"

"I suppose that's fair." Unzipping her coat, she glanced around the room. "So, this is a hotel room, huh? I haven't been in one since I was a kid. They don't seem to have changed much."

"This is a motel," I clarified, thinking about all the things I took for granted. "And no, it's pretty standard. You've got to pay big money for home comforts. All I care about is a place to sleep and hot water."

Someone knocked on the door. Kelly's breath hitched. She grimaced and then inhaled deeply. "I can do this. Go ahead and answer."

I realized I hadn't thought much about how I'd bring Kelly into the situation. I certainly didn't want to introduce her as my computer genius. As if that's all she was.

Still trying to figure out my story, I opened the door and was unsurprised to see Todd. "Were you listening for me?"

He looked more tired than yesterday, bruise-like shadows beneath his eyes. He'd forgotten to shave, and his mustache threatened to creep back. "Something like that. Can I come in?"

I glanced behind me. "I have company."

"Who?" His voice hitched a notch.

"It's not really any of your business, but she's a friend who's come back to offer whatever help she can." I lowered my voice, determined to protect Kelly but unwilling to betray her confidence. "She has space issues, so keep your distance."

Empathy settled into Todd's face, as I knew it would. "Sure, no problem. Can we talk?" Some of the edge in his tone evaporated.

I stepped aside, and he walked slowly into the room, keeping his hands at his sides, visible and relaxed. He'd dealt with enough traumatized victims he no doubt knew how to handle the situation, but I didn't think it would have made any difference. Todd's compassion guided him just as well.

Kelly had retreated to the corner with the small table and two chairs, her knees drawn to her chest, her black leggings showing exactly how tiny her legs were. She looked so small and wary, I wanted to tell Todd to leave.

"Hi," he said. "I'm Detective Todd Beckett. I'm helping search for Chris." He stood calmly by the dresser, allowing her to get used to his presence.

I slipped past Todd and quickly took the other chair, hoping to ease Kelly's nerves. "This is my good friend Kelly."

She gave me a tiny smile and then nodded at Todd. "I know who you are. Thanks for helping Lucy out."

Her steady voice surprised me, and some of the tension in my shoulders eased. "Have a seat, Detective."

Todd sat on the far corner of the bed, respecting Kelly's space. "Snow's coming down hard. I was starting to worry about you."

"It got nasty the last ten miles," I said. "I don't suppose the search party is still out?"

He shook his head. "They covered all the woods by this morning and have canvassed a lot of the county. Lennox is trying to track down the old man, but so far no one knows his name."

"I find it hard to believe he was Mary's accomplice," I said. "Age is bad enough. His physical ailment is another. He's useless to her."

"He's all we've got right now."

Silence descended. Todd's tapping foot made the room sizzle with his irritation.

"Go ahead and say what you need to."

He gritted his teeth. "You went to Chris's apartment after you were explicitly asked not to start your own investigation."

His anger struck me in a way I didn't expect. I squirmed, feeling guilty about omitting the full truth. "I promise, I wasn't investigating his disappearance. I needed to check on something else. It didn't have anything to do with his going after his mother."

Todd still glared, and I realized he probably thought I'd gone to hide evidence of one of the crimes he believed I'd committed. "It's not what you're thinking, either. It's personal with no bearing on anything else."

"I can't keep sticking up for you when you keep shitting on me."

The words sounded funny coming from him, but I caught my laughter. "You're right. I didn't think of it like that. It won't happen again."

He looked unconvinced. The sort of awkward tension I hadn't felt since high school settled in the room. Thankfully, Kelly spoke up.

"What about the records search?" she asked. "Did the FBI's people turn up anything? Any sign of cold cases with similarities?"

"Not yet," Todd said. "A lot of the state records from the seventies aren't computerized. So they've been calling police department after department, sending them to check their storage records." He leaned back on his hands and yawned. "Lennox did find records of John working for the Maryland State Highway Association in the seventies. Some of his paychecks went to an address in Baltimore, but since he worked all along the I-95 corridor and was on the road a lot, most of the time he was paid by the foreman running the crew. And there's zero chance of finding a check cashed thirty years ago."

"What about Mary?" I asked. "Have they turned up anything that points to her real name?"

Todd yawned. "The FBI analysts are looking at public records in Maryland trying to find Mary during John's tenure with the highway association, but there are too many names to go through, and not a single one is Weston."

"It's too much paper to work with." Kelly grimaced, shuddering the way she did when she had to read a paperback instead of her electronic device. She loathed the feel of paper on her skin. "That's pointless. He's never going to find her family, if she has any."

"I don't think she does," I said. "She's too selfish and transient. If she's got family, it's probable she hasn't heard from them in years."

"We're hoping to find some place she might seek refuge. Some place she'd take Chris. After all"—he looked at me—"didn't you say she wanted to show him the truth about his past? That's looking more and more likely after finding out about the custody issue."

I rubbed my hands over my face. "I can't believe they kept that from Chris. All the lies were like a perfect storm, just waiting for Mary to swoop in and mess with his head."

I'd been debating on how much to reveal to Todd. And Lennox, for that matter. But if we were going to find Chris, they needed all the pertinent information. Which did not include my stay at Camp Hopeful and Chris's stalking. "When I was at Chris's apartment, I found evidence he'd been to see his dad at some point. His aunt wasn't aware of this, and I'm assuming the ADA isn't either."

Todd sat back up. "What sort of evidence?"

"Weston's personal effects."

"That doesn't mean they spoke," Todd said. "If an inmate knows he's in for life without parole, he can request those things go to a family member. It's a paperwork issue."

"But Chris has at least been to the prison. He'd have to pick those things up in person, sign for them," I said. "Something he kept from us all, for whatever reason." Todd didn't need to know the other things he'd kept from me. They served no purpose in the case at hand. "I have a hard time believing he didn't at least try to talk to his father."

"I'll tell Lennox. He can call the prison and have the

warden double-check the visitors' log," Todd said. "They'll at least have a record of when those items were discharged to Chris, so we'll get a timeline. But if he's not on the list..."

"He might have used a fake ID," I said. "I wouldn't put it past him."

Todd shot me a look that said he wasn't surprised. "Really? Why?"

"He didn't want his aunt and uncle to know. His uncle's the assistant district attorney—someone might have called him when Chris came around. And getting a fake ID isn't that hard."

"It would have to be a really damned good fake," Todd said. "The offender is the only person who can add names to his visitors list, and only every so often. You can't visit unless your name is on there, and the prison runs a background check." He stretched his legs, wincing as his knee popped. "If the person is approved, then they're sent a notification they have to sign and return. They can deny contact from the prisoner."

"Meaning Chris would have had to have made contact to visit, and then John would have had to approve him?" I asked.

"Yes," Todd said. "And that doesn't happen overnight."

So Chris had planned to see his father and had probably been doing so for a while. He kept it all to himself. At this point, I was more curious than hurt. He told me everything else. Why not about visiting John Weston?

"I think we need to talk about the elephant in the room." Todd glanced at me the same way a child does when he's afraid to ask for another Popsicle but just can't help himself. "The fact is, the guy's got issues. I can't blame him. It's obvious the discovery of Mary posing as Martha Beckett and having another kid messed with him. Then he finds out the people he's always trusted lied too, and Mary's in his head. How much is she influencing him now?"

"He's injured," I said.

"We have no idea how badly," Todd said. "There wasn't enough blood on the snow to make me think he risked bleeding out and no significant trail. Even if the wind covered it, I still think there's a strong possibility his injury was minor and Chris treated it himself. He's certainly capable."

"And then what?" I said. "He goes with her willingly? I just can't believe that, and you don't like him. You're not exactly impartial."

"No, but I'm a good cop, and I can separate personal opinion. He might not have been willing at first—she's got a gun, after all. But you know him, Lucy. You know his head better than anyone else. How easy do you think it would be for Mary to completely twist it around, with all the other things he's found out?"

Not hard at all.

I couldn't bring myself to say the words out loud.

EIGHTEEN

My eyes peeled open sometime after dawn but before the sun made its full ascent. Weak gray light filtered in around the stiff, brown curtains like smoke from a campfire. I'd won the cot, and I'd placed it near the window to ensure the light woke me up. Truthfully, I was surprised I'd slept at all. My mind was a tangled mess of storm debris, and my subconscious the survivor picking through the wreckage trying to figure out what the hell to do next.

I still didn't have the answer, but I figured the best thing to do was to work with what I did know. Chris had been taken by his crazy mother, and he had a serious injury. His head was a thousand shades of messed up right now. Chris lied to me, but he'd also been a good friend. Walking away wasn't an option, and the only way I'd get answers was to find him. So that's what I'd do.

Safely wrapped in her sleeping bag, Kelly slept in an impossibly tiny balled-up position. I didn't want to wake her. She'd handled last night so well, but she needed time to rest and get ready for the next round today. Using what little light my phone provided, I shuffled to the bathroom to get dressed and brush my teeth, and then I slipped out of the room in search of coffee.

At this early hour, the breakfast area was blissfully empty and the television turned off. The motel's continental breakfast consisted of a sparse choice of cereal and bagels. I chose a plain bagel and a black coffee and took too many containers of cream cheese. I sat down at one of the small tables and tried not to let my mind wander to dark places.

It raced anyway. Was Chris still alive? What horrible things was his mother subjecting him to? If we did manage to save him, who would he be when he returned? Not the same. No matter what the outcome, his life as he knew it was shattered.

I wanted to be mad at him for the lies and the creeping—and I was, on some level—but the emotion sitting heavily on my chest was pure pity. I wasn't sure Chris ever stood a chance. I'd retreated so far into my head I didn't even hear anyone else come for coffee, and I nearly choked on my bagel when the voice piped up behind me.

"Are you Lucy Kendall?"

I cranked my head to see a slim woman with long legs, well-fitted jeans, and blond hair pulled into a bun that somehow managed to look stylish instead of messy. Her skin was the kind of flawless usually reserved for Photoshopped magazine covers. She looked down at me with striking eyes. Not for their color, but for the gleam inside them, as if she were a shark and had just happened upon a helpless sea lion pup. "Excuse me?"

"I'm Beth Reid." She offered her hand but let it drop when I didn't take it. "I'm a reporter for Fox 29 in Philadelphia."

My coffee suddenly tasted bitter. I realized she was the woman in the lobby when Kelly and I arrived last night. "Good for you."

Any hope that my rudeness would run her off quickly dissipated. I should have known better. Her kind fed off another person's dismay. She lingered at the empty seat across from me, clutching a Styrofoam cup of coffee and obviously waiting for an invitation to sit. "I've been following your work for a while now."

A familiar fear trickled down my neck before I brushed it off. "My work? I'm a private investigator. We tend to stay pretty... private."

She smiled at the poor joke, revealing teeth so perfectly aligned and white they appeared false. "I meant your contribution to finding Kailey Richardson. And more recently what happened with the sex trafficking ring. You know Senator Coleman's fighting hard not to lose his constituents and backing for his task force. Seems his benefactors can't figure out how someone like Jake worked right beside him for so long and the senator didn't have a clue."

"I can't say as I blame them."

"Getting the full story about what happened to you in that garage has been tough," she said. "We've only been told you defended yourself, and Jake killed his girlfriend. The press has been left to assume he died from injuries inflicted in the struggle with you."

"Assume all you want." I still couldn't believe how well the police had protected me, although I assumed that had more to do with the senator wanting to keep everything about Jake's demise as quiet as possible.

She clearly wasn't deterred, this time resting her right hand on the chair, her bright red fingernails shining. "And now your friend Chris Hale is missing. John and Mary Weston's son."

"How do you know he's my friend?" Stupid question. We'd both been associated with the Richardson case, and police talk, especially in small towns. I cursed myself for the mistake but maintained eye contact, refusing to be intimidated by her. Let her have a glimpse of the person she believed she could coerce.

Something about my harsh glare must have hit home

because she took a step back and then sucked down a hasty gulp of coffee, wincing as it burned her throat. I smiled.

"Is it true he's gone with his mother?"

"Is that what they're saying?" I felt the ridiculous urge to laugh. "That and he and Mary just skipped off into the sunset together?"

"Not exactly. But it's pretty clear the woman's capable of terrible things."

I shrugged. "Doesn't take a genius—or even a good reporter—to figure that out."

She gave me a smile as predatory as a hyena's. "I've got sources telling me the police are worried about Chris's well-being. Not to mention his physical health."

"Sources?" I tossed my empty coffee cup in the trash. "I'll have to mention those sources to Agent Lennox. I highly doubt the FBI wants any kind of leak in this case."

"Every news station in the country needs to have Mary and Chris's faces running at all times." Reid was undeterred. "Are the FBI covering the airports? Are they watching the train stations out of Baltimore and Philadelphia?"

"Why don't you ask Agent Lennox?" The idea of this Barbie questioning his ability to handle the investigation warmed the chillier areas of my cold heart. "I'm sure he'd be glad to tell you exactly what he thinks."

"The FBI doesn't speak to the press unless they feel it somehow benefits them," she said. "He's not aware of what I could do to help."

I stood, feeling the tendons in my knees stretch. In my jeans and sweater, my hair pulled back and no makeup, I felt dowdy next to her. I doubted she ever left the house without her face on. But that's all she had on me. Her pitiful attempt at manipulating my trust made me feel like laughing in her face.

"Why don't you help by searching? Or even better, keeping

your nose out of it and stop trying to make a name for yourself based on other people's misery?"

She did her best impression at looking shocked, as if she'd never been rebuffed. Her gaping mouth and wide eyes made her look like a dead fish with a painted face. "That's not what I'm trying to do at all. The media is a powerful thing. Our viewers are the largest demographic in the greater Philadelphia area, and I've no doubt a lot of the satellite stations would pick up the story. You'd probably even make the national news."

"Is that what you want? Me to sit down and make a plea for Chris's safe return?"

"Of course," she said. "Humanize him. Tell the viewers how you met, how the two of you found Kailey, which led you to the truth about Mary Weston. Through Chris, and I assume Jenna Richardson, you know firsthand what she's capable of. The viewers need to hear that. They need to know what they can do to help bring Chris home."

I'd heard enough. This stupid woman wanted nothing more than to get an exclusive with someone who'd had access to the Westons' survivor, Jenna Richardson, and to Chris. She'd ask gruesome questions the public didn't need to know, and she'd try to convince me to play amateur psychologist where Chris was concerned.

"I'm going to tell you this one time." I leaned closer, lowering my voice as if confiding some snippet of my soul. "If you have questions about the investigation into Chris's disappearance, don't ask me. Ask your police source or Agent Lennox. And if you approach me again about giving some trashy tell-all, I will physically hurt you. Do you understand?"

She blinked, wide eagle eyes with finely fringed lashes. "I just want to help."

"Then go back to Philadelphia."

.   .   .

Kelly was awake and dressed when I returned. She sat cross-legged on the bed, her face a mask of twitching nerves. I gave her a cup of coffee and the last chocolate donut from the lobby. "What happened?"

"Stupid reporter asking even more stupid questions," I said. "How did you sleep?"

"Better than I expected to. How about you?"

"I got a few hours."

She stretched her arms over her head, rolling her neck. "Todd has a point."

We hadn't spoken about Todd's theory of Chris and Mary last night. Kelly seemed to understand I'd reached my limit when the detective left the room. But today was a new day. "I know he does."

"And he stalked you. There's no other way to put it."

"Let's keep that between us, okay? It's not going to help find Chris, so no one else needs to know."

"That's fine," Kelly said. "But I just want you to remember, he's already shown he's capable of doing some pretty bad things —even if they were harmless. If his mother gets her way, he won't want to come back."

"He won't go that far." I wasn't sure where my faith came from. "Chris needs answers, but he also hates her. She's the cause of his problems. I'm not worried about his going along with her."

"You're worried about her killing him because he won't," Kelly said. "Let's hope he's found before it comes to that."

"That's not it," I said, finally able to organize the wretched mess of my head. "I'm worried he'll kill her, and not just in self-defense."

Kelly shivered despite the heat in the room, the single jerk of her head acknowledging she understood my meaning.

NINETEEN

At the Jarrettsville police station, the administrative conference room about the size of a breadbox had been turned into the command center. A coffee carafe and a box of donuts sat on the table next to a pile of napkins that had cascaded over like an accordion. A whiteboard had scribblings from the case, various bits and pieces of evidence I already knew, as well as photos of Chris and Mary, along with the dead girl from the cabin. Seeing Chris labeled "victim" made me feel as if I'd just showered with ice. Kelly walked by my side, her small shoulders hunched, her head low. Todd walked a respectful distance behind. I knew his sharp mind still swam with questions about Kelly. He'd eventually put two and two together, if he hadn't already.

Three sets of eyes turned on us. Lennox, clearly the alpha, stood in the middle of the group. His blazer and tie were gone, replaced with a simple dress shirt and slacks, but his stance still commanded attention. I guessed he served in the military, possibly Special Forces. Those guys knew how to choke fear to death, and even worse, they were pros at spotting it in the enemy.

Next to Lennox stood an equally tall man wearing a

Harford County Sheriff's uniform. His slicked-back hair bordered on using too much product, his nose a bit too big for his face. His lazy eyes scanned the room with little emotion, as if he'd seen this all before and had long since lost hope for a positive outcome. A younger man closer to Kelly's age sat at the end of the table with a laptop. His shaggy hair fit right in with his generation, and his baby face belonged in high school.

"Lucy." Agent Lennox's voice rang with frustration. "Nice of you to join us. This is Detective Adams from the Harford County Sheriff's Major Case Squad." He glanced at the detective. The jurisdictional tension rippled through the air. Technically, the police were supposed to invite the FBI in on cases, but Mary Weston was already an FBI-assigned case, and Chris Hale was from another state. So Lennox was within his rights. But unless I'd blacked out part of that first evening, the FBI had probably been informed long before the Major Case Squad in Harford County. Chief Deputy Frost's being assigned to beat the pavement in the search instead of in here with the big boys was likely punishment.

I cleared my throat, realizing from the look on Lennox's face it was time for my own introduction. "This is my friend Kelly Swan." This was the moment we both dreaded, but Kelly insisted it happen. She wanted to help, no matter the consequences. "She works as a forensic computer consultant for the Philadelphia Police Department, and she wanted to come down to support me."

Behind me, Todd made a hard chuffing sound in his throat. I hated revealing Kelly's identity to him, for purely selfish reasons. Knowing she was insulated from scrutiny, cocooned in her apartment, made me less responsible for her safety. Now, she was in the thick of it, with me. For me.

"I usually work from home." The strength in Kelly's voice surprised me. "And I know this is your operation, of course. But I'd like to offer another set of eyes." As she spoke, her chin raised, as if each word gave her a little more confidence. My self-pity bloomed to pride once again.

Lennox's steely eyes honed in on Kelly, and I fought the urge to block her from his view. "You have credentials? I can't just let anyone walk into this investigation. We've already got a reporter skulking around."

As Kelly handed over her department-issued identification, I told Lennox about Beth Reid. "She knew Chris and I were friends, which isn't a stretch. But she claimed to have sources from the department who said police are worried about Chris's mental and physical health."

"She's bluffing." Detective Adams spoke with more vigor than I expected from his baleful appearance. "Of course we're worried about those things. That's common sense."

Lennox handed Kelly's ID back with a brief nod. "What you see doesn't leave this room, and Ryan is in charge of the technical investigation." The twenty-something with the shaggy hair looked up from his laptop and gave a little wave. I almost laughed at the difference between field and office agents. Ryan bore the casual stance of his generation, more comfortable with his computer than with a gun, while Lennox kept his hand on his weapon while he talked, as if drawing his authority directly from the piece.

"I'm a senior tech agent with the Maryland FBI office," Ryan said. He smiled shyly at Kelly. "I'm happy to have another set of eyes."

She nodded, her whole body moving with the motion, and then looked at her feet.

As for Lennox, he missed nothing. "To answer your reporter's question, of course we're manning the airports—every one within a hundred miles. We've got roadblocks set up. Their pictures are running on every station in Maryland, Philadelphia, and Northern Virginia. I've also got a grainy security photo circulating of the strange old man several eyewitnesses from town have mentioned. Anything else?"

"I told her if she had additional questions to speak with you."

"Thanks." He turned to the whiteboard as if it would yield new answers. "Here's what we know. Mary Weston was squatting in that hunting cabin for an undetermined amount of time. The girl has been identified as Amy Magnum, missing from Northern Virginia for sixteen days. The medical examiner confirmed she died between two and four hours prior to our discovery. That's sometime between five and seven p.m., Tuesday evening, which means Mary doesn't have as much of a head start as we'd originally thought." He turned back to look at our group, eyebrow raised. "You guys might as well sit."

I took the nearest chair, while Kelly sat next to me. Todd positioned himself across the table, his eyes searing into me. I didn't look at him.

"We know from his voicemail messages that Chris Hale encountered someone Tuesday morning." Lennox picked up a marker and tapped the end on the board. "At approximately eight a.m., Chris left the message for Lucy that ended with the gunshot. By the time Chief Deputy Frost was able to zero down the location and find the blood in the snow, roughly nine hours had passed. Amy Magnum's body was found at nine p.m." He looked at all of us, making sure the information sank in.

Frustration burned within me. While we were sloughing around in the snow, that girl was being murdered, damned near under our noses. The same questions from the first night rattled through me. Why hadn't Chief Deputy Frost been aware of the cabin? Wasn't it her job to know the local area? Why hadn't she swallowed her pride and called in the state troopers or the Major Case Squad detective?

"Chief Deputy Frost"—Detective Adams spoke as if reading my mind, his tone sounding more like stock loyalty to his fellow officer than conviction—"handled things to the best of her ability. Maryland landowners are serious about their privacy, and very few people would have known about the cabin. She wasn't able to get ahold of the owner or the real estate agent until it was too late for this young girl. It's unfortunate and unfair, but it's part of the job. That's why we need to find Mary Weston and her accomplices right away."

"Accomplices?" Something simmered inside me. "As in plural? I assume you're referencing this old man who came into town for supplies? But is there any proof he was in the cabin?" I finally allowed a glance at Todd. He shrugged his shoulders, but I could tell from the skittish look in his eyes he knew more than he was saying.

"We're all in agreement at least one other male was in the cabin with Mary," Agent Lennox said. "Toiletry items and clothing left suggest that, and we've already confirmed with the cabin's owner that it was empty when he left it. As for the old man, we found an overcoat resembling the one in the security footage from the pharmacy. It's not an absolute, but it's a start. Given his age and description, we'd hoped to find prescription meds left behind, but Mary's better than that."

"That's one accomplice who sounds pretty frail," I said. "I suppose he could have been the one to shoot Chris, which might explain why he's still alive. Or was, at least in the cabin."

Lennox nodded, but his hard look told me he expected me to move on to the next possibility.

My jaw tightened as I spoke. "You're not suggesting Chris is in on this?"

Agent Lennox put the marker back in its place and walked to the head of the table, resting his muscular bulk on his hands. "We need to look at all the facts and keep an open mind. You know what she's capable of."

I shook my head, refusing to admit I'd been worrying about the same thing.

"As for this old man, three different witnesses from the pharmacy, grocery store, and hardware store said he came in on the same day every week," Detective Adams said. "All described him as acting strangely and in a hurry. No one recognized him, so they assumed he was from out of town, but he never offered any personal information. Yesterday was the day he should have come in for supplies. He didn't show up, which keeps him on my suspect list, no matter how frail he seems. That could be an act."

Lennox took over. "We've gone over the emails between Chris and his mother multiple times. Our staff psychiatrist has read them as well." His eyes remained on me, each word carefully measured. "Given the new information about Chris knowing that his aunt and uncle lied about the custody battle, we're all in agreement Chris is very vulnerable to this woman right now. You even said it yourself."

"So Stockholm syndrome. Or something like it?" I shook my head. "Not Chris. Not this soon, anyway. He didn't help kill that girl. He won't help kill anyone else."

"How do you know?" Lennox asked.

I thought of Chris's pale face as he stared at Preacher, the way his Adam's apple bobbed and his tense face as we struggled with the body. "I just do. Is he in danger of his mother breaking him down psychologically? Yes. But to the point of becoming a killer? No. Chris would die first."

"I hope you're right," Lennox said. "His uncle feels the same way, but we've got to keep all possibilities open."

"Where is ADA Hale?" Todd finally spoke.

"He went back to Philadelphia," Lennox said. "There's not a lot he can do here, and he needs to be with his wife." His eyes slid to mine, and I squirmed. He knew I'd been in the apartment. I'd have to decide how much to tell him.

"So the plan right now is going over a lot of data I've had brought in from various police records," Lennox said. "Detective Beckett, we haven't located your father, but we've searched the entire state of Philadelphia for marriage licenses in 1992, the year they would have been married. There's no record matched to your father."

My stomach sank. I'd been clinging to the hope that we'd find her via the name she used with that marriage.

Todd's mouth twisted. "So you're saying they were never married? All those years, all that trauma, and they never made it legal? And yet she applied for a Social Security card with my father's last name?"

Lennox scowled as though he smelled something rotten. "If she legally changed her name, there's no record of it. She applied for the Social Security number in December of 1992, and she provided the required birth certificate and driver's license. Both stated her name as Martha Beckett."

"Fakes." I stated the obvious. Kelly and I both knew how easy it was to forge documents, and pre 9/11, it would have been even easier. I looked across the table at Todd's angry face and was again hit with the sense of righteous disappointment. Why did so many good people's lives have to be churned through the meat grinder?

Lennox sighed. "It's a low blow, because we know that neither Weston nor Beckett is her real last name, but we don't have any kind of physical starting point beyond those names. For all we know she could have told your father her name was Weston too. It's not like she was on the hook for the murders at the time. I did manage to get John Weston's work records from the Maryland State Highway Association. He worked for them until shortly before he and Mary showed up in Lancaster in early 1980."

He dropped a thick printout onto the table. "We've got one small break. Interstate 95 had a major overhaul in 1978—one of those projects that was supposed to last six months but took more than a year. John Weston worked on the stretch running south from Baltimore to the Virginia state line. We need to cross reference the police data looking for similar crimes near that route. If we're really lucky, we'll find something that ties to Mary."

"Why?" Kelly asked, her voice soft but firm. "This is going to take a lot of man hours, and with all due respect, how does information from so long ago help us now?"

"It might not," Lennox said. "But Lucy seems to think that Mary would keep Chris around to tell him his true life story, especially now that he knows she didn't willingly give him up. It's a long shot, but I'm hoping we'll find someplace they might retreat to. We're also looking for similar crimes in the tri-state area prior to 1978, in case Mary acted alone before she met John, or had another accomplice. Anything that would lead us to someone with information."

He nodded at Adams, and both men grabbed for their jackets.

"What will you be doing?" I asked.

"We've got an eyewitness to talk to, and then we're following another lead. I'm also checking in on the search. See how Chief Deputy Frost is handling that." Lennox zipped his North Face jacket. "But first, I'd like to talk to you in private, Lucy."

I stood up easily, a grim smile on my face. Showing weakness to Lennox was a mistake I didn't intend to make. He waited in the hall, his shoulders even wider in his bulky jacket, and wasted no time getting to the point. "So. Your trip back to the city and into Chris Hale's apartment, this is the personal errand you just had to run. Why? His uncle and I searched it before we left for Maryland. We have everything of interest to the case, unless there's something you're not telling us."

"What I'm not telling you," I said, "is personal and between me and Chris. It has no bearing on the case, and I was upfront with his aunt about why I was there."

"But you're not going to share with me."

"It's not necessary," I said. "I assume Todd told you I found evidence Chris visited his father?"

Lennox nodded. "I called the supermax in Greene County and asked for the visitors' log for the last six months. I'm still waiting. It's possible he visited a long time ago. But I'd like to know how he got in without raising any red flags. We're supposed to be notified if John Weston talks to anyone."

It took me a minute to realize he meant SCI Greene in Waynesburg, Pennsylvania's only maximum-security prison. "I don't know that he did talk to him. But Weston had to sign over his personal effects to Chris. I didn't find any other sign of correspondence between them."

"We're checking that too," Lennox said. "For more than twenty years, John Weston has refused visitors and says very little when some new agent thinks they can break him. After the truth about Mary's involvement broke last fall and the case was handed to me, I went back and interviewed him myself. Same results. Warden says he's a model prisoner, and his mail consists of the usual cross between fan worship and disgust."

Fan worshipping of serial killers—a concept I still couldn't wrap my mind around. "I don't think Chris talked to him."

"He might not have," Lennox said, "but you also didn't know he was communicating with his mother. If I understand things correctly, you haven't been yourself since the events of last month."

"Would you be?" I immediately wished I hadn't asked the question.

"Killing someone is a tough thing, even when it's self-defense," Lennox said. "It takes a bit of the soul, I think." He let the silence simmer, and I suddenly felt like I'd been dropped into the boiling pot. "But there are some really interesting rumors about you. I don't know if they're true or not, but I do know you've taken a strong stand against sex offenders. And those two people in the garage were just more of the same scum, right?"

My throat felt dry. "I'm not sure what rumors you're talking about."

"Let's skip that." Lennox's easy cadence and friendly expression were meant to lure me into giving something away. "I know Detective Beckett approached his superiors last fall about the possibility of your involvement in the murders of Cody and Brian Harrison. There wasn't enough evidence, and for some reason, he decided to drop it. But information like that doesn't go away, especially when you make headlines like you have. After you survived the attack in Jake's garage—against two capable people who both ended up dead—people like me really start to wonder. Especially when the body of Jake's main man turns up in the Allegheny Forest. Preacher. You're familiar with him, of course."

My stomach actually heaved as though Lennox had just sucker-punched me. I struggled to keep the proper mask of confusion and indifference, even as the roots of my hair dampened with sweat and my palms grew clammy. I'd known it would be just a matter of time before Preacher was identified. "I hadn't heard about that. What happened to him?"

Lennox gave me a cagey smile. "I can't discuss the details of the investigation with you, but I wouldn't be surprised if you already knew the answer."

I stared back at him, knowing full well any sort of act I put on wouldn't work on this man. "I don't know what you're talking about."

"I'll let it sit right now, because I've got more important things going on," Lennox said. "But I'm telling you, if Mary Weston—or anyone connected with this investigation—somehow ends up dead and you're anywhere near the scene, I'm opening up a full-scale investigation into your extracurriculars, and I will find out exactly what you've been up to."

"Feel free," I said. "This is nothing but a figment of Todd's imagination, and you said yourself he'd let it go. Although I don't know why you care about Mary Weston's life."

"Because I want the whole truth," Lennox said. "We've got no idea how long she's been operating or how many other victims are out there. She dies and all those families have lost their shot at closure."

"Anything else?"

Another friendly smile, just two buddies catching up. "For now, no. Just remember what I said."

As if I could forget. I just added it to the list that kept me awake at night.

TWENTY

Lennox stalked out, and I allowed myself a minute to gather my thoughts. Not that I could do anything about the situation. Everything had already happened, and standing around stressing out about the past wasn't going to help find Chris. I gathered my composure and re-joined the group.

Kelly had taken part of the stack of folders. A pile sat near my seat. Todd had a third. Ryan looked up shyly from his laptop. "So to recap, we know Mary and John met in 1978, so we're looking for any crime similar to Mary's known ones. Since we know John Weston worked on I-95 in 1977 and 1978, we're starting with these." He gestured to the unsettling amount of folders. "These are police records from along that route, all pre-ViCAP days. Unfortunately, some of the smaller jurisdictions didn't get on the system until a few years later, so we're probably going to have some records in the late eighties and early nineties. Ignore those, at least for now. Stick to the dates we've discussed."

He glanced shyly at Kelly, whose head remained down, her eyes glued to her stack of files. "Kelly has all cases prior to 1977, looking for similar crimes on a tri-state level. Meaning Maryland, Pennsylvania, and Virginia. If we're lucky, we'll find proof Mary was active long before she met John. If we can narrow her pattern to a few places, we'll have a better chance of digging up her real name and possibly finding information leading to where she might be now."

I nodded and sat down next to Kelly, who looked at the folders and paper as if they might give her hives. "And there's no computerized record of any of this?"

"In the bigger cities, there's a few," Ryan said, smiling as he no doubt understood her pain. "But we've got a lot of small towns on the route."

"This is like searching for a needle in a haystack," I said. "I'd rather be out there, actively searching."

"It's probably best you stay here." Todd gave me a hard look. "And you never know, we might find the smoking gun right here."

I rolled my eyes and reached for a donut. There wasn't enough sugar in the world for this job.

By noon, we'd found a number of unsolved murders along the I-95 corridor, but none of them glaringly matched the assaults on the known Weston victims. We found no mention of wooden spoons, a fun fact that turned Ryan slightly green. It looked like John and Mary either had been very careful before they moved to Lancaster, or they didn't kill together before then.

Kelly made a clucking noise next to me, so soft I barely heard it in my half-awake state. Hours of combing through these files, with so many personal details omitted by thick black mark-outs, threatened to put me to sleep.

"Luce." Her whisper possessed an urgency that gave me a thread of hope.

"What?"

She pointed to her file. "Rollins. I remember this name from earlier research."

I glanced at Todd, intent on his own file, but no doubt listening. "What earlier research?"

"Months ago," she said. "Mary Rollins in Harford County is a name I cross-referenced, but I had no reason to tie it to Mary Weston. But here it is again, in 1972. Harford County."

I read over her shoulder. Richard Rollins had died in a house fire in 1972, leaving his widow of one year, Mary, a small life insurance policy. Mary wasn't on the property at the time. She'd been with her father on his truck route.

My heart skidded. "Mary Weston told the Hale family she worked with her father, and he drove a truck."

Todd looked up from his pile, his eyes bleary behind his reading glasses. "You have a name?"

"Kent," Kelly said. "Alan Kent."

The air raced out of my lungs, leaving a hollow burn. "Chris's middle name is Alan." I saw him clearly then, sitting across from me at Cheddar's that first night, so cocky and confident. My throat tightened, and a wave of fear left me mute. Whatever the lies he'd told me, Chris had saved my life. He'd trusted me when few others did. Where was he now? What sort of pain was his mother subjecting him to?

I should have taken his calls. I could have talked him out of it, at least stalled him so I could call the police and give them the heads-up. I never should have brought Chris into my games. But it was too late for him now.

"What else do you have?" Ryan asked. "Harford County is actually one of the few that has gone back and digitized some of their records, but the last one I'm finding is 1975. Nothing in 1972 or for any Rollinses."

Kelly cleared her throat, her neck and face turning red as all eyes focused on her. She pushed the file to me with trembling hands.

"The fire occurred at 22 Stapely Road in Harford County, in Churchville." I looked at Ryan. "Can you pull that up on a map?"

Ryan did as he was told. "It's an unincorporated community about sixteen miles southeast, on the other side of Bel Air."

"The cause of the fire was believed to be accidental," I said. "Several dishrags containing ammonia and other combustibles were left in a cleaning bucket in the kitchen. The fire started overnight. Richard Rollins's body was found in the downstairs bedroom, which was across the hall from the kitchen." I squinted at the small print, wishing I'd succumbed to the need for reading glasses. "It was so badly burned the coroner at the time couldn't tell if he'd inhaled smoke or not. There were no signs of an accelerant on or near his person. Some investigators were suspicious of his being in that bedroom, as he and his wife slept upstairs, but there was no proof of foul play. The corpse was too badly burned to tell if he'd been tied down or given any sort of drugs."

"Wow," Ryan said. "I know it was the seventies, but that's some weak investigation."

"A lot of things have changed," Todd said. "And remember, small towns had less resources—and still do."

"That might not be the only reason." Instinct crackled in the synapses of my mind, almost as though Mary Weston had crawled into my ear and found a way to whisper her secrets. "Richard Rollins was black. He's actually listed as 'Negro.'" I shook my head in disgust. "His wife is white, per the description in the report. So their interracial marriage bothered officers enough to note it on the report. Who knows how well his death was investigated? If they did anything more than the bare minimum, I'd be shocked."

"Shocked might be an understatement," Ryan said. "Interracial marriage wasn't even fully legalized until 1967, so it was still new in the seventies. Especially in the South. There were

*

plenty of rumored lynchings even after the law was passed." He flushed as he realized we all stared at him. "Sorry, I'm kind of a history buff. Continue."

"Rollins had life insurance," Kelly pointed out. "$25,000 of it, which was a lot of money in those days. He was a construction worker, and he got the insurance through the union."

"Does it have any information on his family?" Todd asked.

I skimmed the report. "A younger sister who told the police she didn't trust Mary Kent or her father. But there's no contact information. Just a name."

"Kent," Todd said. "So that's the surname listed in the file?"

"Yes, but there's no copy of the marriage certificate," Kelly said. She pointed to the pathetically small paragraph containing the sister's statement. "They knew her as Mary Kent, father named Alan. There are a few notes in here about the sister calling hysterically after her brother's death, demanding the police look into Mary's involvement. It doesn't appear they ever did."

"Of course not." The idea had already taken root, but I needed to flesh it out for a few minutes. "Back then, police would never question a white woman over a black man's death. Not in small-town Maryland."

"So..." Todd rubbed his forehead. "We've got Mary Weston's real name as possibly being Mary Kent, and her father as Alan Kent. We need to look up birth records for those names between 1950 and 1954. That's a wide net, but with all the lies Mary told, I'm not counting age out as one of them."

"Then I might be able to find something," Ryan said. "Census records are online, and some birth records, depending on the state. Give me an hour and I'll see what I can come up with."

"Ladies," Todd said. "Shall we break for lunch? There's a small diner just down the street with great greasy cheeseburgers."

Kelly looked at me with frightened eyes, shaking her head.

"She needs some rest," I said. "Let's drop her off at the hotel, and then you and I can grab something."

"Greasy" perfectly described the diner. My shoes squeaked against the floor, and the table felt as if it had been cleaned by yesterday's dishrag. The place smelled of fried food and an impending heart attack. And it was nearly full. Todd and I jammed into a two-seater table beneath the window, the quarters so tight our knees nearly touched.

I shook my coat off and sat on it, wary of it falling on the floor. I should have ordered a salad, but the burgers smelled too good to ignore. When our waitress disappeared, Todd pounced.

"So Kelly's your hacker."

It sounded like more of a statement than a question. I shrugged. "She's my friend."

"Who happens to be a forensic consultant for the Philly police. Funny how you never mentioned her before."

"I have a lot of friends you don't know about," I lied. The realization left me cold. I'd never had a lot of friends, preferring to live in semi-isolation, but that seemed sad now, as though I'd missed out on so much of life.

"Fair enough," he said. "What's her story? You said she had space issues."

"She was a case of mine," I said. "You can look her up for details, but let's just say her stepfather screwed her up royally. She was a near shut-in for a long time, and it's only been in the last couple of years she's started to venture out more regularly. I'm shocked she wanted to come with me."

"She's a good friend," Todd said. "You should hang on to her."

"I intend to." I cleared my throat, taken aback by the

sympathy in his voice. He'd leave Kelly alone. "So, do you think we have our name? Mary Kent?"

"I don't know. Obviously she started somewhere, and the stuff with her father fits. But Rollins was black, and I very clearly remember my stepmother using the N-word quite freely. She had a racial chip on her shoulder the size of the state. My father never seemed to mind."

The idea that had first occurred to me in the cramped conference room had been spot on. At least some of my instincts were still reliable. "Exactly. So she seduces Rollins, knowing full well he's got the life insurance policy. She and her father plan it out." I tapped my index finger on the table. "I always wondered how she managed to make ends meet, even when she was married to John. In Lancaster, he worked as a handyman and stayed close to home. Yet they bought that property. Who knows how many times Mary worked the life insurance scam before she met him?"

"The idea of Mary seducing anyone blows my mind," Todd said. "When I knew her, she was a middle-aged, overweight, angry woman with crow's feet."

That's how I remembered her as well. When I'd first entered the home as a concerned CPS worker, she'd struck me as a small giant whose habitat was being threatened. "You also saw her through the eyes of a seventeen-year-old boy who hated his stepmother. Both ADA Hale and his wife said she was attractive on some level when she was young, and you have to understand, women like her have the ability to use whatever they possess and make it work. They're like a virus, able to attack the body's weakest point and infect until the person is fully under their control." Myself and my mother included. But we'd both been blessed with good genes, and people more easily trusted an attractive person. A fact I'd proven more times than I wanted to admit.

"You speak as if you know what you're talking about."

I took a long drink of water. "Maybe I do."

"Hmm." Todd nodded at the waitress depositing plates containing our massive burgers. He waited until she'd moved on to her next table. "I remember the first time I saw Mary, before they were married—or so they said. I can't really remember her face, just the impression. Tall and dark, like her face was sunk into her curtain of hair. It was still long then. Normally I thought long hair was beautiful, especially since my mother kept hers short, but Mary's hair made me think of the things I imagined hiding in my closet. I hated her from that moment on principle." He picked up his hamburger. "And she didn't disappoint."

"I'm sorry," I said, feeling lousy that was all I could muster. "You and Justin both deserved so much more."

"At least we're alive," Todd said. "That's more than a lot of her other victims can say." His eyes flickered between mine, the implication growing between us. No matter what cruel act my own victims had committed, I'd caused someone in their lives horrible suffering. How was I any different from Mary? And how long would Todd continue to dance around the elephant?

Lennox had no intention of dancing, and I wasn't sure if that scared me or gave me some sort of relief. Maybe I wouldn't have to kill again.

"We need to see if we can locate Rollins's family," Todd said. "Maybe his sister is still alive."

"A photo of Mary as a young woman would be even better," I said. "We can show it to the sister—if she's alive—and see if she can identify her."

"Let me ask you something," Todd said. "In all the research you've done the past few weeks, did you come up with anything that suggested she had any sort of close relationship with her father?"

I shook my head. "Do you remember her talking about him?"

"No, but I did everything I could to shut her out."

"And yet we know she worked for him, according to John. We know from the tone of her emails she wanted to tell Chris about her family. And there's this old man Lennox seems hung up on."

"Exactly," Todd said. "Which has me wondering about how many generations of crazy we are dealing with here."

We picked Kelly up before driving the few meager blocks to the station. Walking to the conference room, I felt a buzz in the air, as if a fly had somehow survived the miserable winter and taken root inside my brain. My footsteps quickened; my fingers jittered. Kelly matched my pace. She must have felt it too.

"You guys got back just in time." Ryan stood up from his computer, revealing the rest of his body to be as thin and gangly as his face. "So I found three different birth records that could be our gal. Three men named Alan were registered on birth certificates for daughters named Mary. None of them were Kent."

"Could be another alias," Todd said. "Or she didn't have a birth certificate. If she was born in the fifties and in the poorer part of the state, it's possible."

"I managed to track down current addresses for two of the three women," Ryan said. "Agent Lennox is sending field agents to interview them."

"That's not what has you so excited," I said. "What else has happened?"

Ryan's long body lurched to the left as he paced excitedly. This was likely the biggest case he'd been involved in. "There's been a sighting of the older man from Jarrettsville a couple of hours south."

TWENTY-ONE

Waiting for news made me feel powerless and far more imbalanced than usual. Our small group busied ourselves with more case files, searching for similar victims, but most were robberies and drug deals gone bad. A few missing girls, but no specific tie-in to Mary's known assaults.

"So he and Mary didn't start killing until 1980 when they moved to Lancaster." Todd took off his glasses for the millionth time and rubbed his eyes. "Maybe it took longer to break John into submission."

"Or they changed their MO," I said. "Perfected it. If Mary Kent really is our girl, and she married and then killed Richard Rollins for insurance money in 1972, I can't see her stopping there. Not with the way she likes to torture. She had to be active between then and the time she met John. No way is she able to put a lid on that kind of aggression."

"I don't think she did, either." Kelly spoke for the first time since arriving back at the station. Her hands rested on the stack of records she'd been assigned, all prior to Mary and John Weston's meeting. "At first I didn't see any sort of pattern in these files. There's several missing and murdered girls from two different states, with age their only thing in common. But then I pulled up a map on my phone, and it dawned on me that all of these cases occurred on Interstates 95 and 81, between 1972 and 1978. If her father was a long-haul trucker and she worked for him, is this possible?" Kelly finally lifted her eyes to meet mine and then realized everyone in the room was staring at her as if she'd just dangled a golden carrot.

"I need an atlas." Todd jumped up, his chair banging the wall, and hurried out of the room.

"I can pull it up on the computer," Ryan said.

"Sometimes a real map is better," I said. "He can mark it up all he wants. Kel, tell us about these girls."

She flushed, ducking her head down and pulling her short hair as far around her cheeks as possible. "So far I have four definite murders—meaning their bodies were found. There are four more girls still missing."

"Jesus," Ryan said. "That's a long time to pray for someone to come home."

It was, and it never ended, no matter how much time passed. The family members left behind always clung to the flickering hope their loved one might walk through the door again.

Todd returned with a beat-up map of Maryland and Northern Virginia as Kelly continued. "The four murdered girls were between fourteen and seventeen, three white and one black. From what I can tell, there's nothing else they have in common."

"And they're not linked in the system?" I said. "Some detective didn't make a note thinking this might be a serial?"

Kelly shook her head as Todd plopped down the map beside her. She jerked away, nearly bumping into me, and he flushed red. "Sorry." He took a careful step back. "As for the cops linking these together, remember, this is the early seventies, before sophisticated computers and before serial killers were damned near cliché. It's not a stretch that it didn't happen. Can you tell me the locations so I can mark them on this map?"

Kelly nodded, allowing her body to uncoil. "In 1972, Connie Elway was found in a field about twenty miles from Richmond. She was from Bowie, Maryland. In 1974, Lena Moran's body was found in a ditch just south of Dale City, which isn't too far from D.C.," Kelly said. "She was from Ashland, Virginia."

Todd made his marks on the map, circling the locations with a red marker. "That's close to Richmond. What about the other two murders?"

"Sarah Shelby in 1977, found in Triangle, Virginia. From McLean, Virginia."

"A suburb of D.C.," I said, stretching to see the map. "And it looks like there's a bypass around it that connects to I-95."

"But there might not have been a bypass in '77," Todd reminded me. "Kelly, go on."

"Marie Smith, taken from Arcadia, Virginia, and dumped southwest of Richmond in a town called Tuckahoe."

Todd squinted. "That's almost on I-64. You said there's more on Interstate 81?"

"Yes," Kelly said. "Those are still listed as missing." She read off the names of four more girls who'd all disappeared just off Interstates 95 or 81. The cases stretched out in a pattern that was only easy to spot if someone was looking, but the police working the cases back then didn't have the tools we did now. ViCAP might have saved some of these girls' lives.

"Are there any missing or murdered off Interstate 64?" Todd asked. A fine sheen of sweat had broken out across his forehead.

Kelly flipped through her files. "I don't see any..." She opened up the file on the bottom of the weathered pile. "Wait. I hadn't got to this one yet. Where's Lexington?"

Todd drew a circle on the map where Lexington nearly

connected Interstates 64 and 81. "Right there." He streaked a
red line down one interstate to the next. "From Baltimore to
Richmond on I-95 and then over to 81 via I-64. They took 81
back north and cut over to Baltimore at some point."

He and I exchanged victorious smiles, but the color had
drained from Kelly's face. "What is it?"

Kelly swallowed hard. "Myra Weston. That's the girl's
name. She went missing February 25, 1978."

Cold sweat erupted on my back. Nausea flooded my system
even as admiration for Mary's brazenness sparked. "Tell me
again when John met Mary?" I knew the answer. I just needed
to hear it out loud.

"March," Todd said. "March of 1978."

We all sat in silence for several seconds, letting the information
digest. Ryan, who'd remained silent during the mapping, broke
the tension. "So Mary, who claimed to be working with her
father when John met her in 1978, just happened to have the
last name of one of the missing and presumed dead girls on this
route? And then goes on to kill a bunch of girls? How similar are
the crimes?"

Kelly took her time answering. "All of the murder victims
were tortured and mutilated. Raped with inanimate objects."
She flipped through the files, looking for the autopsy reports,
murmuring to herself. Finally, she looked up to meet my gaze.
"Marie Smith died of sepsis, and one of the other girls had a
similar infection, but she was strangled before it could kill her."

The spoons. Mary's favorite toy, something everyone had at
home. Did she purposely not wash them? Was passing on the
wicked infection just another form of torture?

Todd looked back down at the misshapen rectangle he'd
drawn on the map. "We already know her father was a long-
haul trucker in the seventies, which is the heyday of interstate

commerce and trucker culture in general. Those guys were
everywhere, and police had a hard time keeping up with the
crime rate. Most were misdemeanors, but those trucks were the
perfect traveling torture chamber."

I thought of Aron, the boy I'd saved just a few months ago,
and shivered. "And now we've got this old guy in Jarrettsville
who suddenly appeared an hour south. You think it's possible
Mary and her father hooked up again?" I asked.

"I don't know," Todd said. "She never mentioned family,
but like I said, I tried not to talk to her."

I pushed my chair away from the table. "Right now, the only
way to confirm these murders were done by Mary or her father
is to get a confession. And the only person besides Mary who
might know the answer is John. Someone needs to try to talk to
him again now that his son is missing."

"You think he cares?" Todd asked.

"He gave Chris his stuff," I said. "It's worth a shot."

"You'll have to convince Lennox," Ryan said. "He's tried to
talk to Weston several times with no results."

"Any idea on when Lennox will be back?" I asked.

Ryan checked his phone. "He texted fifteen minutes ago he
was on his way."

Agent Lennox arrived alone an hour later, bringing a gust of
cold air and frustration into the small room. We'd yet to find any
more missing cases, but Ryan had sent a request to all state law
enforcement agencies for missing or murdered females along
our kill line, as we'd taken to calling it, between 1972 and 1978.
"I doubt we'll get anything until tomorrow," he said. "Hopefully
Agent Lennox can light a fire."

"And why would I do that?" Lennox strode into the room,
his dark eyes brooding. He didn't stand quite as tall as he had

this morning, and he walked like a man who'd just lost the race of his life.

"What did you find out?" I asked.

Lennox tossed a grainy, black and white picture onto the table. Obviously printed off security footage, the photo looked as if the printer had been running out of ink. I had to squint to make out the old man in the picture. Short and thin, with a shock of white hair and his weak chin ducked into his chest, he clung to the arm of an equally short woman.

"Mary," I said to no one in particular. Wishing I had my reading glasses, I studied the grainy print. Her black hair had grown since the night I'd staked out her house along with Justin and Chris. That seemed like ages ago.

"This was taken from the security camera in a tiny gas station outside of Dale City, Virginia. That's about twenty-five miles west of D.C.," Lennox said. "The town's near Interstate 95, but this gas station definitely isn't. I can't believe it's still operating. It looks like it hasn't been updated since the Depression."

"So either she knew it was there," I said, "or she's deliberately taking side roads and lucked out and found the station." I didn't think any of Mary's success had to do with luck.

"Either way, this is a break," Lennox said. "She might not have expected the place to have a security camera. So we know she was in Dale City less than twelve hours ago. The convenience store clerk positively identified her from her driver's license picture."

"She's going by Martha Beckett in that one?" My head hurt from trying to keep the names straight.

"Yep," Lennox said. "But of course, she paid in cash. This was taken this morning, and there was no sign of Chris, but that doesn't mean he wasn't there. Detective Adams stayed to mobilize a new search, and I'm heading back down in the morning. What have you guys found out? We're still interviewing the various Mary Kents you located. So far, they're all accounted for and most certainly not our girl."

Todd took the lead. "Kelly found a pattern, and we think it's relevant." He laid out the map and explained each case as we understood it, ending with the final victim, Myra Weston.

"Balls." Lennox slammed his fist on the table, making it shudder. "They took the girl's name. I wonder if they kept her longer than the rest too. Might be why her body was never found."

"The only person who knows that we have access to is John Weston," I said. "We need to talk to him. Before you go back to Virginia."

Lennox looked amused. "Explain to me why you need to see him and why you think you can get him talking."

I felt as if I'd stepped into a pig trough, but I didn't have a choice now. "I can speak on behalf of his son on the chance he does care. And I can understand why he succumbed to Mary. I have an idea of what makes him respond, or at least, what used to make him respond to women."

Lennox studied me with eyes that made me want to sit down and shut up. I felt as if he could somehow strip through the bullshit and get straight to the heart of it: *I'm a manipulative killer just like Mary Weston. John and I have something in common. Let me at him.*

And maybe that's exactly what Lennox did, because after a long silence, he nodded. "We leave at six a.m. I need to be back in Dale City by afternoon."

Kelly and I didn't speak until we'd brought our cold dinners from the greasy diner into the hotel room. She sat down at the small table, staring at the takeout platter. "Are you sure you want to do this?"

"No," I said. "But I'm not sure I've got a choice."

"Lennox is gunning for you," Kelly said. "He looks at you like some kind of conquest. Like he wants to break you down."

I hung my coat in the makeshift closet. "I know."

"And now we're finding out Mary and her father probably killed together." Kelly pushed the tray to the side. "I've been through some terrible things, but I can't wrap my head around that."

"Me neither," I said. "Not until I hear more of the story. And I think I can get it from John."

"Because you keep identifying with Mary," Kelly said. "I see it on your face every time her name's brought up, but you're not like her. Just because you have some skill to manipulate people and you've done some bad things doesn't make you like her. She did those things for her own self-gratification. You were trying to help."

I sat down on the corner of the bed. My head swam, but I needed to confess this sin. "That's just it, Kel. Jake was self-defense. Riley? I felt guilt. Pity. But a rush too." My throat tightened. I could stop there. I didn't have to further mar Kelly's opinion of me. But I needed to purge. "I enjoyed killing Preacher."

The words burned my throat, but I kept going. "His fear was intoxicating. I could have watched him squirm all night. But killing him—that was special. I loved the control it gave me. So what kind of person does that make me?"

Kelly looked at me for a long time, sympathy in her wide, expressive eyes. "I don't know," she finally said. "But you're not her, Lucy. Never allow yourself to believe that."

TWENTY-TWO

I hated flying, and being stuck in a little twin engine provided by the FBI, with Agent Lennox on the prowl like a starving jungle cat, only heightened my dislike. We'd left when the sun came up, boarding the plane for Franklin Township, Pennsylvania. A four-hour plus drive shortened to a thirty-minute flight. I tried to tell myself this was a better alternative than being trapped in a car with Lennox for most of the day, but his constant observance did nothing to ease my nerves.

"So." He sat down across from me. "Before we took off, I heard from my field agents. Most of the Mary Kents we tracked down turned out to be nice, retired ladies. But one of my people turned up an Alan Kent with a very interesting history."

I leaned forward, shoving the foreboding turbulence out of my thoughts. "Is it him?"

Lennox rubbed his forehead, smoothing the deep creases between his eyes. "I think it could be. This guy was born in 1934 and did a six-month bid for assault in 1954 after his wife died in childbirth. 1954 is the birth year for Mary Kent, born in Dale City, Virginia, and the age matches. So we're looking for any DMV records that show an Alan Kent applying for a commercial vehicle license, but again, we're decades ago. We might be grasping at straws."

"Dale City again." I stated the obvious, trying to connect the myriad of dots. "What about Social Security? He's certainly old enough to draw it."

Lennox nodded. "We're checking on whether or not he's been drawing it and where the checks are sent, but it's a paper-work-filled process. I'm hoping to hear something by tomorrow."

He glanced at his phone, his eyes scanning the screen. "One of my people spoke with Richard Rollins's niece. She doesn't remember her uncle or Mary, and her mother's recently passed, so all of her information's secondhand. Mary met Richard in Dale City while he was working at a small truck stop there as a cook. She told him she grew up in Dale City. Her mother died in childbirth, her dad was all she had. He drove a truck, and she liked to ride with him. That's why she was at the truck stop. Her father's name was Alan."

"So pretty similar to the way she met John. But possibly using her real name," I said. "And the story she gave him matches with the information on Mary and Alan Kent. But I don't know how you're going to narrow that down without official records or talking to someone who actually knew them."

"I'm more concerned with the Dale City angle," Lennox said. "Mary went back there for a reason. That's where she was born, assuming that part of the story is true. So why take Chris there? Show him his roots? Her first kill? Where his crazy grandpa first decided to snatch girls and teach her the trade?"

I didn't have a clue. "There's no sign they're using the Kent name right now?"

"Nothing that matches. No credit cards or bank accounts, no major purchases in either state in the last twenty years. No rental property. Nothing traceable. Given our digital age, that's damned tough. And when she lived as sweet baker lady Martha

Beckett, she had a credit record. But it all stopped the night you guys made her."

"She'd been saving her money, and she went right back in hiding after years of moving freely and hasn't made a single mistake," I said. "You'd think she'd be out of practice and slip up."

"She will," Lennox said. "Every criminal does, eventually."

He let the words sit between us, their impact as heavy as dropping a basket of food in front of a starving person.

Lennox leaned forward, his elbows resting on his knees. He'd worn a power suit for the occasion, the charcoal blending quite nicely with the blue dress shirt and tie he'd chosen. "What's your plan here? I know you're a private investigator, and I know you've gotten results. You can deal with people. But this guy doesn't talk. And he's probably bitter as hell."

"I don't think so," I said. "He's in prison because of her, but nothing is forcing his silence. He's never admitted to her involvement—why? Is it loyalty? Did she con him into loving her so much he's happy to waste his life so she can have hers? Does it make it worth it that she's still out there doing her thing?"

"That's one of my theories," Lennox said. "I think he's happier in prison. Safer."

"From her. Or her father?" Lennox's reaction to the kill line had been bugging me since last night. Or rather, his lack of reaction. He hadn't expressed much shock or outrage that these killings had occurred and hadn't been matched to Mary Weston after all this time. And he'd been hung up on the old man the moment he'd heard about him. I debated pumping him for information, but I knew he wouldn't tell me. Not unless I produced something he could use.

He looked out the window as the pilot announced our descent. "Good question. I hope you can get the answer."

TWENTY-THREE

Shaped like a warped pentagon, State Correctional Institution Greene—or SCI Greene—sat on nearly a hundred and thirty acres in Franklin Township, just outside of Waynesburg. As the state's supermax, it housed all violent offenders. As our vehicle drove through the massive, interlocking gate, I turned to watch it glide shut, suddenly queasy.

Heavy-duty fences topped with spikey rolls of barbed wire surrounded the complex. The prison itself was a maze of interlocking buildings and pathways.

Agent Lennox led us through the designated gate and then to the reception area. Outside, the cold morning had been bright and shimmering, with some brave birds who'd decided to weather the winter singing their song. Everything went silent once we crossed the prison's threshold.

As we checked in at reception, providing our credentials and consenting to the weapons check, the somberness gnawed a pit in my stomach. The atmosphere matched every funeral I'd attended, including my sister's. Melancholy saturated the air and seeped its way into the staff. No one smiled, no one joked.

Hysteria bubbled in me until I nearly turned and ran screaming toward the gate.

A round man with a drooping, stern face greeted us. He shook Lennox's hand first and then mine. "Superintendent Robinson. I've informed the prisoner he'll be interviewed today. He said nothing, as usual."

I debated asking Robinson about Chris's visit, but I didn't want to cross any boundaries before I got the chance to speak with John Weston. Lennox would tell me if the prison's records produced anything useful.

We followed Robinson down a well-lit corridor, varying shades of neutrals and gray making me feel even more smothered by misery—probably exactly what the facility was designed to accomplish.

"He's in interview room number one," Robinson said. "You know the protocol, Agent Lennox. He's in restraints, so I won't send an officer in with you, but he'll be right outside the locked door. The entire interview will be recorded." His eyes slid to me. "You sure you want to do this?"

I stood taller, reminding myself I'd faced the worst of the worst and came out on top. Fear did nothing for me now. "I'll be fine."

The door slid open painfully slow, revealing a generic room with a table and chairs. A man faced us, his prison orange the only color in the room. John Weston's salt and pepper hair was cut neatly, his beard only scruff. A thin scar ran from his eye to his chin, likely a result of a prison fight. He sat quietly, his cuffed hands folded on the table. Lennox allowed me to enter first, and as I walked toward the nearest seat, my shoes smacking the floor, my eyes caught his.

They were a very familiar, crystalline blue.

They shined with a glint of knowing, the way an infant reacts to another child without needing to be told he's mingling with his peers. Or more appropriately, the way a predator sizes up competition.

He knows what you are.

His mouth ticked up in the slightest hint of a smirk that made me feel like running away. Instead I moved forward and took my seat. Weston watched every move, those hauntingly familiar eyes possessing the same power of Chris's: instead of looking at me, it was as if John Weston lasered right through the pomp and femininity and saw my true heart. *The heart of a killer, just like him.*

"Hello again, John." Lennox spoke easily as he took the seat next to mine. "How are you doing?"

"Fine." The voice was soft, not at all the sort of thing you'd expect from a man convicted of multiple murders. Then again, we had that in common, didn't we?

"This is Lucy Kendall," Agent Lennox said. "She's a friend of your son's, and a private investigator. Are you aware he's missing?"

"I am." He gave nothing away, and our eyes locked, each trying to feel the other out. I didn't smile, but looking away wasn't an option. Let him see me, let him make his assumptions. I needed information.

"We believe he located his mother, and either she or an accomplice wounded him," Lennox said. "We're operating under the assumption he's still alive and being held against his will by her and whoever she's with." Lennox slid the photo from the convenience store across the table. "Do you recognize this old man?"

John's eyes barely flickered to the picture, his drumming fingers missing just a beat. "Nope."

Lennox looked at me and nodded. I'd been ordered not to mention the kill line or the Kent surname, but I could reference Mary's father as much as I wanted. "Mr. Weston."

"Please, call me John."

"John, then. We really need you to help us. We know Chris communicated with his mother after finding out some disturbing information regarding custody of him as a child. He's not in a good place, and he's vulnerable to her."

John said nothing.

Lennox leaned back in his chair. Sweat dampened my neck. I wished I'd worn my hair up. "I know how Mary operates." My tongue felt grimy, coated with shame. "She makes you feel special. She looks at you like you're the only person in the room, even though you see nothing special about yourself. She makes you feel like her light, as if she can't push forward without you. This is how she gets your guard down. You open up and tell her about all the things you hate about your life."

John remained silent, looking at me with those eyes that seemed strong enough to slice through my skull.

"She listens and understands. She's got the innate ability to tell you everything you need to hear, and the next thing you know, she's in control. But you're all right with that, because she makes you feel so important. And then you'll do whatever she asks. And you did, right?"

Sweat began to shine on his forehead. Bolstered, I continued. He might see me for who I really was, but I also saw him. Tit for tat. "It was always about Mary and her needs, wasn't it, John? And she let you take the fall. She set you up.

"Chris is in danger," I said. "He's in danger because he's completely lost. He feels abandoned by his family, just like you did. And he's physically injured. With Mary and her father talking in his ear about their family history. Is that what she did to you?"

John's jaw clenched as if he'd bitten into a rock-solid walnut.

"She's going to do the same thing to Chris. This guy who put the demons of his childhood behind him, who helps people.

He's a paramedic, and he saves lives. Do you want your son to end up another one of her victims?"

"Stop."

"Chris told me you used to taking him fishing," I pressed. "He remembers you being a good father, the affectionate one when she was silent and cold. You've spent all these years in prison and allowing her to run free. Why, John?"

"It doesn't matter."

Lennox shifted beside me, and I prayed he'd stay silent. "Yes, it does. It matters for your son." I leaned forward, feeling the snap of frustration. "You can't tell me Mary Weston has such a hold over you that you've pined all these years. You took part in killing those girls for her, but some part of you enjoyed it. You relished the control and the adrenaline rush." My entire scalp felt soaked, as if I'd been running. "Those things made you feel powerful—something you craved. And Mary made you feel like that's the only way you could be the man she needed. But she used the spoons, John. She took part. And then she let you rot in prison while she married another man and started over. Why, John? Why are you silent?"

"You're just like I pictured you." John's quiet words hit me with the force of a bullhorn.

"I'm sorry?"

"Chris said you were strong. That you knew how to get things done—the right things."

My vision blurred. I blinked, all hope of keeping a poker face gone. I looked to Lennox for guidance; he sat stone-faced, staring at John with an expression so carefully blank it told me everything I needed to know.

Lennox knew Chris had spoken to his father. He'd kept the information from me.

The shock eased, fury taking its place. This was why Lennox had given in to my interviewing Weston so easily. He'd played me like some stupid girl, and I'd fallen for it.

Murderous rage flowed through me, as powerful as the force that drove me to kill. I wanted to stare daggers at Lennox and make him see exactly who he'd double-crossed, but I needed to gain back control of the interview if I had any hope of getting information from John.

I forced myself to look back at the prisoner, and his smile drowned my frenzy. It reeked of self-righteous, all-knowing arrogance. "He said you liked to win. I guess you didn't know he visited me."

"That doesn't matter. What matters is—"

"Don't be mad at him for not telling you," John said. "He was worried about you. Thought you were losing your edge."

"The visit was recent." My voice sounded much more calm than I felt.

"About a month ago," John said. "You'd have to check the prison log. It's easy to lose track of time in here."

"Did Chris talk about Mary at all?"

John threaded his fingers together. "He remembers her as a woman who liked to be in control. She ran the house. I allowed it. She ran our lives. I allowed that too. She made the decisions, I followed. It was easier somehow, not having to think so much. And she knew more about life than me. Knew what kind of people existed in this world and how to take care of them."

"Is that why she chose innocent girls as her victims?" I couldn't stop the sarcasm leaking.

"They weren't innocent," John said. "Not in Mary's mind."

"What did they do that deserved the torture and abuse you inflicted on them?"

He shrugged. "I allowed her to make the judgment. As I said, she knew better than me."

"Or so she convinced you," I said.

His smile stretched from ear to ear, revealing two missing teeth. "You're just like he said. You don't pack any punches. Just like Mary. I liked that about her. Telling the truth meant something to her."

I felt sick all over again. But it was there, the weapon I needed. It was just a matter of wielding it properly. "You met your son. He's a good man. A paramedic. He's volunteered with troubled kids. He's done a lot of things to fix the issues in his life, and all he wanted is answers. Mary has him now. Remember Chris?"

I felt the momentum shifting. John leaned away from the table; I leaned forward. "He's got your eyes. He sat across from you just like I am and tried to tell you about his life so that you'd tell him about yours. He tried to bond with you, didn't he?"

John said nothing, but I saw enough in the shadows that crossed his eyes.

"And you failed him," I said. "You let him walk out of here with nothing, and he turned to her. But you can fix that now. Tell us how we can find Chris."

John cleared his throat, the sound loud, as if he'd gone years without speaking. "I cared about my son. I still do. But before I say anything else, I want to know something about you."

Sweat trickled between my shoulder blades. Panic blazed in my chest. He was going to ask a question I couldn't answer, not in front of Lennox. But my choices were nil. "Go ahead."

"Chris said you're a good person. That you understand right from wrong when it counts, and you do the right thing no matter how hard it is. Is that true?"

What had Chris told his father?

"He never said your name, you know." John read my expression. "Just that a woman he knew had the right idea about things, that he'd worked hard to become a part of her life. He said she understood the torment he'd gone through."

The room twisted as if we'd been dropped into the middle of a cyclone. I barely managed to answer. "Yes."

"So, is Chris right about you?"

Whatever Chris said to him would have been recorded. He'd have spoken in code, hoping his father would decipher. Or maybe he was just referring to his hope that I could save him from being a sociopath, an idea he'd voiced when we'd first met. Either way, he'd admitted to his father he'd worked to be a part of my life. I couldn't allow myself to think about that right now. "Yes."

John stared at me for several long seconds. I gave it right back, even as Lennox shifted anxiously in his chair. Keeping silent had to be infuriating for him. Good. Served him right for this stunt.

Whatever John wanted to see, he must have been satisfied, because he nodded. "Alan's crazy. He warned me that if we ever got caught, I'd take the blame or he'd kill my son. And after the things I saw him do, I believed him."

The air left my lungs in a searing breath. Lennox flexed like a nervous animal. "What name did they use, John? What are their aliases?"

"Weston is the only one they gave me."

"And they came from where?" I said. "Virginia? Maryland?"

"She said she grew up in Virginia until her dad took her on the road when she was around seven."

"Is that where she learned her killing trade?"

John shrugged.

"Do you know of any property they might have, any place they might hole up?"

"It's been nearly thirty years since I spoke to her. How would I know that? The only place they'd ever stayed in for long was the house in Lancaster. That's all I know."

He folded his arms over his wide chest. We would get nothing more out of him, but at least he'd confirmed our suspicions. Lennox stood, and I followed his lead. "Thank you for talking with me, John. You've been a big help. When we find

Chris, I'm going to tell him what you told me. He needs to know you still care."

He looked up at me with those unsettling blue eyes then. "You know it's too late for him. If they've got him, he's as good as dead, even if he keeps breathing."

TWENTY-FOUR

Nausea rolled through my stomach and into my esophagus, cold sweat slathering my arms and back. My face burned. Each step felt unsteady, as if my ankles were weak and ready to roll beneath me. And then I'd be trapped in this prison forever, with all of the other murderers.

Right where I belong.

Lennox communed with the excited superintendent while my mind tumbled. Apparently John Weston had spoken more to me than anyone who'd ever interviewed him. As if that made me special. I guessed it did. He saw the same thing inside my heart he did in his ex-wife's, something black and bleak and unforgiving.

"You all right?" Lennox's hand touched my elbow, the motion grounding me just enough to stop the room from spinning.

I jerked my arm away. "Don't touch me."

He didn't seem to notice my anger. "Give me a few minutes, and then we're out. I've got to get to Virginia." He turned back to Superintendent Robinson, and their voices rose as they went over strategies.

I no longer cared. John Weston had given us all he would, and it was enough. Mary Weston had been raised to be a killer by her father. Her bond with him superseded any with her sons, and John Weston had given his freedom so that his son could live.

Was Chris still alive? And if he so, was he dead to me?

Lennox led me out of the prison, through the various clanging gates and security checks, into the cold, fresh winter air. I breathed deeply, realizing I'd been truly afraid I wasn't coming out of that place. *Maybe another day.*

"I'm going to have Ryan search Virginia and Maryland for any more activity with the name Weston," Lennox said as we got into the SUV. "But I doubt we'll find anything. They dropped that as soon as the shit hit the fan in Lancaster. He's already checking for Kent, but I have zero hope for that."

I said nothing, walking briskly to the car. Lennox caught up with me, two quick beeps from the SUV indicating he'd unlocked it. I jerked open the passenger door and sat down, making sure to slam it shut.

Lennox slid into the driver's seat. "Look, I'm sorry. I should have told you that Chris visited his father last month. But to be fair, I only found out this morning. I thought if I told you it might mess with your head."

"You wanted to get my reaction," I said. "To make sure I didn't know."

"Not at all," Lennox said. "You were so sure Chris hadn't spoken with his father that I was afraid finding out might throw off your game. And yeah," he sighed, starting the car. "I knew he talked about you—or a woman I assumed was you. Weston wasn't lying. Chris didn't name any names. I thought if he actually talked, things might go better if you didn't know Chris had been here. And I was right."

"You threw me to the wolves," I said. "Chris hid more things from me than I realized. You didn't tell me because you want to be able to say 'I told you so,' if it turns out Mary breaks him."

"You're wrong," he said. "I want to find Chris and his mother. And his grandfather. I don't care whose feelings get hurt in the process." Lennox hit the gas. "And my plan worked. Weston connected to you, somehow."

I didn't bother to explain why John Weston connected to me. The agent would eventually figure it out for himself. "Fine. Then I want some answers."

"Go ahead. I'll do my best."

"Yesterday, when we showed you that kill line, the route we thought Mary's father might have taken. We were all bouncing off the walls, and you took it in stride. And today, Weston's confession didn't shock you."

Lennox drove out of the gate, waving at the guard. His silence only proved he had something major to tell me. I tried to remind myself that he was the FBI agent, and I was just a private investigator here because he allowed it, but my ego and personal investment mucked up my ability to rationalize.

Once we entered the highway, he spoke. "I've had my suspicions about a father-daughter team since the Mary Weston/Martha Beckett case hit my desk last fall."

"Why?" How could he have possibly known about Alan?

"First, we knew Mary was a killer. And when I started going over the Lancaster stuff, I saw something that freaked me the hell out." Lennox gripped the wheel, obviously still affected by the memory. "My first year as an agent, I worked a lot of cold cases. Some of the very same ones Kelly looked at yesterday, although not Myra Weston's. That never came up, and if it had, I would have made the connection sooner. But I saw the pattern, and I considered a long-haul trucking route. Those files you all saw, they were minimal. You didn't see the crime scene photos."

"Bad?"

"Horrific. Multiple sexual assaults, torture. The girls were bound and two of the autopsies showed it had been several days since they'd eaten. But it was the sepsis that rang a bell."

"Mary and her unwashed foreign objects," I said.

"Some of the torture marks were similar to those found in Lancaster," Lennox said. "Lighter marks, flesh wounds from a pocketknife in specific places. Possible signatures. When I spoke to Assistant District Attorney Hale last fall and heard about how Mary and his adopted brother met, I started to wonder. Because like you, I believed Lancaster wasn't her first go around."

"Alan was in Lancaster," I said. "For all we know, John Weston did very little of the crimes. Alan might have been the main male perpetrator."

"Did Chris ever mention his grandfather being around?"

"Not to me," I said. Which meant exactly zilch at this point. "I'm sure ADA Hale would have told you if he had. But there's quite a few things Chris hasn't told me."

Lennox took the exit for the airport. "He definitely doesn't have genetics working in his favor. And with the position they've got him in now, assuming he's still alive, he's vulnerable. How far can they push him? What will he do to survive?"

"He won't kill anyone." I didn't know if I believed that anymore. People could be pushed to do terrible things in the heat of stress.

That's what I had done, and where had it gotten me? Is that the person I wanted to be? Because my chosen path would certainly land me in a supermax before it was all over, and with how many deaths on my soul? Or even worse, on the run like Mary, using fake names and constantly looking over my shoulder, wondering if today was the day I'd finally be caught.

Kelly's words drifted back to me, and I thought again about the job opening with the National Center for Missing and Exploited Children. Maybe I could make a difference there. I could carve out a new life, reinvent myself. Make peace with the bad decisions of the past and focus on the future.

The idea sounded like a fantasy, but after being inside the prison and seeing the pale, worn countenance of John Weston, one I very much wanted to cling to. At least I still had the opportunity to try to fix my life.

Thanks to his own foolish decision—something I was certainly guilty of—Chris had everything against him.

On the plane, awaiting take-off, Lennox made calls and barked orders. I sat down and tried to come to grips with everything I'd learned today, but the understanding wouldn't come. I felt as if I'd stepped into the middle of a movie and had no way to orient myself. No clue what to do next.

Lennox was about to make it worse. He stopped at my seat. I'd already buckled in and closed my eyes, hoping for sleep. "What is it?"

"There's been a second sighting in Virginia. With Chris."

TWENTY-FIVE

Lennox left me at the station with a cursory goodbye and a promise to update me on the sighting. In the conference room, more files and case jackets had arrived. Kelly's and Ryan's heads were bent at painful angles, each of them lost in their own work. Todd stood at the whiteboard, scrawling more notes.

"There's been another sighting. This time Chris was with them." My voice sounded scratchy. "In Virginia, the gas station outside of Dale City. Lennox is on his way." I sank into the chair next to Kelly and scooted as close as I dared. Somehow sitting next to her cleared some of the mottled air in my head. "John Weston talked. Mary's father was with them in Lancaster, and he threatened to kill Chris if John didn't take the blame."

All three of them stared. Kelly squeezed my hand, and without thinking, I leaned my head on her shoulder.

"We're searching for anything on Mary and Alan Kent," Ryan said. "So far it's pretty scarce, which isn't surprising since they probably haven't used the name since the early seventies. We also found a few other unsolved cases in both Maryland and

Virginia that might be their work." He paused, his shaggy bangs nearly in his eyes. "Or his. Alan's, I mean. We're not sure, but it fits what we know about the other cases. Just a different interstate."

"We don't know what he did before 1972," I said. "Other than taking his daughter to ride with him on the road. Stands to reason he started killing in his truck then."

"She was just a kid," Todd said, his trademark empathy seeping through. "If he killed them in front of her, it's no wonder she turned out this way."

"I have no doubt he did." I assumed I didn't need to explain why. Surely they could see all of the signs: Mary's inability to bond with her sons, her stone-cold killing, her skill at making any situation work for her. She'd been groomed to be a killer.

"Now they've got Chris." Emotion snagged in my throat, and I stumbled away from the table. "Excuse me."

I couldn't allow them to see me cry. Especially Todd, although I knew he understood. Whatever lies and games Chris might have played with me, my heart ached for the torment he must be enduring. Mary wouldn't stop until one or both of them were dead. The thought left me cold and shaking. Leaning against the wall, clammy with sweat and outright exhaustion, I searched for the ladies' room, but my legs gave out a few feet away. I slipped to the chilly floor and put my head on my knees.

Dry sobs wracked my chest. I rocked back and forth, unsure if I cried for Chris or myself or something more. In that moment, if I could have ended it all, I would have.

"Lucy." Kelly sat down beside me, her delicate arm wrapping around my shoulders. "It's going to be all right. Somehow."

"No, it's really not." It hurt to talk through the tears. "No matter what happens, none of us are going to be all right. Not like we once were."

"Well, no," Kelly said. "But I accepted that a long time ago."

Shame heated my face. "I'm sorry, I wasn't thinking."

"It's fine." She gave me a squeeze. "I think it's about the new normal, you know? Like you go through this period of agony and then denial, telling yourself you can just deal with whatever happened. And then you slam the bottom—for me it was running away from that last foster home and nearly dying of exposure, you remember that?"

I shoved the hair out of my face and tried to stow the tears. "You scared me to death. That winter was so cold, and I thought for sure you'd lose a foot. Not to mention the pneumonia."

"You know being in that hospital was the safest I'd felt?" she asked. "Even when CPS originally rescued me from my stepfather, and I spent a few weeks at Children's Hospital, I still believed he'd find a way to come for me. And if he didn't, one of his buddies would."

"I would have never allowed that to happen." Kelly had still been a teenager when she'd been rescued, and CPS's hope was the light atmosphere of Philadelphia's Children's Hospital and its highly trained staff would make her feel safe. She'd spent the entire time curled in a ball, refusing to look at or speak to anyone.

"I know that now," she said. "But the second time, with the pneumonia, something changed. I realized I wanted to live, and that just maybe, I had some kind of shot at a different life—a decent life. Even if I had to learn to accept my baggage."

Even after all these years, I couldn't fathom how Kelly had found the strength to do more than simply exist. Her struggles made my problems seem woefully small, and I finally found my composure. "Sitting there with John Weston, I knew he'd talk. You know why?"

"Because you convinced him you understood Mary."

"That was only part of it, and more for Lennox's benefit," I said. "I knew he'd talk because, like any good psychopath, he can read people. Smell his own kind. He picked up my scent as soon as I entered that room. I saw it in his eyes. Almost like we bonded."

"Still, why give you anything?"

"Because he still cares about his son." I told her about Chris's conversation with his father. "Lennox kept it from me because he wanted to preserve the situation. I'm still pissed, but I get it."

"Chris didn't tell you," Kelly said. "I guess that's par for the course."

I nodded. "But this was in the last month or so, when I started losing it. Chris is feeling abandoned again, so he goes to his father and ends up telling him all about me. I guess John Weston sees me and thinks, maybe this one is deranged enough to defeat Mary and her father once and for all. Either way, he's got nothing to lose. He practically asked me right in front of Lennox if I had the stuff to best Mary. Meaning could I kill her and save Chris."

"I think you might be reading into things," Kelly said. "Projecting."

"I love you," I said, "but you weren't there. Trust me, he sensed it. That's the only reason he talked."

"All right then. So what are you going to do about it?"

I looked at her through still-leaking eyes. "I have to find a way to stop Mary. Without becoming any more like her."

"You're not."

"But I could be," I said. "How many shades off am I, really?"

She tapped her fingers against my wrist. "That's the difference. You're aware of it. You see your flaws. She used hers to the worst sort of advantage."

"I've done the same."

"But you won't anymore," Kelly said. "You can embrace

those flaws and use them without making certain choices. And we can find her before Chris is too far gone."

"You really believe that?"

"I have to. How else do you think I managed to make this trip?"

TWENTY-SIX

Kelly and I returned to the conference room to find Todd and Ryan buried in the files. Todd glanced up when we entered, questions in his eyes. I ignored them and sat down. He sighed, pulling off his reading glasses and tossing them onto the table, where they skidded to a stop. "My eyes are about to start bleeding from all this data. I don't think we're going to find anything more."

My mind remained on the sighting in Virginia. Chris had been alive as of roughly three a.m. this morning, able to walk on his own. That's all Lennox would tell me without looking at the security tape himself. It could be hours before he decided to update us, and by then I might lose whatever vestiges of sanity I had left.

The shy officer manning the station's entry appeared in the doorway. "Detective Beckett?"

"Yes?"

"There's a man on the phone who claims to be your father, a Josh Beckett. He was told to contact you here."

Todd's face hardened into smooth stone. "Please patch him through."

Less than a minute later, the phone rang. Todd took his time approaching it, circling the black device as if it might blow up. Finally, he hit the speaker button. "This is Detective Beckett."

A scratchy throat cleared in the room, the sound of phlegm and sickness echoing between the walls. "Son? This is Dad."

"Right. You're on speaker at the Jarrettsville, Maryland police station. I assume someone tracked you down about Mary?" Todd might as well have been speaking to a stranger. No, that was wrong. He treated strangers with much more respect. Not that I blamed him.

"Er, yeah. Can we talk?"

"I need to know anything you can tell me about her," Todd said. "What name did she give when you met her?"

"Mary."

"Her last name." Todd dropped his chin to his chest, hiding his face.

"Weston."

"That didn't ring any bells for you?"

"Why should it? It's not exactly an uncommon name, and several years had passed." The man's tone flared, and I hoped Todd reined in his emotions enough to keep his father on the line.

"All right, then. What about her father? Was he around? Did she talk about him?"

Josh coughed again, the sound coming from deep in his chest. Hopefully he had a place to stay in this bitter cold. "You don't remember?"

"No," Todd said. "I wasn't around that much, and I tried my hardest to forget."

"Look, I'm sorry," Josh said. "I was all sorts of messed up after losing your mother and then my job. Mary was just there, and she was messed up too. We kind of gravitated towards each other."

"Right," Todd said. "Again, her father? And messed up how?"

"She'd been in that accident a few months before we met. Her father had been driving. Wrapped the car around a tree, and she got the worst of it. Messed up her brain for a while. That's why they didn't speak."

Todd looked at me as he spoke. "They weren't speaking?"

"Nope," Josh said. "She hated him when I met her. Or said she did. I always figured it was more like anger and wanting him to ask for forgiveness. Anyway, she'd just come out of the hospital for depression when we met."

"She was hospitalized?" I couldn't stop myself. "Do you know where?"

Josh didn't seem to mind the intrusion. "Somewhere south of Philly, that's all I know. She spent about three months there, and when she came out, she was loaded on antidepressants and anti-anxieties and whatever else they gave her." He paused. "I shouldn't have dipped into her stash. That's where all my real troubles started."

Todd scowled, and I knew he wanted to say more. Remind his father that hooking up with Mary in the first place was the real trouble. "Did she ever ask you to kill for her?"

"What? No. I'd have gone straight to the police. That's why I still can't believe this. I mean, sure, she got to be a real bitch after Justin was born. More and more of a meanness came out, and I think that's 'cause she went off the meds and never went back on. I might have worried about her beating the shit out of him. But never anything like what the police are saying now."

"What about her father?" I asked. "Did she reconcile with him?"

"Not that I know of," Josh said. "But near the end of our marriage, I was pretty far gone. Even before Justin's problem. I spent too many hours out drinking, just to get away."

"Justin's problem," Todd spat, "was that Mary beat and

raped his friend with a spoon and then let him take the blame for it. He lost a decade of his life because of her, not to mention the emotional trauma. And you just walked away."

Kelly squeaked beside me. Ryan's eyes went wide. The room heated with awkward tension, the already too-close walls threatening to close in.

"That was her fault too," Josh said. "Any time we'd argue or I'd ask too many questions, she'd throw stuff in my face. How I couldn't keep a job, that I was a bad father—anything she knew she could zing me with. And then she'd offer me one of her anti-anxiety pills and a drink, talking about how we just needed to chill out and relax. I didn't want to fight anymore, so I gave in. You give in enough times, it becomes a habit."

Mary controlled Josh Beckett with drugs. I'd done the same thing to more than one of my victims.

Todd had regained his composure. "Do you know of any land they might have owned? Any other names she used? Any place she'd run to now?"

"She was a penny-pinching miser, I can tell you that," Josh said. "She worked in the school cafeteria, and then she did side jobs cleaning houses, even though her arm and shoulder bothered her for a long time. She never gave any of the house-cleaning money to the family. It all went into her emergency savings."

"She was always ready to run," I said. "She and her father lived on and off the grid for so long she knows how to hoard cash."

"The name thing, though. Nah, it's probably nothing."

"Let me decide that," Todd said. "What do you remember?"

His father coughed again, wet and harsh. "Her medication from the hospital. It had the name Mary Kent. I questioned her on it, and she said it was for insurance purposes and none of my business. To be honest, I didn't want to know."

Todd and I stared at each other, my pulse pounding. Mary Kent.

"You're sure you don't remember seeing the name of the hospital or a doctor on her medications?" Todd said.

"She never told me," Josh said. "And I figured that was none of my business."

Todd's tight expression warned he'd had enough. "All right, thanks for the call. You've been some help."

"Son, don't hang up." Josh's sick-laden voice took on a note of plaintiveness that pulled at my conscience. "I'd like for us to get together when you're back in town. I'm staying at the men's shelter on 58th; I'm sure you know the place."

"We'll see," Todd said. "I've got to go. Thanks for your call." He smacked the button to disconnect and stared down at the receiver, his arms shaking from the weight of his body. No one spoke until Ryan's uncertain voice piped up.

"There's four different mental health facilities south of Philadelphia that would have been in operation during that time," he said. "I can call and ask whether or not they had a patient named Mary Kent. If we get a hit, we'll need a subpoena for her records."

"Do it, please."

We spent the next hour painstakingly going over the files while Ryan used the FBI's resources to locate the hospital Mary Kent had been admitted to. The drone of his voice as he made phone call after phone call, combined with the sound of files rustling and the anger still seeping off Todd, made me feel like climbing the station's concrete walls.

"I'm going outside for some air." I exited the room before anyone could stop me, shrugging on my coat. My sluggish system welcomed the bracingly cold air. I blinked against the afternoon sun glaring off the snow.

Before I could sink into my thoughts, I heard a nauseatingly familiar voice.

"Hi, Lucy." Beth Reid shut the door to a red Honda Civic and approached me with a friendly smile. The reporter had evidently been squatting outside the station, just waiting for information.

"Leave me alone."

"I think we got off on the wrong foot." Her smile didn't waver, but she kept her distance. "I really do just want to help."

"You want a career story," I said. "And you want to get it before the rest of your flock catches wind of this and flies down. Time's probably running out on that."

"Time's running out on a lot of things." Her false sincerity made me steam. "Have the police found the Chevy?"

Stupidly, I stared at her. "What Chevy?"

"The one the local guy reported seeing Tuesday night, the night the cabin was found."

Had I gone crazy? I flipped through my memory, but I knew I'd never heard of the Chevy before. Why would Lennox keep this from me? Or Todd? If he knew about it, he would have told me.

"You don't know?" Reid's eyes lit up. She no doubt relished having the upper hand. I braced myself for her attempt at an information exchange. She'd learn very quickly that I got what I wanted without giving anything back.

"Around six Tuesday evening, a farmer living on a dirt road adjacent to the property that cabin is on saw a navy, four-door older model Chevy race past his house. The car was going so fast they skidded on the ice and nearly hit his mailbox."

I waited, staring at her with my coldest expression.

"He said a woman with dark hair was driving, and there was an old man in the passenger seat. He didn't see any more than that, but he got a partial plate. The first two letters were BC."

I took my time, compartmentalizing my anger into something useful. "How did you find this information?"

Reid smirked, raising her eyebrow. "I've got my sources. Sounds like you're being left out of the loop."

I bit my tongue hard enough to draw blood. The taste of copper filled my mouth, and I latched on to it. *Remember the end game.* Fortunately, I still knew how to play.

"Give me your source, and I'll answer one question."

Her eyes darted between mine, her chin lifting with arrogance. Let her think she had the upper hand. My ego wasn't so fragile I couldn't give her that fantasy.

"You answer my question first."

"All right."

"Is Chris Hale a suspect in the murder of the girl found in the cabin? Does Agent Lennox believe he's working with his mother?"

"That's two questions. He's not a suspect," I said. "I can't tell you what Agent Lennox believes. But he hasn't said anything like that to me. Your turn."

Reid's smile turned into a grimace that aged her. "You didn't give me much."

I stepped down off the curb so that we were closer to eye level. Reid backed away, just as she had before. "But I answered your question."

"I need more."

"There's been another sighting," I said. "An hour away. Hanover. The FBI thinks they're heading north."

She cocked her head, debating. Searching my face to see if she could spot the lie.

Keep looking, bitch.

"I overheard Chief Deputy Frost talking to the witness on the phone last night." Reid hooked her thumb toward the section of the parking lot where the patrol cars parked. "She was over there, on her cell. I figured she was keeping the information to herself because I've heard rumblings the big boys think she screwed up by not calling in Major Case right away. I figured she was trying to redeem herself."

So Reid had guessed. Frost hadn't shared the information. Instead of passing it on—because she cared so much about justice—she held on to it until she saw the opportunity to use it to her advantage.

"Thank you. Hanover." I left her standing there, hurrying into the warmth of the station. As soon as the doors closed, I called Lennox.

"I'm on my way back with the security footage from the gas station," he said. "I'll be there in fifteen minutes. We'll talk then."

"Fine. But I've got information you need now. Chief Deputy Frost has been holding out on you."

TWENTY-SEVEN

Lennox strode into our makeshift headquarters with the grace of a bull after a cow. His suit pants were wrinkled from the drive, and the energy drink he clutched made it clear he'd dipped to running on fumes. "Lucy, did you mention your information to the others?"

I shook my head, feeling everyone's gaze on me. They'd find out soon enough.

"Good," Lennox said. "She's coming in now. Let me do the talking."

Footsteps soon revealed the she in question. Chief Deputy Frost walked carefully into the room, a doe in the forest during hunting season. Like the rest of us, her face revealed the stress of the past few days. Her skin had lost some of its glow, and strands of hair were coming loose from her ponytail. She smelled of coffee and clothes that had gone too many days without being laundered. I wanted to admire her working around the clock to make up for her bad decision the first day, but I couldn't get past her selfishness.

"Agent Lennox, you wanted to see me?" Her cool tone gave no sign of distress.

Lennox leaned against the back wall, arms folded over his broad chest and his feet crossed at the ankles. But he looked far from relaxed. The tension rippled off him, his jaw set hard and his brown eyes fierce. "Do you have something you want to tell me?"

Frost's eyes flickered around the room, seeking answers from one of us. Her gaze landed on mine, and I stared back, feeling the anger heating my entire system. She swallowed. "Not that I can think of."

"That was your one chance." Lennox drained his energy drink and slammed it into the trashcan. "I hope you've enjoyed your career because it's about to be over."

Her mouth opened, and I saw the debate in her eyes. She still believed she could lie her way out of trouble. "I don't understand."

"Let me spell it out for you," Lennox said. "You have a witness who claimed a navy, four-door older Chevy drove past his house on a dirt road that runs adjacent to the property the hunting cabin is on. Our crime scene," he emphasized, his voice deadly soft. "This person remembers a dark-haired woman driving, with an older male in the passenger seat. The car skidded on the ice and nearly hit his mailbox. You received this information early Wednesday, correct?"

Frost looked like she'd been punched in the gut. What little color she had drained from her face. Her hands jammed into her pockets, her tall body slouching until I thought she might fall over. Disappointment flooded me. I'd hoped she would fight a little harder.

"I can explain," she said.

"There's no explanation that would excuse your decision not to pass this information on to me or Detective Adams from Major Case. You know this isn't some goddamned small-town criminal. This is an FBI-wanted fugitive." His cheeks puffed as he spoke, his voice sharp enough to cut glass. "Yet you chose to be selfish and stupid in an attempt to redeem yourself."

"I've put out a BOLO for the car," she said meekly. "The witness couldn't remember what state the license plate was from, but he got the first two letters. I'm having our people run all possible combinations in Pennsylvania, Maryland, and Virginia. And I notified the state troopers about the car."

"But you left me out of the loop," Lennox said. "I'm the one making the decisions. Detective Adams is in Virginia right now, where we've had two sightings. Don't you think it would have helped us if we'd known to look for the Chevy? The Maryland State Troopers are checking their own roads—they don't know about the Virginia sighting, which means they didn't know to pass the information on. And I'm sure the car's been dumped now."

"I just wanted to show that I could handle a big case." Frost looked down at the floor.

"I don't care what you wanted." Lennox pushed off the wall, standing straight. "You made a mistake by not calling Major Case when Detective Beckett and Lucy told you exactly who you were dealing with. A bad judgment that was forgivable, chalked up to inexperience. But this was pure selfishness, and it's going to cost you."

"I'm doing everything that you would have done," Frost tried.

Lennox slammed his hands down on the table, making the entire thing tremble with his rage. "Do you have access to our FBI analysts? Do you have the same resources we do? Don't you think it's possible we could have found the car when you couldn't? And doesn't the chain of command mean anything to you? The rules exist for a reason. And because of your stupidity, we might have lost our chance to bring closure to a lot of hurting families." He pounded his fist on the table. "That's what you have to live with now. If we don't find Mary Weston and her accomplices, part of the blame is on your shoulders. And if I have my way, you'll go to each family waiting for answers, starting with the dead girl in the hunting cabin, and explain to them why the bitch who murdered their child is still at large." He breathed heavy, spittle forming at the corner of his mouth.

Tears stained Frost's flushed face. "I'm sorry."

"I don't want to hear your excuses. I want the name of the witness so I can go talk to him, and then I want you out of my sight. Your superior is expecting you in his office."

Frost slouched farther, scrubbing the moisture off her face. "Earl Evans."

"Dismissed." Lennox glared at her as if he'd prefer her to stay and let him chew on her a little longer. She turned and walked away, her shoulders rounded.

I still didn't feel sorry for her.

No one spoke. Lennox's anger had sucked all of the normalcy from the room and replaced it with white-hot tension. Kelly trembled beside me, and I squeezed her hand.

"Now." Lennox took a deep breath, turning to Ryan. "I got your message about Mercer Hospital."

"In Allentown." Ryan nodded. "It's a state-funded facility, which would explain how Mary could have afforded it. Here's the interesting part: even though Mary gave Todd's father the name of Martha Weston, that's not the name she used to check into the hospital."

"She used Kent?" Lennox bounced on the balls of his feet.

Ryan grinned. "I managed to get the administrator to tell me that a Mary Kent was treated from January 1992 until the middle of June of the same year." He checked his notes. "But he refused to give me anything else. He said I'd need a court order."

"You'll get it," Lennox said. "You guys should have Mary Kent's records from Mercer Hospital by tomorrow morning."

"Thank you, sir."

I cut him off before he could say anything more, my mind already past Frost's demise. "What about the security video? Did you find any witnesses?"

"I've emailed Ryan a copy of the video." Lennox's gleaming eyes turned to me. "Employees at the gas station confirmed Mary and the older man came in early yesterday and purchased basic necessities: toilet paper, dried food, that sort of thing. This morning around three a.m., the same elderly man came in along with Chris and another unidentified male. He appears to be roughly the same age as Mary, and judging by the security tape, he thinks he's in charge." Lennox's gaze remained on mine, making a hollow pit in the bottom of my stomach. "You'll see that Chris stays close to the old man, and it's obvious the guy needs help walking. Whatever's wrong with him looks to have affected his basic motor skills. Go ahead, Ryan."

Ryan cued up the video, and we all leaned over his scrawny shoulder. My heart beat hard enough I could have sworn I tasted the blood in my throat.

"It's plain-ass luck on our part that the station's camera is well hidden. It's the only modern thing in the entire store," Lennox said. "You'll see the unknown man come in. He's wearing a plaid overcoat." His words came just as the man entered the frame. The low-quality tape did little for facial recognition. The man looked to be around six feet with a beer belly, beard, and shaggy hair. His pants sagged around his butt, and one of his shoes was untied. He kept his gaze left, and it quickly became apparent why.

Despite the low quality, I'd recognize Chris's profile anywhere. The set of his jaw, the slope of his nose. He wore the gray, wool coat I'd seen him in so many times. And he looked straight up at the camera, as if he knew someone might be watching.

Good. Relief slipped through me. *He wants to be seen. That's good.*

An old man—the same one from Jarrettsville, judging by the coat and the shock of white hair, along with the unsteady, painful-looking gait—clutched Chris's left arm. Chris ducked his head, putting his ear to the man's mouth, and then nodded. Together they shuffled to the medicine section, picking out bottles. Their watcher stood closely the entire time, shifting nervously from foot to foot, holding a forty-ounce beer, a loaf of bread, and a bag of nacho chips. He paid in cash, and the three men left. I bit back the shout that raced to my lips.

Don't go, Chris.

"They're getting careless," Todd said. "Going to the same place twice. But where's Mary?"

"We don't know," Lennox said. "I'm thinking she stayed behind, figuring she could trust whoever this new guy is not to make any mistakes. Good thing he's not that smart. We've got a manhunt down in Dale City, and I think we're getting close. Of course, we might have them if we knew about the damned Chevy." He took another breath, blowing it out hard. "I've got the local police searching for it, but she probably dumped it long before Dale City."

"This is more than twelve hours ago," I said. "They could have been on their way out of the area by then. Did the store have any outside cameras?"

"None that caught anything. I don't think they left the area," Lennox said. "Call it instinct, but I think they're running on fumes. The old man is obviously sick—they bought over the counter flu medicine—and assuming he's Mary's father, she's probably worried about him. Could be his health's thrown her for a loop, and she's decided to lie low. Ryan, you find any medical records for Alan Kent yet?"

"No sir," Ryan said.

"What about vet hospitals?" Kelly asked, her voice still shaky from witnessing Lennox's anger.

Ryan's eyes widened. "Shit. I hadn't thought of that."

"If he's Alan Kent and he was born in 1934, he might have served in the Korean War," she said.

"That's 1950." Lennox sounded doubtful. "He'd have been sixteen. Even if he enlisted in '52, at eighteen, he'd have been lucky to have made it to Korea before the conflict ended the next year."

"Unless he lied about his age," I said. "That happened a lot back then. Boys wanted to go to war, especially after seeing the vets come back from World War II. They wanted to be heroes."

"You might be right," Lennox said. "Ryan, go ahead and check the vet hospitals in Pennsylvania, Maryland, and Virginia. Look for any one of them treating an Alan Kent as far back as their records go. For Christ's sake, try to find an address."

"Okay," Ryan said. "But this guy's eighty years old. How in the hell is he still killing?"

"I don't think he is," Lennox said. "But he wants to. And he enjoys seeing it done. Believe me, these guys develop a taste for pain and suffering like some people get addicted to crack. They never quit unless they die or they're caught. If he can't perform the act, he's got his daughter to do it for him and find a way to get his jollies."

It made perfect sense, especially if father and daughter had spent decades killing together. "But according to Todd's father, the two of them fell out after this wreck that landed her in the hospital. And for all we know, he had severe injuries too," I said. "I guess after she left Justin and their dad, Mary reunited with her own father."

"Moths to a flame," Lennox said. "They couldn't stay away from each other."

Despair crept up on me for what seemed like the hundredth time today. "There's not going to be an address. They're transients. Everything we're doing is running in circles. We're filling in part of the puzzle that answers why, but it's not getting us any closer to finding Chris. You know that."

He looked at me for too long. "Let's you and I speak privately."

For the second time, the energy of the room drained. The look in his eyes was too dark, too knowing. Too much like the one he'd given Frost.

But I didn't have a choice. I followed him into the hall and then stopped, angling for some sort of control over the situation. "Go ahead."

"You're giving up on me," Lennox said. "On your friend?"

"That's not it at all." I knew he was just warming up, but I played along. "We're chasing two different timelines, and the only thing it's telling us is that Mary and her father are a couple of psychopaths who attacked girls on his long-haul routes."

"And what else?"

"Mary learned her trade from him," I said. "The two of them are probably co-dependent. I don't know if sexual abuse was involved, but he definitely brainwashed her from an early age. She was taught to kill."

Lennox had wandered over to the coffee pot. He sniffed the remnants of this morning's coffee and quickly set the pot back on the burner. "And now she's taking care of an aging father. We know that's her weak link. No matter what details we don't know, that man is our ticket. We get our hands on him, Mary folds. Tell me, why do you think they're back in Dale City?"

"Because that's where she was born," I said without thinking. "Her father might have first killed there. Isn't that where she lived with her grandmother until Alan took her out on the road?" I asked.

"As far as we know right now, yes."

"But again, what we're doing isn't getting us anywhere."

"Sure it is," Lennox said. "You're finding out the psychology we need to use as a weapon. If the time comes to barter for Chris's life, everything you're finding out will help me."

"I see." I took a chance, hoping my finding out about Frost had gained me a few brownie points. "And you're also keeping me busy. Out of your hair of the immediate investigation."

He smiled, that same fake, friendly smile that made me want to punch him. "That too. But aren't I doing you a favor?"

"I'm not sure I know what you mean."

"Sure you do." He kept smiling. "What happens if you run across Mary and her little family? How long would you allow her to survive?"

My blood chilled. "You're wrong."

He stepped forward, pointing his long finger at me. "I'm not, but the thing is, right now, I don't care. I don't care about some slime bucket named Preacher who helped traffic kids. I don't care about the Harrison brothers or whoever else you might have targeted. All wastes of space. Believe me, I get the temptation. But what I do care about is answers from Mary Weston. I want to know how many girls she and her father killed over the years. I want to be able to close case files for as many families of missing persons as I can. That is my focus, along with saving your friend before he gets sucked into the family fold. If you don't prevent me from doing that, your past just might stay there. Are we clear?"

I'm sure he could hear my thunderous heart, and if he couldn't, the sweat on my face was a dead giveaway. "Crystal."

TWENTY-EIGHT

Evening fell with no new information. I couldn't stand the thought of one more greasy dinner from the local joint, and I wasn't sure I could keep the food down anyway. Lennox had essentially called me out, dangling a carrot: play nice, or I'll ruin your life. Not that my actions had earned me anything less. Lennox executed a perfect pass, and it was up to me to either run out of bounds yet again or take it into the end zone.

Neither option appealed to me. Right now, I wanted nothing more than to climb into bed, hide beneath the covers, and forget all the messed-up things I'd learned. But my brain wouldn't allow it. Like a prizefighter, it slung itself off the ropes and staggered back into the ring for the next round. But no opponent waited for me. At least none I could see. Flashes of people, first Mary, then the shaggy male, and then her aging father leaning on Chris as though his life depended on it. Who was the real enemy? If Lennox actually caught up with the group, would Chris try to play interference? He might not be aware of the things his grandfather had done. For all we knew, Mary and Alan had convinced Chris he was no more than a dying old man who just wanted to get to know the grandson the Hales had robbed him of.

Was Chris foolish enough to believe it?

Kelly emerged from the bathroom, face pink from her shower, her wet hair still clinging to her head, its darkness contrasting with her pale skin. "You want to talk about it?"

"Lennox knows what I did. What I've done. He can't prove it, and he doesn't care. As long as I don't screw things up with Mary."

"He wants to make a name for himself," Kelly said. "Closure to the families is just a bonus."

"Either way, it might give me the chance to start over, just like we talked about."

Never mind that I wasn't sure if I could do that. Until now, I hadn't really dared to believe it was an option, and I still doubted Lennox's sincerity. What was to stop him from using this on me time and time again?

Kelly tightened her robe and sat down on the bed. "Can I tell you something?"

I nodded.

"This whole experience has been scary as hell, but it's also really freaking fascinating," she said. "I mean, a father-daughter killing team that spanned decades? This is the kind of thing you see on televisions shows. It's not supposed to happen in real life. And yet here these two are, still going in some capacity. How does that happen?"

"Crazy breeds crazy," I said. "Nature versus nurture. Most people—including myself—believe it's a combination of both. But nurture is also about the perception of the bad guy. It's a weakness in their own mind. How many people withstand horrible abuse and get through it, like you have? A lot more than the ones who go on to kill. Even if they have lifelong problems, they're not killing people. So there's some component of their minds that doesn't process like everything else, and the nurture is like a disease." I rolled over to face her. "And before you ask me where that leaves me, I have no idea. I'm probably a case for crazy breeds crazy. It's not like my background is Americana."

Kelly smoothed her hair back. "Crazy breeds crazy. Where does that leave Chris?"

We looked at each other, neither one of us wanting to voice the answer. My phone dinged with a text from Todd.

Turn on the television, channel 9 out of Baltimore.

I scrambled for the remote, my stomach lurching as though I'd gone ahead and eaten at the diner anyway. The television came on, the artificial light flashing in the darkened room and making my eyes hurt. Finding the station and the source of Todd's ominous text took less than a minute.

Beth Reid stood shivering in a royal blue overcoat in a snow-covered field. A distance behind her was the supermax in Greene County. Wind lashed at her, but her pulled-back hair remained immobile. Makeup layered her face, her red lipstick horribly gaudy against the prison backdrop.

"What in the everlasting hell?" I said. "She moves fast."

I turned up the volume.

Reid looked into the camera with a sparkle in her eyes that seemed meant for only me, her smirk a challenge. "Sources close to the investigation claim FBI Agent André Lennox and Philadelphia private investigator Lucy Kendall visited notorious killer John Weston in SCI Greene early this morning. Weston's only son, Christopher Hale, is believed held against his will by his biological mother, a woman known as Mary Weston and Martha Beckett. Recent events in the past several months have brought to light Mary's involvement in the famed Lancaster killings, but her ex-husband maintained his silence, refusing to implicate his wife. Rumor is that changed today when Lucy Kendall, the private investigator involved in a recent takedown of a high-profile sex-trafficking operation in Philadelphia, spoke to Weston. We're still trying to find out what exactly John

Weston told Kendall, but reports from the prison indicate he gave them valuable information regarding a possible location for Mary Weston."

I felt the blood vessels in my face pulse, my hands digging into the cheap motel sheets. "That freaking bitch."

"Who would have access to the information?" Kelly asked.

"The superintendent made it clear the interview was recorded. For all I know it might be property of the prison, but I assume he and Lennox discussed the need for privacy. I've got no idea how many people might have seen it. Lennox is going to blow a gasket. This compromises the entire investigation."

"Why? She didn't give specifics."

"It doesn't matter," I said. "Mary needs to think she's invincible to screw up. That's when we make our most ridiculous mistakes—when we think we've outsmarted everyone, and there's no way we've left anything unchecked. No way she expected John Weston to talk. This is going to screw with her confidence, make her more careful."

"Stop saying 'we,'" Kelly said. "The difference between you is huge."

"Not right now." I sat up, too angry to feel sorry for myself. "We both know how to hide from the police, live a secret life. She might have years of experience on me, but I know what it feels like to have something like this happen. It freaks you out and sucks you right back into your shell."

"Maybe that's a good thing," Kelly said. "Especially if her father is sick and she's already worried about him. Maybe this will cause her to make a mistake."

"Either way," I said, "this information should not have been leaked. This girl is looking for fame and nothing else." My blood pressure spiked again, making my pulse race and my face sweat. I wiped my damp hands on my jeans and reached for the bottle of water from the nightstand. God help that stupid girl if I ran into her in the dark of night. I didn't think I'd need poison to kill her. My bare hands would do, squeezing the life out of her until her eyes popped right out of her mascaraed sockets.

"Lucy." Kelly's shrill voice halted my backslide. "Whatever you're thinking, stop."

I didn't want to. The wickedness that burned inside me wanted to snatch justice back into my own hands and make the reporter pay for interfering with us—with me. For putting my name out there for all the world to see. What would the National Center for Missing and Exploited Children think now?

My gaze shot to Kelly's concerned one. I cared about the future. About the path I might still be able to take. I couldn't let the frustration win. Not this time.

I let Todd inform Agent Lennox of the reporter's stupidity.

"He didn't take it too well." Todd leaned in the doorway of my and Kelly's motel room, shifting on his feet. "He's going to find out who talked at the prison and hang him up by the balls. His quote."

"I believe him." I looked at the duffle bag slung on Todd's shoulder. "You have to take off tonight? It's dark and more snow is coming."

"I've got cases piling up," he said. "And I'm not sure what more I can do here."

"Babysit me," I said, only half-kidding. "I'm sure Lennox charged you with that. He seems to think I'm going to take off and go rogue."

Todd smiled. "Because you've never done anything like that before."

"Only once or twice."

He tried to laugh, but it came out fake and tired. "I'm worried about you in all of this. You've found things out about

Chris, and he's coming back changed. If he comes back at all. Where does that leave you?"

"I'm still figuring that out."

"I think you should go to New York," Todd said. "If the NCMEC wants you, take the shot, Lucy. Start over. The right way, while everyone is still ignoring the forest for the solitude of the trees."

I wished I had the meanness to push him away. Grabbing on to the frustration of his supporting me when I didn't deserve it was much easier than feeling grateful and beholden to him. "I don't know what to say to that."

"Just think about it," Todd said. "The medical examiner thinks Preacher died of a drug overdose. Working theory is that Jake offed him for causing problems."

I couldn't look him in the eye, so I concentrated on the small mole on his left cheek. "Sounds plausible to me."

"It does," Todd said. "But how many times do you get to pass go without heading to jail?"

Smiling, I shook my head. "Be careful driving back, please."

"I will be." He glanced behind me. "Goodbye, Kelly. It was nice to finally meet you."

She blushed and waved. Once again I knew things would never go back to the way they were, and I was starting to wonder if that might not be so bad. "I think you should see your father."

The humor evaporated off Todd's face, leaving him looking washed-out and angry. "Why?"

"Because you guys have unfinished business," I said. "He's part of the cause of your problems, and Justin's. You actually have the chance to talk to him about that. Don't you think you might feel better if you did?"

"Would you?"

The root of my problems? What exactly was it? Once upon a time, I would have said it was the bitter injustice of the system, but now I realized my inability to deal with that harkened back to the darkest event of my life. "Yes," I said. "I would tell my sister how angry I was at her for leaving me and how much I hated myself for not being able to help her."

Todd shook his head. "That's different. She was a victim."

"Your father was too. Of life, of Mary. Probably of things you don't even know about. I'm not saying anything he did was right, or that you should suddenly start having Sunday dinners together. But a single conversation might change your life."

"You're better at reading people than you think, Lucy, and not just the bad ones. Remember that." He ducked forward, brushing a kiss to my forehead so quickly I almost missed it. Then he left, walking down the hall with a straight back and no intention of looking back.

TWENTY-NINE

"Some guard at the prison ran his mouth." Lennox dropped his briefcase into one of the rolling chairs sitting next to the table that had become our workstation over the last few days. His eyes were bloodshot from lack of sleep, and he moved stiffly, stretching his neck. "My people are trying to stow it, but most local stations in Maryland and Virginia picked it up, and then it ran on CNN at four a.m. this morning. I'm praying Mary was passed out."

"She probably never sleeps." I thought of Mary's face, inflexible and unrelenting, her expression solid ice. When I'd first met her, I'd assumed this was a result of her true self, her nasty disposition leaking to the surface. And like everyone else, I'd wondered how anyone could have tolerated calling her his significant other. But what about Mary before the accident? How much softer had the planes of her face been? Had some other emotion besides sour indifference shone in her eyes? Surely it must have. She had to have charm by the boatloads, even if her face was more interesting than attractive. That's the only way she could have sucked her victims into her trap. Accomplices included.

Mary had to adapt after the accident. She might have taken years to realize she still had the capacity to kill—and maybe the desire even fell dormant with the medications—but something had gradually awakened within her, and she started all over again.

Unless she'd been active the entire time she lived as Todd's stepmother, and so far, very little evidence pointed to that. Ryan hadn't been able to find any cases that lined up with any kill Mary had been known to commit. Of course, that wasn't solid proof, but whatever strange companionship I had with Mary insisted I was right.

But then again, maybe I really am just another product of crazy breeds crazy.

"I tracked the reporter down in Baltimore," Lennox said. He rubbed his eyes. "She was filling in for the morning anchor and almost refused to talk to me. I didn't get the impression she took my warning very seriously."

"The First Amendment is a bitch sometimes," Kelly said.

Ryan, shielded by his laptop as always, laughed. Kelly blushed and focused on her steaming coffee.

"Did your manhunt turn up anything else?" I asked.

Lennox sat down across from me, his eyelids threatening to close. "Nothing around Dale City. Early this morning, there was a possible sighting in some tiny town about thirty miles northeast of Dale City. Troopers are on it."

"Why would they head north?" Kelly asked. "You'd think she'd be running as far south as possible, crossing state lines and complicating the search."

"Why'd she go to Dale City in the first place?" Lennox countered. "It's not that far from here. Even if she and her father are on some pilgrimage, it's risky."

"Alan's sick," I said. "We all know that. Chris shows up and gets shot, and tells Mary I'm coming. She's got to know the police and the FBI will be called in. She doesn't want Chris to die—at least not yet—and she's got an ailing father. Maybe she just throws them all into the car and starts driving. She knows she's going to have a hard time walking into a hospital now, especially once the word is out about Chris." The more I spoke, the more right the theory sounded. "Her father's a different story. If he's using his veteran's insurance, he can still walk into a hospital and get treated. They'd just have to hope no one put two and two together."

"I'd bet Alan Kent is too smart and too stubborn to go anyway," Lennox said. "Dale City is specific. There's a reason she went down there and a reason she's coming back this way. We've just got to figure out what those are."

He opened his briefcase and tugged out a package. "Judge came through. This was waiting for me this morning."

I sat up straight. "Mary's medical records from Mercer Hospital?"

"And Mercer is a psychiatric facility?" Kelly asked.

"State-funded," Lennox said. "Which means they see it all, and a lot of the people have been struggling for years with mental illness and depression because they didn't have the financial ability to get help for it. Some of them are pretty far gone, like schizophrenic and bipolar patients, but others are able to learn how to manage their chronic depression with meds and therapy. They get less government money now, but back in the nineties, that's about all they took."

Lennox began reading the various reports. "Looks like she admitted herself in January of 1992 for severe depression and suicidal thoughts. She'd been in a car accident with her father several months before. He was driving and lost control of the vehicle. Mary received the most injuries: nerve damage to the side of her face, a broken clavicle that wasn't healing correctly, and a fractured wrist."

"What does it say specifically about her state of mind?" I asked.

"At first she didn't say much at all," Lennox said. "She talked about the accident and its effects making her feel useless, but she didn't want to open up to the counselors. It basically got the to the point where if she didn't open up and start talking about her issues, they'd have given her medication and sent her on her way."

"And she started to talk?" I asked.

"Looks that way."

"If she and her father had a falling-out over the accident, maybe that scared her because she didn't have any place else to go," I said. "She'd been with him her whole life. I wonder if that's why she used her real name instead of Weston, at least until she remarried."

Ryan perked up. "That was a big case—all those girls, and the little kid discovering them. Mary's hospitalization was only a few years later. Maybe she didn't want to have to explain her association to John Weston."

"Possibly." Lennox continued to skim the report. "But she eventually did—I assumed she decided sharing the information worked to her advantage. She told the doctor she was the ex-wife of notorious killer John Weston, and he'd ruined her life and her chance at raising her son. She talked a lot about losing custody of the child and called his uncle a bitter man who used his position as a lawyer to make Mary look even worse."

"Christ," I said. "And this is what Mary's filling Chris's head with—after he finds out his aunt and uncle lied."

"Why'd she want him, though?" Ryan asked. "She didn't treat her next son very well. Seems to me they were burdens."

"It's not always about maternal instinct," I said. "Some people view kids as having their own little corner of the world to mold and control. And I'd bet Mary's main issue with losing custody of Chris was more about losing that opportunity than any love she felt for him. Does she talk about her father?"

"Not much," Lennox said. "Which is interesting. The

doctor noted she seemed to grow highly agitated when her father was mentioned. She refused to talk about the accident. The few times she did mention it, her explanation didn't make sense."

"How so?" The accident still bothered me. Ryan hadn't found any record of it, which wasn't unusual since we didn't know the surname they'd used, but he hadn't found anything in the tri-state area that matched the circumstances or known timeframe.

"'My father took things too far.'" Lennox read from the file. "'He's more experienced than that, he knows how to keep control of the situation. But he wasn't paying attention, and then everything happened at once. I paid the price. He barely got scratched.'"

My mouth went dry. "Does that sound like a car accident to you?"

"Sounds vague," Kelly said. "Have you found any other living victims besides Jenna? Are there any other girls out there with a similar story? What if her father got cocky and made a mistake, and Mary fought with the girl and lost? Any one of those injuries could be explained by a fight, even the nerve damage, if she was hit hard enough with something."

I'd been thinking the same thing. "Or they could have still been in a vehicle and had an accident. But it revolved around a victim and not just failure to control."

Lennox pointed to Ryan. "Get into ViCAP and check Maryland, Pennsylvania, and Virginia for anything matching Mary's known MO in 1991 and 1992. Maybe we'll get lucky and find something unsolved."

"The girl might not have succeeded in escaping," I said. "She may have just delayed the inevitable. What about visitors? Did her father ever come to see her?"

"No," Lennox said. His breath caught, his large hands tightening on the paper. "But there's a cousin. Lionel Kent. He visited once a month, for four months." Lennox flipped through the pages. "He's also listed as the emergency contact. And his residence was in Dale City, Virginia."

Ryan was already furiously pecking on the computer. Kelly's fingers twitched, the tension rolling off her. I knew she wanted to be the one digging up the information.

"Here we go," Ryan said. "He's still listed as a resident of Dale City as of last fall, when he renewed his driver's license." He swung the laptop around so we could all see it. "Look familiar?"

The face was vague and average, the eyes too far apart and his thick chin covered with beard. But he had the same shaggy hair of the man on the gas station camera, and the height and weight matched.

Lennox grabbed his phone. "I told you she went to Dale City for a reason."

Lennox had the local sheriff's deputy at Lionel Kent's front door. He lived in a small one-story ranch a few miles outside of Dale City, and according to his workplace, lived alone.

"I made some calls on the way over." The deputy's voice cracked through the speaker. "Lionel Kent worked full a full shift Monday. He called in and took the rest of the week off for illness."

"Which means he wasn't in Maryland when everything went down," I said. "Mary and her father might have shown up on his doorstep and given him no choice."

Lennox scowled. "There's always a choice."

"This place is empty." The deputy's voice filled the room again. "No vehicle in sight."

"Virginia DMV has a 2003 Jeep Grand Cherokee registered in Lionel's name," Ryan said. "Black."

"That matches the description from the eyewitnesses at the

gas station in Dale City," Lennox said. "Give me the license plate, and we'll get an ABP on it."

Ryan rattled off a series of numbers while Lennox furiously jotted them down.

"What about his cellphone?" I asked.

"His work gave me the number, but it's off right now," Lennox said. "Of course. He turns it on, we can track the ping off a tower. In the meantime, I'm trying to get a warrant for his phone records. Deputy, can you guys go back and see if any of them recognize Lionel by his picture? Check with his work too. See if he's got any known spots he likes to go: a hunting cabin, fishing shack, whatever. Any place they might hole up. We're pulling his financials. He paid in cash, but if he's been dragged into this, he might slip up and use a credit card we can track."

"Sure thing," the deputy said. "I'll call you as soon as I know something."

Lennox ended the call. The hangdog look had evaporated, replaced by a jittering brightness. "We're getting close. Whatever Lionel's story is, he's not the pro Mary and her father are— or were. He's going to slip up."

"He didn't look ready to slip on the video," I said. "He looked disgruntled, maybe. But not out of his element."

"He might not have any idea what's going on," Lennox said. "I'd hope he's unaware of the monsters in his family. Who knows what he's been told? Either way, we need to find out all we can about him."

"I don't think that's going to be too hard," Ryan said. "He's got plenty of stuff on public record. Looks like he's spent most of his life there, decent work history. Married once in the eighties, divorced. Couple of arrests for public intox a few years ago, but nothing beyond a citation."

"So unless he's really good at hiding it, he's no hardened criminal."

"But he knows about John," I said. "At this point, how can

he not realize she was involved?" Lionel Kent looked nervous on the security video. He might be stuck in the middle of Mary's mess, but he knew Chris was there against his will.

"That doesn't mean he's not going to open his door if she showed up," Lennox countered. "We have no idea what their family dynamic is." He reached for his coat. "But it's time for you to pack up."

"Why?"

"Because you and I are going to Virginia, and we're going to find out."

THIRTY

Kelly didn't want me to go. But I didn't have a choice. Lennox had me right where he wanted. Deputy Frost had been bumped all the way down to desk duty, and most of her colleagues thought she'd be out on her butt by the end of the month. Lennox had pull, and he moved quickly. So I promised Kelly I'd be fine and back by tomorrow, feeling like a jerk for leaving her by herself.

Now, my newest worst nightmare rose frightfully to life. Trapped in a car with Lennox.

"We're going to get them," he said. "I can feel it. Every available cop in two states has that license plate number."

I hoped he was right, but my doubts far outweighed it. Switching plates wasn't exactly hard. And Mary seemed to have a knack for hiding in plain sight. Our best chance was that some member of her patchwork entourage screwed up and left some kind of trail.

Lennox drove too fast, causing the SUV to slide on the snowy roads. I double-checked my seatbelt.

"I wouldn't have pegged you as a nervous rider."

"Only when the driver is putting my life in danger."

He laughed. "You know how many hours I've put in on the road? I started out as a sheriff's deputy in Virginia, Hanover County. Big area with a lot of spread to cover. When I put in for the academy, I spent my first year as an agent in Columbia, South Carolina. My job as the new guy took me to all the rural cases. Part of our jurisdiction was the Catawba Indian Reservation, and they had a high assault rate. Mostly sexual. I spent many hours on those roads."

"Is Philadelphia your final choice?" I knew enough about FBI agents to know they submitted a list of state offices they'd like to work at, with a ranking order, but there was no guarantee they'd ever get it. And if a shot at a promotion came up, most seized it, because they'd have to wait seven years for the next shot if they said no.

"California," Lennox said. "Somewhere out of this miserable muck of snow and ice. But Philly's all right. We're never slow, that's for sure."

Was this the part when I was supposed to ask what made him want to be an agent? If I was supposed to shower him with praise over his bravado? Probably so, but instead I voiced the thing that had been bugging me since the night ADA Hale showed up with Lennox in tow.

"Why'd it take you this long to get serious about finding Mary? Because Chris Hale's a pretty face and his uncle is a major public figure? Is that what it takes to get the ball rolling?"

Lennox grimaced, his eyes narrowing. "I've been looking. When she burned the house in Lancaster last fall, we found jack shit that could help us. We still haven't managed to identify the man's body she left behind. She vanished, and as we've discussed, she's damned good at it. We've been watching for more girls to go missing, trying to narrow down a profile. But like I said, we're always busy. We're dealing with sex trafficking and gang murders, drug cartels—you name it. Sometimes you have to prioritize and wait until something bad happens. It sucks, but it happens."

"One of the many hallmarks of our justice system."

"No, it's a simple cause and effect situation," Lennox said. "You've got a sixty-something woman on the run, with no financial activity as far as we can tell. And yeah, maybe we missed something. But I like to think I'm better than that. In the meantime, you've got three runaways being prostituted and two fresh murders, and they've all got active information. Now you tell me, which one are you going to choose?"

I shrugged. "I see your point."

"Sure the system is full of red tape, and not a day goes by I don't want to bang my head against the wall because of it. Criminals have too many rights, and politicians have too much say. But what can I do against it? Spend my valuable time barking up a tree that's never going to change its colors, or get out there and do the job I was hired to do?"

"It's easier for you," I said. "You have the law working with you. When you're in CPS, there's a hundred other factors."

"Maybe we've got a little better budge," Lennox admitted. "Some people are genuinely afraid of jail, and a few of them still think the FBI has more rights than the average citizen. It's bunk, but I use it to my advantage when I can. But it's not that much difference. We still have to follow the law or risk everything getting thrown out by some criminal defense attorney with a fat wallet and a blind eye for what's right and wrong." He glanced at me.

"That's why I get the idea of going rogue," he continued. "Black and white is cozy. Easy. Eye for an eye and all that. Black and white sounds like it would help everyone sleep at night, but you know what? That's just an illusion. There's no such thing as black and white in the world, Lucy. Not with skin color, not with personality, and certainly not with right and wrong. In the end it's all shades of gray that don't look much different from the other, and it's my job—and sometimes yours—to figure out the best match."

"And that makes you feel good about your life?" I asked. "You feel like you're making a difference, choosing your battles based on what you can and can't win?"

"That's not what I'm doing," he said. "If I think I've got a snowball's chance in hell of finding out the truth, I'm going for it. But sometimes that's just not an option, and there's always another victim in the wings. And to answer your question, I know I make a difference."

He shrugged his phone out of his pocket, driving with his left hand and nearly running us off the road again. He handed the phone to me when he found what he was looking for.

"It's a wall with a bunch of pictures I can't really make out," I said.

"Every one of those people, I've helped in my career. Every one of them represents a closed case, one way or another. And when the days hit where I wonder what in the hell I'm still doing this for, I look at that picture and remind myself. I gave them closure." His voice caught on the last word —not the first time I'd sensed that particular emotion from him.

"Who is it?" I asked.

"I'm sorry?"

I cleared my throat. "Your lack of closure. Who did you lose?"

A single muscle in his jaw flexed, and then he sighed. "My younger sister. She got in with the wrong crowd in high school, turned to drugs. Ended up on the street. I thought being a cop, I could help her." His laugh sounded hollow. "I even arrested her for prostitution once. She was out in less than a day."

"Is she dead?"

"I don't know. She disappeared two years ago. I've used every resource I have, but she's just vanished into thin air."

"Maybe she decided to start over." I felt stupid even saying it.

"She wouldn't have done that to our mother," Lennox said. "I keep hoping she'll turn up, but I know in my heart she's dead. Probably killed by a john or a pimp and dumped somewhere." He stopped, his throat drawn so tightly the cords in his neck bulged. After a minute, he managed to speak again. "That's what the cop in me says. But the brother still holds out hope. So yeah, I believe there's something to be said for closure. And being able to do that for some other family makes it easier to sleep at night."

It was a nice sentiment. Lennox might be more of an idealist than I thought. One of the good guys, I supposed, even if he believed in playing by the rules. Part of me hated how much his rationale made sense. It only pushed me further to the conclusion that all my previous choices were made for my own personal inner demons instead of for my burning sense of justice. I was starting to think I'd made that all up. "I'm sorry for your loss."

A call made his phone vibrate in my hand. He snatched it away. "Lennox."

The air in the SUV changed then, like a whisper from the backseat from a surprise guest we had no interest in hearing from. My toes flexed in my boots; my legs suddenly jerked. Lennox said nothing, listening to the voice coming from who knows where, the agent's expression turning into thunderclouds.

"You're sure?" His tone said he already knew the answer, but he'd ask one last time, just in case he'd imagined whatever fresh nightmare we were about to run into. "On the state line?" Lennox hit the brakes, and this time we did slide, nearly rear-ended by a compact car. My fingers dug into the dash as he skidded to a halt on the shoulder. He reached for the GPS and started punching in coordinates. Northeast of Dale City, towards Delaware.

What the hell was Mary doing?

"Don't touch anything, and don't call anyone," Lennox said. "We're about forty miles away. I want to make all the notifications. Just compile a list of people I need to talk to."

Death. That's what he was talking about. But whose? Panic tasted like metal shavings on my tongue. I tried to breathe normally, but I felt the swell in my chest, that fast gasp for air as if someone had been holding a pillow over my face and given me one blissful second to try to breathe.

"Who is it?" I asked the second he hung up.

"Lionel Kent."

THIRTY-ONE

I wasn't prepared to be hanging on the edge of a crime scene in the middle of winter. Granted, I had the right sort of coat and boots, and death certainly didn't make me squeamish, but standing on the side of the road, with my hands shoved in my pockets and my head ducked down against the wind, while a small group of police officers encircled a dead body wasn't something I'd planned on today.

Lennox stood next to a man wearing a coat that looked to weigh at least twenty pounds. From the way the man approached the body, his eyes knitted and his movements methodical, I assumed he was the medical examiner. Sheriff's deputies and state troopers flanked the other two men. Snippets of conversation drifted back to me in cold gusts, but I couldn't make out enough for details.

The SUV's engine hummed; Lennox had been gracious enough to leave it on for me. But I couldn't stay inside. Lionel Kent's remains held little interest for me, but even so, my body seemed compelled to be a part of the scene, even if I had to stand on the fringe.

We were exactly six miles across the Delaware state line,

and not much farther from Maryland and Virginia, in a pocket of fields off the kind of gravel country road that might see half a dozen cars in a day or none at all. Lionel lay some thirty feet off the road, cut down in the snow. Last fall's weeds poked out from the white drifts, as if the plants refused to be forgotten, soaking up whatever winter sun they could until the snow melted and they could begin their cycle all over again. This place had loneliness locked up tightly. The flat field stretched as far as I could see, and Lionel's blue plaid shirt looked like a bruise against the white.

Lennox moved towards me, his tall frame bent against the wind. "You should have stayed inside the car. It's damned cold out here."

"Too anxious." I wanted to ask him for details, but he'd either provide them or he wouldn't.

"Single gunshot wound to the head." Lennox pointed to the snow where one of the responding officers had left evidence markers. "Looks like he was led right out there and executed."

"That cold bitch."

"You're not really surprised, are you?"

"I don't know." Maybe I'd hoped Mary's twisted sense of family might save Lionel. Some kind of duty she felt she owed him, since he'd been the one to visit her in the psychiatric hospital. But her loyalty only lasted until it no longer served her purposes.

"Weapon looks like a nine-millimeter. I'm assuming it's not registered, but we're checking anyway," Lennox said. "His wallet's gone, but the county boys have already found next of kin."

I waited.

"His mother, and she lives in Dale City too."

I got back in the truck and fastened my seatbelt.

. . .

Lennox insisted on being the one to deliver the bad news to Margaret Kent. This was an experience I really wanted to stay in the car for, but he opened my door and waited until I'd stepped onto her icy sidewalk. She lived alone, on the east side of Dale City, in an inexpensive but well-maintained duplex. Recent snow covered the walk and the porch. I assumed her son had neglected his duties in clearing them.

"She's never married?" I asked Lennox as we picked our way up the walk.

"Not that we can find. I'll take any break we can get at this point."

I half-expected an elderly version of Mary to open the door, but Margaret Kent looked more like a frail baby bird. Barely five feet, with hands twisted from arthritis and decades of wrinkles around her eyes, she trembled in her doorway. "Can I help you?"

"Margaret Kent?" Agent Lennox's voice and demeanor changed, his tightly controlled persona shifting into one of camaraderie and compassion. As if they were old friends, and he was just the person to deliver the worst news of her life, because he'd be able to support her through it.

A lovely illusion.

"I am. What's this about?" Margaret's eyes shifted from Lennox and then to me. Did I look properly compassionate? I certainly felt it, although righteous anger seemed to dim my empathy. Another person had died at Mary's hands, and I was sick of being too many steps behind her.

"I'm Agent Lennox of the FBI, and this is Lucy Kendall, a private investigator working with me on a case involving your niece, Mary Weston, née Kent. May we come in?"

Margaret's brown eyes burned with the brightness of a freshly sparked fire. "It's my son, isn't it? She's gone and got him into trouble."

"Why don't we come in, and I'll tell you everything I can," Lennox said.

The old lady shifted out of the way, although either one of us could have brushed her aside with a single arm. Her small front room was filled to the brim with a lifetime of knickknacks and memories. Collectibles I'd never seen the point in spending money on. Photo after photo of her son through the years. The temperature suddenly felt like we'd been dropped on the equator. I didn't want to draw attention to myself, didn't want to be the one Margaret honed in on, demanding news about her son. I wanted to fade into the background and observe, so I kept my coat on and started to sweat.

"Is Lionel dead?" Her voice wavered only a single note.

"I'm afraid so." Lennox reached out an arm, as if he expected this frail-looking lady to faint, but she simply walked to a recliner that needed new upholstery and sat. Her hands folded into her lap, her head bowed. Her shoulders—no bigger than some children's—trembled.

Lennox sat in the chair nearest her; I hovered by the couch. I didn't know what to say or touch or even think, so I kept my mouth shut.

"Is there anyone we can call for you?" Lennox asked.

Margaret shook her head. "It's just me and Lionel. Or it was. Now it's just me." She looked up, her face crumpled as though she'd been sucker-punched. "I'm old. Everyone I know is dying or dead. I just never thought I'd outlive my child. That's not supposed to happen."

"No, it isn't." Lennox gave her a minute, the silence stretching me like a guitar string. How could he be so patient? How could he mask the anger I knew he felt and channel it into something gentle and understanding? He'd seen the mess of Lionel Kent, knew what his evil cousin had pulled him into. I wanted to rage against everything, and I knew Lennox did too. I saw in the tautness of his hands as we drove to Margaret's house, the grinding of his jaw and the way his eyes narrowed at the road, as if daring something to get in his path.

And yet here he sat, calm and collected, whatever turmoil he felt completely masked.

"Was he with Mary?" Margaret broke the silence.

"We have reason to believe he was," Lennox said. "They were spotted at a gas station in the last forty-eight hours. Were you aware Mary had contacted your son?"

"I suspected it," she said. "He called me early Tuesday morning, upset. It had snowed again, and I needed him to shovel. But he said he couldn't, that he was too sick to get out."

"But you didn't believe it," Lennox said.

She shook her head, tears standing in her eyes. "Lionel doesn't believe in being sick. And I heard something in his voice, even though I can't really say what it was. Fear, I suppose. Something wasn't right."

"Why'd you assume it had to do with Mary?"

"It was only a matter of time." The old woman reached behind her for a faded green, crocheted blanket. She wrapped it around her shoulders, and fresh sweat broke out across my upper lip. Her wrecked hands fisted the blanket in her lap. "When I heard the news about her this winter, that she'd been involved in all those killings in Lancaster, and that she was probably still doing it, I wasn't surprised. I told Lionel to stay away from her if she came calling, but it had been years, and he didn't think she would. Not now."

"Did he believe she was involved?" Lennox asked.

"He didn't want to think about it," Margaret said. "He still sees her as the cousin he wanted to look out for their whole lives." She chewed the corner of her mouth, rocking back and forth, her hands still clutching the blanket. "And she got him killed. My son is dead." Her tears fell onto her hands, looking like great puddles against her paper-thin skin.

"You're Alan Kent's sister?" Lennox offered her another tissue. I held my breath even though I knew the answer.

"God help him, yes." Margaret shuddered, pulling the blanket tighter. "I wish he'd left Mary with our mother and me, instead of taking her on the road so much. But he was never right after Korea, and even worse after Mary's mother died. He didn't think about what was best for Mary as a child, you know? A stable environment with some kind of education. He only thought about all his losses and being alone on the road. He wouldn't listen."

Lennox and I glanced at each other. We'd both heard "Korea." Kelly had been right. And if Alan Kent was using his benefits as a veteran, then he had to be using his real name.

"When did he start taking her?" Lennox prodded Margaret.

"Why does it matter?" Her frail voice pitched high. "She needs to be stopped before she gets anyone else killed. You don't need a history lesson on her."

"Actually, we do." Lennox's gentle voice never wavered. "It will help me understand her, which in turn gives me a better shot at locating her."

Margaret's teary eyes looked doubtful, but she sniffed and continued. "Just after her sixth birthday," she said. "Right in the middle of kindergarten, and they were gone for three weeks. And it just got worse from there." Margaret grew more agitated as she spoke. "How's a girl supposed to learn to be a girl when she spends all that time in a semitruck on the road? How's she supposed to learn to be social? Alan always took her homework, and for some reason the school never really argued much, but I thought it was awful."

Lennox made a sympathetic noise. "Was she always a different child?"

"Not until then." Margaret wiped her eyes with the soaked tissue. I wanted to hand her another, but I couldn't make myself move. "She was bright and outgoing. And then year by year—

no, trip by trip, really—it got worse. She withdrew and became moody. I thought part of it was just adolescence and girl stuff. You know that poor thing got her period on the road? She was thirteen, and her father hadn't said a thing to her about it. She didn't know what was going on." Now she looked at me, and I wanted to hide beneath the hood of my coat. But Margaret didn't seem to notice. "1967! Those things weren't exactly advertised the way they are now, but mothers warned their daughters. I'm the one who sat her down and talked to her about sex, told her how she could get pregnant now. I tried so hard to get her father to just leave her with me, but he wouldn't listen."

"I'm sure you did," Lennox said. "She was a watcher, then?" Lennox asked. "An observer?"

"As she got older, yes. You could see it inside of her—she'd sit there, unsure of how to join in with the other kids. She didn't fit in anymore." Margaret shivered. "It's like she was suddenly an adult trapped in a little girl's body. Gave me the shivers."

"And yet she and Lionel were close?"

Margaret jerked at her son's name. She brought the blanket to her face, inhaling deeply. "Lionel loved this blanket. He used it when he was over here the other day. Sometimes he stayed with me, especially when the weather was bad."

Lennox waited, allowing the woman her moment of heartbreak. I fidgeted, wishing I could run away. Her pain dredged up memories of my sister, and I needed a clear head today.

Finally, Margaret took a deep breath, as if to steel herself. "As much as she'd allow it. He's only eighteen months older, and he always felt protective of her. So he tried, every time she came home, to draw her into normal things. But it never really worked." The sadness in her eyes turned to pure hatred. "I should have made him stay away from her. I knew she was no good for him."

"What about the accident in the nineties?" Lennox said.

"Mary suffered serious injury and eventually checked herself into a hospital for depression. Lionel visited her."

"Yes, he did." Pride drifted into her eyes, and she raised her chin. "She didn't have no one else, then."

"What about her father?"

"Alan just disappeared. Mary never would tell Lionel what happened, but she was damned hurt. The two of them were so unnaturally close. Those terrible things happened in Lancaster, and Alan was right by her side, taking care of her. At the time, we all felt sorry for her being so taken up with such a horrible man. And then losing her son." She made a sound of disgust. "I hope she burns in hell."

"Did you ever meet Chris?" This was the first time I'd spoken, and my throat itched with the effort.

Margaret jumped again, evidently having forgotten I was there. "No. Mary never brought anyone in her life around to us. She went back on the road with Alan, and I'd heard they were living downstate. Then the accident happened. I don't know if she blamed him for the accident or vice versa, but the story I got was that he dropped her off at that hospital, and that was it. It devastated her for a long time. We hoped she would get better, but I guess evil always remains evil." Margaret's small body shuddered. "Now she's taken my son. How could she be so evil?"

Lennox took his time, the subtle shift from empathetic listener to skilled investigator altering the mood of the room. I wondered if the woman guessed that Mary had killed Lionel, or if she just blamed her for getting him involved. I hoped I wasn't in the house when Lennox gave her the details.

"If I can speak frankly," Lennox said, "I believe she learned it from her father. We have evidence that suggests Alan kidnapped and killed several girls, dating back to the early seventies. And possibly before that. We're still putting the pieces together, but the scenario is looking more and more likely."

Margaret stared, swallowing as if she gone days without a drink. "He was never right after Korea. And after Judy—his wife—died, he never dated that I knew. But I always figured he must have someone, even if she just passed in the night. But Mary never talked about another woman. And oh! Mary was with him. You think he did this with her, when she was a child? Is that why?"

Lennox reined her back in. "That's one of several scenarios. Would you mind looking at some evidence photos?" He reached for the briefcase I'd forgotten he'd brought with him. "These are from a murder in March of 1964. A fifteen-year-old girl disappeared walking home from school not ten miles from here. Alan was on the road then, right?"

"He was a trucker, yes. But I don't know if he was here or halfway across the state in March of 1964. And please, for all that's holy, don't show me any dead girls. I can't take it."

"Of course not." Lennox retrieved a black and white photo, and I leaned over the couch to get a look at it. A weedy area, probably in the woods, with spring shoots struggling to come through the still melting snow. Beneath a still naked bush lay a doll, with scuff marks on her face and tattered dress.

"Do you recognize this doll?"

Margaret looked everywhere but the photo for a moment, her hands twisting and clasping in her lap, but the temptation proved too great. I felt the recognition before I saw it on her face, felt the zing in my ears and the prickling on my scalp.

"That's Mary's," Margaret said. "I gave it to her for Christmas, and she lost it. I remember because she didn't even seem to care, as if she'd outgrown such things—or never been interested in them in the first place. I always wondered if she just threw it away."

Had she? Had a desperate child tried to leave something

behind as a cry for help from her demented father? Or had she simply forgotten about the doll?

"When was the last time you spoke to Alan?" Lennox asked.

She closed her eyes for a minute, her jaw working as if she were chewing leather. "More than ten years ago, after he had his stroke in 2003."

"Did the stroke leave him with any lasting side effects?" Lennox had shifted to the edge of the couch.

"I think it affected his driving," Margaret said. "When he called me, he was looking for Lionel. I had a hard time understanding him. After all that time, there wasn't much to say."

"Do you happen to know where Alan was living at the time? Or where he's been living since then?" Lennox's legs twitched, his feet tapping the worn carpet. "We know Mary lived in Philadelphia for several years, free and clear as Martha Beckett but we can't find any trace of Alan anywhere."

She shook her head, running a hand through her thin hair. One of the strands caught in her twisted finger. "The last time I spoke to him, he was living somewhere in Pennsylvania. That's all I can tell you." Her eyes still glistened with tears, but a steely resolve steadied her voice. "Now I want you to tell me exactly what happened to my son."

I wanted to run out of that house and throw myself in the glittering snow, as if it could somehow wash off the secondhand misery I'd been painted with after spending another thirty minutes with Margaret. She cried over her son, talked about the child he'd been and the man he'd become. He'd made his mistakes, but he was mostly good—a hard worker who took care of his mother and tried to do the right thing. My skin itched with every word. Lionel was nothing like the men I'd killed, and yet somehow he'd been elected their representative in my mind.

Witnessing Margaret's grief felt like I'd been forced to sit and watch the Harrison brothers' family cry, or Preacher's. Or one of the others.

I didn't think I'd feel clean again if I stripped and bathed in the virgin snow.

Lennox already had his people searching for Alan Kent in Pennsylvania, combing hospital, tax, property, and whatever records they could dig up. He'd relayed the news about Alan serving in Korea to Ryan as he drove one-handed, barking orders into his phone, while I struggled to figure out what bothered me most about recent events.

"What is it?" He tossed the phone on the dash and glanced at me. "Something's eating at you."

What could I say? That I actually felt remorse and couldn't handle watching a loved one grieve? That my brain felt on the verge of exploding with guilt and self-awareness?

"Why did she kill Lionel?"

"She didn't need him anymore."

"But it's a mistake," I said. "Because his death is going to be noticed. And it's brought us to his mother. Now you've got a possible lead. She's got to have known that would happen. It's not as if she hid the body."

"I was thinking the same thing," Lennox admitted. "And I don't have much of an answer. Just a theory."

"I'm all ears."

"We know Mary's a twisted piece. Groomed by her father since she was small. If she witnessed the murder I just asked Margaret about, she was less than ten years old. She didn't stand a chance, and she and her father spent their lives learning how to be the best at the game they played. But the running, the looking over the shoulder—all of that takes a toll on the mind. Especially when you have a safe period like Mary did."

"You think she's just wearing out?"

"It's possible," he said. "Everything's catching up to her.

Add a sick father and her long-lost son into the mix, and she's probably wrecked. How easy do you think Chris would make this for her?"

"What do you mean?" Chris was becoming more and more like a stranger.

"No matter how messed up his head is right now, he's going to resist for a while, right?" Lennox asked. "He's going to fight her and question and demand answers. He's not just going to be all meek and mousy and afraid of her, is he?"

"I can't answer that," I said. "A few days ago, I'd have laughed at his going after her at all. There are things about him I didn't know and I'm wondering..."

"If the Chris you know is real?"

Shamed, I looked down at my cold hands. "Something like that."

"He might be," Lennox said. "But no one's one-dimensional. And it's the other bits and pieces a person's got to worry about."

THIRTY-TWO

Evening had descended by the time we arrived back in Jarrettsville. I dozed during the drive, caught in a semi-lucid state filled with images of Chris bleeding and his mother's creepy childhood doll wielding a knife. Lennox dropped me off at the hotel and headed to the station where Ryan still pored over newly pulled records.

"I'll call you if we get a hit," Lennox said. "Thanks for going with me today."

I tried to smile, but I'd used up whatever acting skills I still possessed. "I'm not sure I was any help, but I appreciate your letting me tag along." I got out of the car, my feet slipping on the ice. Cold rushed me, but I needed to say one more thing. "Listen, about your sister. I get it, the need for closure. And it's a wonderful goal. But you can't deliver it to everyone, no matter how hard you try."

"Very true. But I'm not going to let that stop me."

I waved goodbye and picked my way back to the motel. Kelly jumped up from the bed, her eyes still drowsy from sleep. "How'd it go?"

Exhaustion turned me to jelly, and I collapsed on the bed.

"She killed Lionel Kent, and Lennox thinks we're getting closer. I'm not sure we'll ever see Chris alive again."

"You can't lose hope," she said. "Not yet."

I made my head move up and down, but my heart wasn't in the sentiment. "Do you mind if I just crash for a while?"

"Of course not." Kelly slipped to the far side of the bed, holding her sleeping bag like a talisman. "But you're not lying down on that cot. The bed's big enough for two."

This time, I didn't argue with her.

My phone rang somewhere near midnight. For a terrifying second, I didn't know where the hell I was, panic burning my chest. Then the memories of the days crashed down on me, and I grappled for the cell.

"Yeah?"

"Sorry to wake you." Lennox sounded positively cheerful. I sat up, rubbing my eyes.

"That's okay. What's going on?"

"We've got something. You still have that rental?"

I was already out of bed, looking for my keys. "I'll be there in fifteen minutes."

A sheet of ice, glistening beneath the hotel security lights, covered the parking lot. With midnight closing in, the frigid air seemed to have a life of its own, dense and relentless. It cut through my coat and invaded my bones until they screamed for mercy. I tried to ignore it, instead focusing on the clear night sky. Millions of stars glittered, their brightness making it hard to imagine they were nothing but gas.

The warning surged through me seconds before I heard the footsteps. The little parking lot suddenly seemed miles long, and the silence pressed down on me as though I'd suddenly become the only living person in this small town. *Stupid*. A few days away from the city, and I'd forgotten every safety precaution. The pepper spray was back in the hotel room, my other weapons burried even deeper. No matter. I could fight.

My rental was parked at the end of the row, beneath a security light that hadn't fired on. The muscles in my legs jerked with the need to run, but no one had bothered to use any ice melt. Moving any faster would likely result in my landing on my ass. My heavy boots smacked against the frozen pavement. *Weapons*. I could pack a good kick if I had to.

"Lucy, can I speak with you?"

The fake honey in her voice sent a wave of disgust through me. I whirled, my gloved fingers digging into the palm of my hand. Reporter Beth Reid materialized from behind a big SUV. Wearing dark, warm clothes, she looked like she'd been waiting for the prime opportunity to jump out at me.

"No."

"Please, I just have a few questions. And you owe me, since you gave me false information. After I helped you and Agent Lennox." She had the gall to sound offended.

"I don't have any answers for you."

"What did John Weston tell you?" Beth ignored my denial. Her breath wafted into the cold air in great white puffs. "Did he give any details about Mary's involvement in the Lancaster killings? Did he say why he let her get off free and clear while he sat in prison all these years?"

"Are you stupid?" Unlike Lennox or any other cop, I didn't have to play nice with the media. "I mean, seriously? Is there something wrong with you?"

"I'm just trying to get the story."

"Why?"

She blinked, still trying to look genuinely surprised. "Because people deserve to know."

"Bullshit." I was too tired to dance with her. "You want the story because you want to make a name for yourself. When this is all over, and Mary is caught, then the public has a right to some of the details. Beyond that, every time you stick your nose in where it doesn't belong, you run the risk of helping her evade authorities. And killing more girls."

"That's not true."

I rolled my eyes, no longer freezing cold but warm to the core. "Don't you realize going public with the story about John Weston talking to us gives Mary an edge and makes her more cautious? Or did you think she didn't watch television?"

"I followed the story."

"You followed your selfish desires." My head pounded, my face heating as if I'd been running on the treadmill. "People like you are a big part of the problem, hiding behind the First Amendment and screaming about the right to know, but you don't give a damn about helping anyone but yourselves. You'd endanger someone's life without thinking twice if it meant you could get a career-making story."

"That's not fair," Beth said. "You don't know anything about me."

"I know enough," I said. "You're all the same. Vapid and self-absorbed. As far as I'm concerned, you're worthless." I turned to walk away before the rage could burn any brighter. It flowed through my veins and into every nerve ending, making me dizzy and my thoughts hazy, as if I were peering through a gray veil. But the voice of my rage, booming in my head, begged to lash out at Beth. I bit my tongue and trudged forward.

"What about the friend staying in your room?" Beth tried again. "Would she say the same thing? Or does she have the sense to realize how much the media can help?"

I stopped cold, turning back to face her. "Leave her alone."

"People are talking about her, you know." Beth's voice told me she knew she'd hit a nerve. "I found out she contracts for the

Philadelphia police. And that she's been through some real hell in her life."

My vision clouded. I saw nothing but anger and Kelly's face —not the one she presented to the world now, but of the abused child. An eye swollen shut, half her face the color of a ripe eggplant. A dislocated shoulder. Lighter burns. A ruined womb. All those details had been filed away, carefully protected by the state because of her age.

But now she was free game—a friend of someone a fame-hungry reporter had deemed newsworthy. Kelly wasn't going to get hurt again because of me.

Beth smirked, the wisps of her hair sticking out from her hat fluttering in the wind. "My contact with Child Protective Services told me some really interesting things about Kelly. You were the social worker who discovered her chained up in that basement room, right? What was that like? Is that the first time you thought about going rogue?"

"Going rogue?" My quiet voice should have warned her. "What are you talking about?"

Her smile widened to Cheshire Cat levels. "You know cops gossip, right? Rumor is, some people think you've taken the law into your own hands, and more than once. If you're really killing pedophiles, more power to you. But given your work on the sex trafficking case, you had some kind of help. And since Kelly is the computer geek, according to my source, I'm thinking it's her."

My heart blasted in my ears. The cold air no longer pierced my skin; in fact, my body felt heated from the inside out.

"What would Kelly say if I asked her about that?" Beth said. "Does she know anything about this Preacher, whose body was just found in the Allegheny National Forest?"

"Stay away from Kelly."

"I'm sorry, I can't do that. Whether you like it or not, the

First Amendment gives me the right to ask as many questions as I'd like."

I closed the distance between us, forgetting about the ice and the cold and whatever future I'd been hoping I could still have.

Beth backed up until she smacked against the vehicle she'd been hiding behind. Now we were nose-to-nose, although I had several inches on her. Our breaths gusted together like white ghosts tangled in battle.

"What are you doing?"

"Listen to me." I pitched my voice low, but it still seemed to boom over the wind. "I don't like threats. And I don't play games. If you bother Kelly in any way, I promise you will live to regret it."

"Is that a threat?" Her eyes danced.

"Take it as you will," I said. "But remember that while you're chasing stories and trying to put together pretty words to make people understand what happened, I've already been there. I've seen the abuse and pain and death in a person. I know what it feels like to see a child who has been used and thrown away. I've smelled it. Tasted it. I've watched dead kids being brought out of homes. Listened to parents lie even as their stinking sweat gave them away. All the horrors you're playing house with, I've experienced. And that makes people a little crazy. Fearless."

She swallowed.

"Remember that the next time you try to sneak up on me in the middle of the night." I paused, giving her time to think. "And if you do anything that bothers Kelly in any way, we'll have another talk. And I won't be so conversational the next time."

I walked to my rental with a slow confidence, shoulders drawn back.

THIRTY-THREE

My head still buzzed from the altercation with Beth.

I dragged myself out of the car, trying to focus on the task at hand. The front desk officer looked at me warily, leaning back in her chair as though I might be contagious. I hadn't thought to check myself in the mirror. Too late for that now.

The energy from our conference room steamed into the hall in great, rolling waves. Everything seemed hyper-focused, from the plants in the hallway to the various pictures and plaques on the walls. Even the emergency exits map looked brighter than it had yesterday, the red escape routes the color of fresh blood.

"What took you so long?" Lennox stood at the head of the table, his dress shirt wrinkled and his sleeves rolled up. Ryan manned his laptop, a cup of coffee in his hand. Two officers I didn't know were busy doing something with the map.

"Ran into Beth Reid."

Lennox's eyes narrowed. "Where?"

"In the motel parking lot. She wanted to know what Weston told me."

"What did you say?"

I dropped my bag on the table and braced my hands on the

back of one of the chairs. "I told her to go to hell, more or less. What's going on?"

"Alan Kent's military paper trail, that's what." Lennox's eyes gleamed. "He served in Korea with the United States Army 121st Transportation Truck Company. He was stationed at Uijeongbu from December 1950 until May 1952."

"So that's where he learned to drive a truck," I said. Had we finally caught a real break? "Anything in his military record?"

"Nothing dishonorable," Lennox said. "He was discharged two months early because of severe pneumonia. According to his records, he and his crew broke down and were stranded overnight. He developed pneumonia after that. But that's not what really stands out. Like we thought, he lied about his age and entered the army at sixteen. By the next winter, he was in Korea."

"I'm sorry, but my military history is sketchy. Why is that relevant?"

Lennox nearly leaped around the room. "Because of his benefits. The winter of 1950–51 in Korea was brutal on troops, and cold weather accounted for a huge number of casualties and evacuations. A lot of times, those guys weren't able to get care for their injuries because of battlefield conditions. Alan Kent got sick twice—the first being in January, shortly after he arrived. As far as we can tell, he stuck it out and stayed on the front lines."

"Then how do you know he was sick at all?" I asked. "There wouldn't be a record if he wasn't treated."

Lennox looked at Ryan, smiling with the pride of a new father. "Because this guy is aces at his job. Korean War veterans who experienced cold injuries are now dealing with medical conditions because of that very winter. We're talking diabetes and vascular disease, arthritis, cold sensitization. The list goes on. Because of that, they're eligible for a wider variety of benefits in addition to the regular military benefits."

"Alan couldn't lie about his name if he wanted to collect," Ryan said. "And he did. So once we found out he was in the service, tracking him got a lot easier."

I sat down, heart racing to the same beat of Lennox's silly pacing. I felt it now—the adrenaline rush that blooms when a case was breaking wide open.

Ryan continued. "He's dealt with cold sensitization since the sixties, according to his records. He was hospitalized for pneumonia several times over the years, and he was diagnosed with vascular disease in 2002. That's what caused his stroke. The Philadelphia VA Medical Center treated him on and off since the eighties—which is, of course, when he and Mary first moved to Lancaster. He was hospitalized there with his stroke for several months."

"And the benefit trail continues," Lennox said. "He started collecting disability in the nineties after his arthritis kept him from driving long hours. Those checks went directly to Mary's residence in Philadelphia, but in 2004, after he recovered from his stroke—which was bad enough to make him retire but still able to live on his own—he got his pension. Along with home assistance." He paused, catching his breath. "Which he applied to a farm in Oxford, Pennsylvania."

I didn't want to hope, but the seed started to grow anyway— just a tiny, frail stalk deep in the pit of my stomach. "Is that still listed as his residence?"

"The government just mailed him a check a week ago." Lennox grinned. "Even better, the place is about an hour from Philadelphia, easy for Mary to visit."

"And just for kicks," Ryan said, "I searched for missing girls matching Alan's assumed tastes within a hundred-mile radius of the Oxford house, and I got a hit on four different teenaged girls going back six years."

"Mary would have had to take them for him," I said. "And if she's got this place in Oxford, why did she go back to Lancaster last fall?" I still felt the heat of that fire and smelled the charred bodies.

"Maybe she had a new partner and a separate operation," Lennox said. "For all we know, she could have been selling those girls for extra money and getting her kicks from the ones she brought to her dad. We won't know until we ask." He reached into his pocket for his keys. "You up for another ride?"

THIRTY-FOUR

After a mad rush back to the hotel and a hasty explanation for Kelly, I was back on the road with Lennox. The SUV shot up I-95, Lennox moving in and out of the light traffic with the ease of someone who knew he wasn't going to get a ticket. I drank my coffee and wished I had some caffeine pills.

Lennox didn't need them. Like every other cop I'd been around, he came alive on the chase. His entire body vibrated in the seat, his hands drumming against the steering wheel in an annoying pattern that gave me a headache.

"This is it," he said. "We're going to nail her now. I can't wait to see the look on her face when I bring her down. And her father. I don't give a damn if he served. What he's done to these girls is worse than an animal."

Something in the tone of his voice cut through whatever fatigue I labored under and awakened my earlier euphoria. Lennox, with his ego and need for justice, his need to see the shock on Mary's face at finally getting taken down, wasn't much different than my desire to see the fear on any of the men I'd killed. We'd both been stewed in the same pot of ingredients, and somehow he'd come out on the right side of the law, pristine and good. And I'd ended up in the trashcan full of bad decisions and lost hope.

How had that happened?

"Don't worry about that reporter," Lennox said. "She's a pain in the ass, but I'll make sure she doesn't bother you anymore."

He couldn't possibly do that unless he knew what she'd tried to accuse me of, and I wasn't about to discuss that. "I can handle myself. But she was asking questions about Kelly, and I won't let her be harassed."

Before I left, I'd warned Kelly about the reporter, cautioning her to not to open the door for anyone. "I'll feel better when I can get her back home. This has all been very hard on her."

"She's a good friend."

"She's the strongest person I know."

Lennox cleared his throat. My defenses immediately shot back up. "Have you thought about what we're going to do here? What you might find?"

"Chris could easily be dead. I'm prepared for it." A lie, but it didn't matter.

"Or he could be worse than dead."

"He's damaged. And there are things he and I need to discuss. But he'll be all right." Another lie. For all I knew, being trapped with his mother's and grandfather's lies and cruelty had already made him feral. But I would see this through because he'd come for me. He hadn't turned his back when I needed him the most. I would return the favor.

Lennox checked his phone. "The state police's SERT team will be in place to breach the farm soon."

"Are they waiting for you?"

"Yeah," he said. "These guys train for this, and they don't really need me. But this case is my responsibility, and if something goes wrong, I want to be there."

"And you want to make the bust," I said. "To see the moment Mary knows she's finally been caught."

The corners of his mouth ticked up. "That's just a bonus."

"What if she catches on and takes off again?"

"These guys are better than that. She won't see them. And if she does, the local police and the state troopers are in place. There's no way out for her."

Or the rest of us. We were forever sewn together with this experience, some of us more so than others. Catching Mary and Alan would change Lennox's career. Chris's life was in tatters, mine in flux. Todd and Justin finally had justice within their grasp, and Kelly had conquered one of her demons. No matter the outcome, all of us would remember the past few days as one of those very clear moments in life when everything changed.

Lennox's phone rang, the noise ripping through my thoughts like a serrated knife. "Agent Lennox." He put the phone on speaker.

"We're in position. How far out are you?"

"Twenty minutes," Lennox said. "Any movement?"

"None," the SERT officer said. "Lights on in the farmhouse. Place looks like it's falling down around them."

"Be careful. We know they have a nine-millimeter, and who knows what's been stored in that house."

"Copy that. My commander is about a half mile south of the house. You'll come to a four-way stop at an intersection, and you'll see our setup. He'll rendezvous with you there."

It was almost over.

Just outside of the Oxford city limits, Lennox exited onto a badly paved road that soon gave way to gravel. Within minutes, two Pennsylvania State Trooper vehicles came into view, along with a very large SERT truck that reminded me of the food trucks driven in the city.

"Don't worry," Lennox said when I freaked out over the attention the group was drawing to itself. "We're in a remote area, and every way out of this place is blocked. Even if they leave on foot. The local police are on top of it."

I twisted in the leather seat. "Let me go with you. Please."

"Absolutely out of the question. You're a PI, not a cop. And you're not trained for something like this."

"I don't care. I want to see her face too." I *needed* to see it. I had to know what it was like to finally have every bad thing you've done catch up to you. If I could witness that moment and freeze it in my memory, then maybe I'd have a shot at redeeming myself.

"I can't allow it." Lennox spoke gently. "I wish I could, because you've done everything I've asked you to do, and you've been a major help to this case. But even if I wanted to risk my job, it's not my call. It's the SERT commander's, and he'd laugh us right out of the county."

Disappointment blazed through me. It must have showed on my face because Lennox reached over and patted my hand, his skin smooth against mine. "I promise I'll bring you on the scene the absolute second they're in custody. I'll take responsibility for you and make sure you don't contaminate evidence."

I nodded, too frustrated to speak. He jumped out of the vehicle, slamming the door and greeting the SERT commander, who'd been pacing at our fender.

Lennox gestured to the truck, and the SERT guy shook his head. Lennox kept talking, his head bobbing up and down, hands gesturing. Finally, the SERT commander held up his hands, pointing at Lennox.

He returned to the truck. "The rest of the team is already on the perimeter of the house, ready to go. The commander and I will join them and then make the move. When things are secure, I'll send an officer back for you."

I didn't have a hope of changing anyone's mind. "Thanks."

Lennox dug around in the back of the truck and produced a SIG Sauer nine-millimeter. "You know how to handle a weapon, right?"

"I've gone to the range with Chris several times."

"Good. Safety's on, and you shouldn't need it. But just in case." He left it on the driver's seat and locked the SUV.

And then it was just me and my thoughts, my festering fears, waiting for his return.

As Lennox departed with the SERT commander, I focused on the gray sky. A heavy blanket of clouds refused to allow the sun to filter through. Jersey cows waddled through the pasture to my right, their velvet-like coats tacky with snow and ice. Several ambled to the fence line, their long tongues lolling out to touch their wet noses while they surveyed the intruding cars. I'd never touched a cow before, and in a moment of pure insanity, I debated getting out of the truck and going up to say hi.

But I'd probably be able to hear any gunshots from inside the vehicle too.

A series of loud honks made me jump. Several brave Canadian geese skimmed past, their leader at the front of the V-formation calling back orders. I realized they fled from the direction of the house. I'd kept my head turned from that line of winter-brown trees, but it turned of its own volition now, my eyes searching for something.

But the staging area had been set up too far away from the farmhouse. My scenery was a choice of dead trees or nosy cows cleaning their noses.

I watched the digital clock. Ever mindful of keeping me warm, Lennox had left the SUV running. I supposed if Mary came hoofing up the road in some outrageous escape from the SERT team, I could run her over and end things for good. Lennox couldn't be mad if I prevented her escape.

Minutes ticked by. I released my seatbelt, settled back. Then I sat forward, checking the horizon. Still nothing. Another glance at the cows told me things were still slow and steady; they'd gone back to chewing their hay. My fingers traced the SIG Sauer, its cool steel warming my hands. I'd rather shoot Mary in the head and watch her brains splatter on the road.

But Lennox was right. We had too many questions and too many families desperate for answers.

My nerves ticked back and forth. I turned the radio on to a cheesy Top 40 song about love and then promptly turned it off. I checked the glove box, but Lennox hadn't left anything juicy or interesting in there. His briefcase in the backseat had a lock.

I went back to watching the cows. The leader had a white splotch on her forehead, as though she'd gotten into paint. She angled her head over the fence, straining her neck, an ear cocked. What did she hear? Or was she just debating about what sort of steak she'd like to be?

I started to laugh and then felt terrible. Her sweet eyes blinked accusingly. I might end up a vegetarian after this experience.

My phone rang. Suddenly limbo seemed a hell of a lot more appealing than whatever came next. "Hello?"

"It's Lennox. I've got an officer coming for you."

"Is he dead?" I couldn't bring myself to say his name.

Lennox didn't answer right away, and my stomach turned to acid. My right hand groped for the door handle. I didn't want to vomit in the FBI's vehicle.

"Chris is asking for you."

THIRTY-FIVE

I didn't catch the name of the SERT officer who retrieved me. He still wore his gear, the adrenaline bleeding from him. I kept his quick pace down the dirt road, my heart rooted in my throat.

A two-story house emerged at the end of the drive. Its wood siding, once painted gray, rotted in numerous places, making the curtainless windows look like ruined teeth in a drug addict's mouth. A slanted porch ran along the front, one end of it supported by two cinder blocks. A fresh wave of cold swept over me, pulling my senses into high alert.

Where was everyone? Only two SERT officers stood in front of the house, their weapons at the ready. Another formation of geese swept by, their calls sounding like an urgent warning this time.

"Where's Agent Lennox?"

"He's in the house." The SERT officer who'd escorted me took my elbow as we reached the porch. "Watch your step. This thing is unstable."

The steps groaned and sagged under our weight; the porch shuddered. Still, I paused at the open door, hit with the stench of rotting wood and dirt and something far worse.

"They're in the front room," the officer said.

Forcing my legs to move, I crossed the threshold. To my immediate right, a death trap of a staircase led to the second floor. The fifth step was completely busted out. Mouse droppings littered the bottom step. I tried to breathe through my mouth, but I'd already inhaled the house's sick air.

"Lucy?"

His voice was weak as an infant's, but I recognized it and forgot to be on guard or angry. I rushed to the middle of the front room, where Chris sagged on a chair. Fresh bruises covered his handsome face; dried blood caked his plump lips. Lennox's heavy winter coat was draped over his shoulders; he'd been wearing nothing but a dirty, white T-shirt and jeans. Scratches in various stages of healing decorated his arms, and one looked infected. A thick coating of old rags wrapped around his right shoulder.

But his eyes were the same bright, perceptive blue.

I knelt in front of him, afraid to touch. That's when I realized his shoes and socks were gone, his right foot covered in dried blood and bandaged.

"What did she do to you?"

He licked his split lip, trying to smile. "Last night, Mary tried to cut my toe off to make sure I didn't run. She didn't get the bone, but the damage is done."

I tried not to react, but my legs wobbled. "Jesus. Your arm— is that where she shot you?"

"He shot me," Chris said. "I got the bullet out and cleaned the wound. Same with my toe. But I think I've got an infection." His body shook, and I realized it was as cold inside as out. My breath showed white, my fingers half-numb.

I looked up at Agent Lennox, who stood behind Chris. "Why is it so cold in here?"

"Heat's turned off," he said. "Windows are open. They left him to freeze."

"Where are the paramedics?" I pulled the coat tighter around Chris, who shivered and leaned against me, resting his head on my shoulder. He smelled unwashed and bloody, but I couldn't push him away.

"Five minutes out," Lennox said. His eyes were grim, and I replayed his words.

"Mary left him to freeze to death. Meaning she's not here."

A single shake of his head confirmed what I'd somehow known would happen. "He said he wanted to talk to you first."

Gently, I lifted Chris's head off my shoulder. His eyes were dilated, his skin cold. "Tell me."

"You know about Alan, right?" Chris tried to glance at Lennox, but his eyes only rolled. "He said you did."

"We found out, yes. And we saw you with him on the security tape from the gas station."

Chris smiled, making his lip bleed. "I looked up on purpose."

"I knew you did. Where's Alan? Did he leave with Mary too?"

"No," Chris said. "He's got health problems from the war. Heart issues. And he got the flu."

"That's why you went to the gas station with him," I said. "Because they needed you to treat him."

Lennox made a sharp noise in his throat, catching my eye. I read his expression easily. *Stop putting words in his mouth.*

"I wanted to help him," Chris said. "I didn't know what he'd done. She didn't tell me until after she killed Lionel."

"Why did she kill him?" Lennox asked.

Chris licked his lips. I wished I had some ChapStick. "Because he was going to take Alan to the hospital. The flu meds were helping, but he was really bad off. Mary wouldn't go, and she and Lionel got in an argument. He called her crazy, said he was going to turn her in." Chris closed his eyes, caught in the nightmare of his memories. "She pulled the car over, told him they should take a walk and sort it out. Then she shot him."

Tears tracked through the dirt on his face. "He was a decent guy. I knew she was up to something, but my hands and feet were zip-tied." Red welts on his wrists and his feet said as much. "Then we came here, and Alan got worse."

"What happened?" I asked.

"She told me to take care of him. But I didn't have anything to help him. He needed to be in the hospital, on an IV and oxygen. He needed his heart monitored and probably new medication. But I don't even think that would have helped."

I waited, letting him gather his composure. Watching him speak physically hurt; the tender skin on his lips cracked with every other word.

"He died this morning, and she flipped out. She tied me up here and left with him."

"By herself?" Lennox said. "Why didn't you fight?"

"I don't know," Chris said. "I think I'd lost all hope at that point. And I've been in and out of it the last day or so, from fever I think. Part of me kept wondering if I was hallucinating the entire thing."

I searched his face, trying to see past the injuries and the now glazed eyes. The part of me still very much attached to Chris wanted to ignore the warning tick in my brain.

Something isn't adding up.

And it hasn't from the beginning.

Lennox chewed his lip, staring at Chris. "I know she's a big woman, but how'd she get his body out of here?"

"She's strong," Chris said. "And you didn't see Alan without his coat on, did you? He couldn't weigh more than a hundred and ten. Skin and bones, and even worse since he got the flu. She dragged him out the back door."

"This was how long before we arrived?"

Chris tried to shrug and then winced, reaching for his

injured shoulder. "I have no idea. It seemed like a long time. The sun was up when she left. Although there's no sun today. But it was light."

"She's still driving Lionel Kent's Jeep?"

"As far as I know. That's what we came here in, and I didn't see any other vehicles."

Paramedics arrived, stomping their way across the beaten-down floors. I stepped out of the way, and Chris reached for me, but I stayed back. "They need to take care of you."

"Will you go to the hospital with me?"

I didn't want to. I wanted to be here, digging for Mary and finding out more of her lies. And I didn't want to be alone with Chris. Not yet.

"She'll be along a little later." Lennox saved me. "I need her here."

Chris closed his eyes. "See you soon, Luce."

I watched in silence as the medics stabilized Chris and then carried him out of the house, struck by how little I felt. Relief he was alive, disappointment Mary was gone and Alan dead, but yet... no earth-shattering emotion. No urge to thank God for Chris's safe return, no overwhelming desire to throw my arms around him and never let go.

Why didn't I feel more?

"Walk with me."

I followed Lennox to the back of the house into a dirty kitchen. No plates in the sink or rotting food, but black filth covered the counter like a fine sheen of gloss. Even more lined the sink, mold seeping up from the drain. So much grime covered the window I couldn't see outside. Sections of tile from the floor had been ripped out and discarded, revealing a stained subfloor.

"No wonder Alan could afford this place."

"I'm not sure he ever lived here," Lennox said. "I think they just used it for the victims."

The kitchen floor took on a whole new meaning. "Are there signs she buried them in here?"

"No," Lennox said. "But that doesn't mean she didn't kill them here and then remove the evidence. But having them in the house isn't Mary's style, is it?" His gaze drifted out the open back door to the storage shed. The SERT team and a state trooper waited.

"The shed's clear," Lennox said. "Of anything living, at least."

THIRTY-SIX

Newer than the house, the shed was long and low, probably twenty by ten feet, all metal and no windows. The SERT commander nodded at Lennox.

"We found the remains of two teenaged girls. We'll need the ME to give us time of death, but there's been insect activity, so I'm guessing they died in the fall and then froze. Winter's preserved them."

"How many of you have been inside?" Lennox asked.

"Just me."

"Good man." He pulled a pair of white paper booties from his pocket and handed them to me. "You can help me confirm Mary's handiwork."

As if he couldn't do it himself. When we were both protected, he opened the door.

"Drawstring light on the immediate left," the commander said.

Lennox yanked the string, and a dim yellow light flooded the building.

The perfect killer's lair waited.

Three wooden benches sat in the middle of the space.

Along the walls were knives, hammers, pliers. Lighters were scattered around the floor. Two wooden spoons sat by themselves on a shelf, right at eye level.

After years of traveling and hiding their trade, Mary and her father finally had the perfect place to enact their terrible deeds.

The dead girls were on the floor against the wall, piled one on top of the other, the way a slaughterhouse disposes of carcasses. Both had blackened skin and nails, but only the bottom girl's face was visible. Her right eye was gone, either ripped out or eaten by the same insects that had devoured part of her cheek. They were so frozen the scent of death had been driven away.

"No sign of the old man?" Lennox called back over his shoulder.

"Nope," the commander said.

"What's she going to do with him?" I asked. "It's too cold to bury him, and she can't exactly drive up to a funeral home or hospital and ask for help."

"Maybe we've got a female Norman Bates on our hands," Lennox said. "She's going to keep him with her, keep driving, keep killing." He rubbed his hands together. "Let her. She'll make a mistake for sure."

I opened my mouth to remind him he'd said that before, but an old steamer trunk near the door distracted me. Whatever color it once was had faded to the color of the dead trees surrounding the property. The wooden slats had cracks between them, and the lid was so warped it wouldn't shut completely.

That's why I saw the blanket.

No more than two steps and I stood in front of it. My wool gloves protected the evidence, so I reached with shaking hands and lifted the aging lid.

At first I thought it was just a worn white hospital blanket, covered with various yellow stains, bunched together. But then

I saw the shape of the knobby knees, the roundness of the head.

Lennox appeared at my side. I allowed him to pull back the blanket.

An old man with sunken cheeks, liver spots, and no teeth stared at us with dead, milky eyes.

THIRTY-SEVEN

"She left him here until she could figure out where to bury him," I said.

"That means she's still out there, driving Lionel's Jeep." Lennox's teeth ground together. "I will catch her."

"Good luck with that." I walked outside, past the SERT guys, sucking in fresh air. The shed was the only other building on the property. The driveway ran west, the opposite direction we'd come from. I knew the troopers had satellite maps, and Mary's back was pinned against the wall. She'd just lost everything, and if I were her, now would be the time for mistakes.

I think I'd kill myself.

Mary's insatiable need for control would give her the strength to end her life if she truly believed she was out of options. Mine too.

Is that what Chris had seen in me at Camp Hopeful? The thing he journaled about but couldn't quite name? That my need for absolute control of my own life would be the thing that separated me from everyone else, the thing that would eventually drive me to take justice into my own hands? Or had he simply recognized the same kind of monster he'd spent the formative years of his childhood with?

Some people thought suicide was a sign of weakness, but it wasn't. It's the ultimate show of control, and sometimes, the only time a person had it. That's exactly what happened with my sister. Chris could have turned out the same way if his aunt and uncle hadn't intervened.

All the confusing threads strung together then, just as an icy breeze swathed my face.

I hurried around the front of the house, heading for the driveway and the SUV. Lennox caught up with me, and I realized someone had given him a police jacket. "I'll take you to the hospital to see Chris. One of the local guys said that damned reporter was snooping around town too. I'd like to know who in the hell she got her information from."

I almost said no. Because the future—my future—stretched very clearly in front of me then, shining on the horizon like a perfect mirage. No more death and destruction. No more lies, no more Marys. Something different. Something real.

But I had loose ends to tie up.

Chris didn't wake until several hours later. I sat dutifully beside him, watching over him until his aunt and uncle arrived. But my motivations were no longer altruistic. I needed my answers.

He'd been treated for infection in both his shoulder and toe, which had been severed with precision and the bleeding staunched by someone with experience. Most likely Alan, whose war records showed he'd had to do something similar for a member of his squad in Korea, to save him from gangrene. Is that where his love of torture sparked?

First troopers and then Lennox questioned Chris before the painkillers took effect. Alan had approached him at the Maryland property, acting every bit the part of a frail old man. Then he'd shot, and Chris passed out from the pain. When he'd woken, he was in the cabin, with Alan treating the wound. He tried to plead with the man, but Mary appeared. She refused to answer any questions and tied Chris back up. The girl was already dead in the bedroom. Lionel arrived at some point, and a shouting match ensued. Chris realized he'd been given some kind of painkiller. His memories were hazy, but he recalled being carted from the cabin and then stuck in the car with his twisted family.

He'd told Lennox that Mary didn't talk much.

I wasn't so sure I believed that.

Chris began to stir, and my lack of patience took over. I gripped his hand, softly calling his name until his eyes flickered open.

"Hey." His torn lips still looked painful, but the blood had been cleaned off his face. "I'm glad you're here."

"Me too." I wanted to be nice. Or at least, I thought I should be nice. But the stress had taken its toll. "Tell me why, Chris."

He blinked a few times, clearing his throat. "I don't know. When my aunt told me my mother had tried to keep me, I snapped. All this time, I thought she didn't want me. And she did."

"Because it was always about winning," I said. "Did it ever occur to you that she and her father would have trained you to be just like them? That even if they were wrong to lie, your aunt and uncle saved your life?"

"It did, yeah. After I got shot."

I didn't return the sarcasm. "Did you have any kind of plan?"

"To kill her."

"With what?" I asked. "You didn't have any weapons, did you? The police didn't find any evidence of that, and you never fought back."

He closed his eyes, his chin jutting out, jaw tight.

"You wanted her to kill you." I couldn't keep it inside any longer. For days, the idea had only been a vague notion tumbling through my mind, something I couldn't put my finger on. "You didn't have the guts to end your own life, and you wanted answers. So you figured she'd give you both." Chris didn't fight because he didn't want to come back to the real world that failed him.

"Does it matter now?"

"It matters to me, because I blamed myself for your actions. I felt like I failed you. And I probably did. But you would have done this anyway, right? From the moment she answered your email, this was the plan." The compassion drained out of my voice, and I tried to keep from talking any louder. Chris would withdraw if I started yelling.

"No," he said. "Not until my aunt told me the truth. And then I just didn't care."

I wanted to ask him what it was like to be in Mary's presence, what sort of horrible things she'd filled his mind with, but it didn't matter.

"I feel sorry for you," I said. "But not because of what you've gone through. Because you can't see how much you have going for you. Because your fear is so paralyzing, you can't let the past go. I guess you forgot everything you learned at Camp Hopeful." I said the words casually, my eyes hard on his.

He swallowed. "I can explain. It's not how it looked."

"You stalked me."

"Only because I was afraid to say anything," he said. "How was I supposed to approach you? Hey, I remember you from the summer we were at a special camp and I've tracked you down thanks to my uncle?"

"How much was true?"

"All of it," he said. "I did hear your name from him, when he was talking about Justin's release. And I remembered you. I swear I didn't intend to follow you. I just couldn't get the guts to say anything. And then I realized what you were doing, and I was so stunned. And jealous. I remembered your story, that your sister had killed herself. I knew that's why you were doing it. And I wanted to do that too. I wanted to wash away all of my memories just like you did."

"Why didn't you just tell me the truth?" Hypocritical question, but I asked it anyway.

He shrugged. "I didn't know how to."

"I wish you had figured it out." I didn't know what else to say. I stood up and stretched. "I'm glad you're all right."

"Where are you going?"

Cold worked its way through me as I slipped on my coat. It settled into the pit of my stomach like a rock, and I wasn't sure I'd ever feel real warmth again. "Your aunt and uncle will be here soon, and you need to work this out with them. It's between the three of you."

He tried to sit up, his eyes wild. "But where are you going?"

"Home, Chris. I'm going home." I zipped up the coat, pulled on my gloves. "I'll see you when you get there."

"What about Mary?" Chris said. "She's still out there. She got away, after all of this."

"She's Lennox's problem," I said. "And believe me, he wants to find her. He's got the best chance of any of us."

"Prison's too good for her."

"You don't believe that."

He stared at me, as if I were really stupid enough to believe him.

"Chris, you could have fought her. You could have tried."

"I did." He stretched out his arms. "How do you think I got these?"

Maybe. But he hadn't tried hard enough. I'd refused to allow those thoughts to surface during the investigation, but Chris needed to understand that he hadn't fooled me. "In the gas station, why didn't you say anything to the clerk? Or to

Lionel? You knew he wasn't fully on board. You're a persuasive guy. The two of you could have outmatched Mary and Alan, even with the gun. You just didn't want to."

"That's not true." His head whipped back and forth, his pupils dilated, his lips trembling.

"It is," I said. "When it came right down to doing the right thing with Mary, you couldn't do it. Because you didn't have the will to survive, but you didn't have the guts to kill yourself." A viciousness welled up inside me. "That's the difference between you and me. You didn't stop her because you were afraid. I would have killed her because I want to live."

He fell back on the pillow, feebly shaking his head. "I didn't know what to do. She gave me painkillers, messed with my head."

That much was true—he'd tested positive for a combination of oxycodone and Vicodin. "Maybe you're right, and I'm just tired and angry because you stalked me. That's why I need to leave."

"But you'll come back, right? And my mother—you promised. You promised!"

I reached for the door. "I'll see you when you get back in town."

THIRTY-EIGHT

Lennox had ordered another rental car for me, and it was supposed to be parked in the second level of the Oxford City Hospital's parking garage. Cold night air rushed me, and I shivered. I needed to drive back to Maryland and pick up Kelly. Then she and I would go back home and figure out what we were going to do next.

Chris's words about my sister had struck a nerve. He'd known from the moment he saw me drop cyanide on someone that it all went back to my sister, while I remained clueless. But he'd made one misinterpretation. I clung to my memories like a starving child, uncertain of how to navigate life without them. I couldn't even blame my actions on the piece of trash who destroyed her life and walked away with too few consequences. But a bigger, more selfish person had to be held accountable for Lily's death. Me. I'd been old enough to know something was wrong, and I should have gotten help. She even begged me to stick up for her to our mother, but I didn't. I didn't even know why anymore. If my sister had gotten angry with me, I might have been able to forgive myself. But she'd understood, even consoled me, while I betrayed her.

If I killed enough of the same kind of monster who hurt her, then maybe I would obliterate the part of me who'd stood by and done nothing while Lily's life was ruined.

Instead I'd become a whole new kind of fiend, and I couldn't escape. All of my prior bad acts scarred my soul, driving me to do it again and again, helping to wipe the scum off the earth one sexual deviant at a time. But they were just symbols, because I finally realized the person I wanted to kill was myself. The coward, the control freak, the liar.

I'd keep going in this vicious circle until someone did it for me. Just like Chris tried to do.

I'd find a way to succeed where he failed.

Kelly would mourn me. Or visit me in prison, whichever came first. But she'd eventually understand that this was the right choice. I didn't deserve any kind of redemption. I'd done too many bad things. I should have fought harder for Lily. Everything would have been different if I'd just stood up to my mother or I'd gone to someone else, like my grandmother. She would have done the right thing.

But I stayed silent.

I didn't deserve to start fresh.

Half asleep, I attempted to sneak into the motel room in Jarrettsville, but Kelly shot up from the bed, hair sticking out, her hand already reaching under the pillow for my gun.

"It's just me." I dropped my bag by the door and then my coat. I nearly face-planted on the carpet in the battle to remove my shoes. My body begged for sleep, my eyelids weighted down like anchors.

"It's over?" she asked as I crawled in next to her.

"Chris is safe," I said. "Nothing's changed from the last time I texted. The manhunt's still on for Mary. Lennox says he's got leads on the Jeep. I told him we're going home in the morning. I'm done with all of this."

She lay back down, her slim hands folded over her chest. "What about Chris? Did he tell you what Mary was like? Or even better, what the hell he was thinking?"

"He didn't say much." I'd tell Kelly my theories on the drive home tomorrow. Right now I wasn't sure I had the brainpower to articulate them. "He's still in shock."

I felt her eyes on me, sensed the curiosity in her. I forced myself to pull back my eyelids and try to smile. "I'll tell you more tomorrow. I'm beat."

"All right. I'm just glad you're back safe." She didn't buy it. That was fine. We had plenty of time on the road.

Sleep pulled me down within minutes, as powerful as an ocean wave. I didn't dream for once, seeing nothing but pure blackness. I wasn't even sure the phone was actually ringing until Kelly's voice answered, and she started nudging me.

"There's a call for you at the front desk."

"You've got to be kidding." I took the receiver, my mouth dry as a cotton ball. If that freaking reporter was calling, she wouldn't get another free pass from me.

"This is Lucy Kendall."

"Hello, dear." A woman's voice, soft and controlled. Every nerve ending in my body fired at once. My legs jerked, my arms spasmed, my throat locked up. She could have been any relative, anyone off the street. But she was the devil incarnate, standing less than fifty feet away, at the shabby motel's front counter while the barely legal and completely clueless night shift worker tried to stay awake. "You and I have a lot of things to talk about. Why don't you meet me outside?"

I reached for my cellphone. "What about in the morning? Can we talk then?"

"That will be too late. For everyone." Her voice dropped to

a whisper. "I prefer Mr. SIG Sauer to the Glock. How about you?"

How many people would she take out before she killed herself? Surely she knew I'd call Lennox.

But he was back in Pennsylvania, believing that Mary couldn't have gotten past the state line in the Jeep. Maybe she hadn't. She could have stolen a car or taken the bus. It didn't matter. She had a gun, and I didn't have a choice.

"I'll meet you outside in five minutes."

"Make it two, dear. Beth Reid is waiting for us. She can't wait to say hello. You know how the sirens scare her."

The call ended.

I should call the local police. To hell with Beth Reid.

But this is your chance. If you can save this bitch and take Mary down, maybe that wickedness in you will die too.

"Lucy, don't." Kelly's face had gone white. She must have read my expression, caught the scent of fear and adrenaline revving in my system. "Just call the police."

"She's got that reporter. She'll kill her."

"She might be lying. It's a pretty big coincidence to have run into her."

Lennox's words from this afternoon came back to me. "No. She was snooping around Oxford today. Lennox thinks someone from here is giving her the information. Mary probably recognized her."

"She's going to kill you." Kelly's voice pitched high, her thin fingers digging into my arms.

Possibly. But I no longer feared death. I didn't know when or why that had changed, but a peace settled over me—an eerie calm that must be similar to what people experience when they know their end is imminent. "I want you to call Agent Lennox. Tell him exactly what's going on. Let him know we need help, and the locals probably aren't able to pull it off without getting Beth Reid killed."

"He's too far away," Kelly said.

"He'll know how to handle it. He'll choose the right people to call, and help will come. I just need to stall her." I put my coat back on, laced up my boots. "Give me the Glock."

THIRTY-NINE

I couldn't trust the locals. Chief Deputy Frost might be on duty, and she'd no doubt try one final time to save her career. Lennox would be able to reach Major Case and bypass her much more quickly than I could.

What a liar you are. You're doing this for you, and you only.

With the gun hidden in the pocket of my coat, I tread down the hallway on tiptoes, feeling light. Weightless. Unburdened.

As I'd suspected, the desk clerk didn't have a clue. She reclined in the chair, eyes closed and her headphones blocking out the world. She didn't even notice me as I slipped out the front door.

Instinct led the way to the same hiding spot Beth Reid used the night she accosted me about an exclusive, beneath the burnt-out security light. Mary Weston leaned against a white, four-door sedan—the same one Beth had been driving.

"You caught up with her in Oxford." I stopped about ten feet away.

Mary was shorter than me and at least fifty pounds heavier. Her black hair, streaked with gray, hung to her chin. A knit cap covered it, making her look as normal as any middle-aged woman. She watched me with glittering eyes as black as the long, wool coat she wore. Her skin seemed unperturbed by the cold, perhaps from the nerve damage. It remained paler than the snow piled around the parking lot.

"She shouldn't have been snooping for a story." Mary's voice sounded much less sweet than it had a few minutes ago and more like the cold woman I'd remembered as Justin's mother.

"Agreed."

She regarded me for a moment, and I realized something that had always bothered me: her eyes were truly black, without any color. Maybe it was nature's way of warning a person Mary had no soul. "You took both of my sons away from me."

"You sent Justin to prison. I guess that was easier than caring for him. Why did you hate him so much?"

"Because he wasn't Christopher." She spoke as if we were old friends, with no need for preamble or pleasantries.

"I had nothing to do with you losing Chris. That happened long before my time."

"I don't mean then. I mean this time. I thought he'd come back to me."

"You weren't afraid he'd call the police?"

A lunatic's smile lifted the left side of her mouth. "I know how to avoid them. My father and I watched from the woods for a long time. He didn't make any calls. He wasn't expecting anyone. He came for answers, just like he said."

Like mother, like son. "And you thought that by giving them, you could somehow bring him into the family fold? Give yourself a new killing partner?"

"I hoped," she said. "I knew my father was dying. His cold injuries got worse every year, and if something didn't kill him this year, it would have next year."

I kept our discovery of his body to myself. "I'm sorry for your loss."

"You're not."

"He was a prolific killer."

"Thank you." She took the words and held them for a moment. "Life without him might have been bearable with Christopher."

"Don't blame me for that," I said. "Agent Lennox found you."

"No one found me. I found you. And that's not what I'm talking about." Her eyes narrowed, and the left side of her face twitched with normal movement, but the right stayed immobile. Looking into that semi-frozen face while you died had to be terrifying. "But Christopher was never going to join me. Because of you."

"Is that what he said?"

"You're all he talked about." Jealousy deepened her already rough tone, making her sound like a lifelong smoker with throat problems. "How you took the righteous path, how he wanted to follow you. To be like you. That taking another life was only right if a person had a good reason." She laughed now, a deep belly roll chilling me far more than the bitter night. "A fool's lie. People kill because they like it. Because it makes them feel better about themselves. Because there's no better high than watching another human being suffer at your hands. But you know that, don't you?"

"How would I?" My body felt numb from the cold. Or maybe her words. Wind cut through the parking lot, bringing the putrid scent of a paper factory bordering the western edge of town. A car drove down the main highway—a mere two streets away, close enough the headlights cast a weak glow over us. Lennox must have bypassed the local deputies, or they'd have come in with sirens blaring by now.

"Don't play coy with me," she said. "The way Christopher

talked about you, you're some kind of patron saint of justice. And I know you killed at least one person in that garage in Philadelphia. Although my money's on you killing them both and enjoying every bit of it. No need to pretend it was self-defense with me."

Chris hadn't betrayed me. Not with enough information that could hurt me if Mary ever spoke to the police, anyway. She sensed the killer in me just like John Weston had. Which meant she also sensed my weakness.

"We're not all that different."

"No, we're not." The idea no longer ignited fear. I accepted it, just as I accepted my fate. "But you're far more skilled than I am."

She flashed me another twisted half-smile. "That's true. But practice makes perfect. Which brings me to why I'm here."

"I would love to know the answer to that," I said.

"I won't be incarcerated. I'm sure you can understand."

"Of course."

"And the only way I know how to live is to kill. It's my heritage. But I'm getting older, and going it alone is tough."

The growing pit in my stomach burst open. Bile whipped up my throat; I swallowed it down. "You could always retire."

"Killing's in my blood. If I stop, it's because I'm dead. I'm not quite ready for that. It's a last resort for me." She shook her head, real emotion in her throaty voice. "I'd hoped Christopher would be my new partner and maybe have some time with his grandfather, getting trained up."

"Which is why you tried to break his spirit," I said. "Bring him in close, emotionally isolate him. Tough to do with an adult, but he was ripe for it."

"See, you understand me," Mary said. "That's why I think we could work together. You're very good at what you do. You just haven't accepted your true self yet. I can help you with that."

"Thank you, but I'll have to decline. I'm retiring after tonight."

She laughed again, that hideous expression searing its way into my brain. "You'll never be able to stop. You might go a year, maybe even five or ten. But the need will crop up again. But don't kid yourself. It's not about justice. It's about taking a life to give yourself one."

And there it was. "You're wrong."

"Stop lying to yourself, girl. That's the real travesty here. Who cares if you killed men who like babies? Who cares if you've killed anyone as long as you wanted to do it? Don't be a wimp and label it to make yourself feel better. Accept who you are, and show it to the world."

Fear rocketed through me, not at her words but because they made such pure sense. Because a part of me wanted to take her advice and forget everything else. I bit my tongue until I tasted blood and then took a long breath of the cold air until my throat burned. "Thanks for the advice. I'll keep it in mind."

"The reporter wronged you," she said. "First she brings your name into the public eye, and then she tries to use it to worm her way out of trouble with me."

"Did she?" I kept my voice level, my body relaxed. My right hand still ghosted over the gun, but it no longer clutched the Glock.

"She said you'd promised her an exclusive after I was captured. That the FBI had granted you the opportunity to interview me since you'd managed to get John to tell you about my father."

"And you believed that?"

"Of course not." She snorted, the sound cutting through the silent night. "But it is interesting, don't you think? Clearly, Agent Lennox has a leak. Because John didn't know my father had served in Korea or about his cold injuries. Yet this woman does."

My money was on Chief Deputy Frost for the leak. "I'll pass the information on to Agent Lennox."

"Beth Reid told me where you were staying, of course."

"I assumed as much."

"She's in the trunk. We can drive away from here and have some fun. Did you knife the girl in the garage?"

Yes, even as she begged me for mercy. "Her boyfriend did it."

"And you hit him with the shovel," she said. "That's what the newspapers claimed."

"I was trying to save myself."

"And you succeeded," she said. "But you'll slip up one day. Maybe you'll be tired, or sick, or going without sleep. Either way, you'll screw up. That's when having a partner comes in handy. They can pick up the slack."

"Is that why your father trained you to kill with him?"

She shrugged. "I was only six years old the first time he dragged a girl into the sleeper. He raped her and then cut her. I thought it was normal. He eventually explained that society didn't agree, and we had to keep our secret."

"And now he's dead." My time had to be running short. At least thirty minutes had passed since I left the motel. Harford was a small county—whoever Lennox was mobilizing had to show up soon. "The only person you've ever bonded with is rotting in a trunk on his farm. Or he was. He's probably locked in an autopsy room right now."

Pure hate rippled over the half of her face that still worked. "He wouldn't want that."

"I don't think anyone cares what he wanted. I even over-heard Lennox talking about donating his brain to science as part of the study of serial killers. He doesn't think your aunt will have any trouble signing the release."

"Stop talking about him like that." Spittle bubbled at the corners of her mouth. "My father was a great talent. He could do things no one else even thought about. Much less had the balls to do. He didn't care how loud a girl screamed. He kept hurting them. He never stopped until he was fully satiated."

"Until his cold injuries caught up to him," I said. "Is that how you got hurt? Did he make a mistake?"

"What do you mean?" Her confidence wavered for the first time, her eyes settling on me with chilling calm.

"The nerve damage to your face and arm. I don't think it was from a car accident. I think a victim fought back and dear old dad screwed up. You paid the price."

She glared at me, the good side of her face twitching. "I told you, having a partner is a good thing."

"I suppose it's good the two of you made up," I said. "Because I don't think you would have been caught otherwise. He's your weakness."

"Caught?" she said. "You consider this caught?"

"It's going to happen," I said. "Agent Lennox has been notified. Even if you take off with that woman still in the trunk, he'll figure out a way to find you."

"No, he won't."

I glanced east. Sunrise would come soon. Already a thin stream of light pink skimmed the horizon. "Thank you for the offer, but I'll have to decline."

She wavered, clearly thrown by my lack of fear. But her need for control and complete submission drove her to recover quickly, as I'd known it would. "You don't have a choice. You took my son from me. If you won't join me as a partner and help me to continue my father's legacy, then you'll die."

"Go ahead and shoot, then." I no longer feared the veil or what waited for me at the bottom of the pit. Again, I felt peace. And a smattering of arrogance, because I'd managed to do what Chris couldn't: his mother would kill me, ending my suffering. No more looking over my shoulder, waiting to get caught. No more sleepless nights convincing myself I was doing the right thing. No more angst.

"You think I'm bluffing," Mary said. "Or that someone's coming to save you. But this is all very real, and this is your last chance. Get in this car, or die."

I shook my head. "I know you're serious. But you made the mistake of thinking I valued my own life."

"I'm not going to shoot you," Mary said. "You'll get in the car. I'll drug you. I'll tie you up. I'll take you with me and do all those terrible things you've read about. You'll die of infection. Suffering more than you can possibly imagine."

"The spoons," I said. "The sepsis was intentional."

She smiled. "You understand me."

"I guess I do." Disappointment washed out the brief flash of hope. Death I could handle. The torture would force me to kill Mary, and we'd end up right back here. But killing her meant Lennox would lose his chance at answers, and I wanted to give him his chance at closure. I supposed I could stall her a little longer. Once I got in the car, I would be relying on my own strength and quickness. If she drugged me, I could be in trouble. My hand closed around the Glock again.

"But not well enough." She pulled her own gun out of her pocket with her left hand. She held it awkwardly, her fingers fumbling for the right position. "Because if you did, you'd know I do my research. Even if I have to hurt someone to get the information."

I waited.

"I know about Kelly. Our little reporter did all the legwork for me. I bet that child's got some demons I can have fun with. And you won't be here to save her."

My teeth pierced my bottom lip; I tasted blood. My fingers held the Glock so tightly my knuckles cracked. The air in my lungs tasted stale, as if I'd breathed in something acidic and contagious. How dare she threaten Kelly?

Kelly, who still believed in me and trusted me to keep her

safe. The only person in this life I completely trusted. My family.

"I'm sorry to hear that." Shadows moved around the dumpster sitting in the parking lot behind her.

I pulled the Glock out of my pocket and fired.

FORTY

The shot pierced her left shoulder, just as I'd intended. She staggered back, dropping the gun. It fell with a thud and slid a few inches away on the ice. She tried to move for it, but I was quicker. I slammed the butt of my pistol into her head. Mary fell to her knees, screaming. I snatched her gun and pointed it at her temple.

"You could have won," I said. "But you threatened the one person I'm willing to keep fighting for."

"Just kill me." She rolled to her right side, trying in vain to reach her bleeding shoulder. "I won't make it in prison."

At the sound of my shot, the shadows behind the dumpster turned into solid masses barreling toward me. "Harford County SERT," a man screamed at me. "Put the weapons down."

I held up my hands, backing out of Mary's reach, and laid both guns on the pavement. The SERT surrounded us, weapons still raised.

"I'm Lucy Kendall," I said, keeping my hands raised. "Mary Weston called me in my motel room. She claimed to have a woman in the back of her car. I had my friend call Agent

Lennox, and I came out to stall Mary. She was going to shoot me."

One of the SERT members knelt over Mary, applying pressure to the wound. "It looks like she mostly hit flesh."

"I just wanted her to drop the gun."

The SERT officer in charge retrieved the guns. "Our orders are to take you back to our command vehicle to wait for Agent Lennox. He's en route."

"As long as there's heat, I'm good."

Lennox arrived forty-five minutes later, long after I'd called Kelly to tell her it was over and Mary had been taken to the hospital. He stalked out of his SUV, his coat trailing behind him. He yanked open the door to the SERT's truck and glared at me.

"You shot her."

"I had to," I said. "She was going to shoot me and then take me with her. How's Beth Reid?"

"Shaken the hell up," Lennox said. "She told the responding officer Mary caught up with her outside of town, where she had pulled over and was making notes. She'd just been told by her source in Jarrettsville that we'd got a lead in Oxford."

"Chief Deputy Frost."

"She won't say," Lennox said. "I'll get it out of her, though. Why'd Mary come after you?"

"She blamed me for taking Chris away from her," I said. "She thought he could be trained as a new partner, but apparently I instilled too much hope in him." That version would suffice. Mary would never talk to the police, and if she did, she didn't have enough on me to cause many waves. "I'm sorry."

He cocked his head. "For shooting her? It's all right. She's alive, and we got her, thanks to you."

"For your missing the look on her face when she went down." I smiled at the memory of her eyes widening in shock, the perfect "o" of her mouth, and the way her body rocked backward at the impact. "It was priceless."

He groaned. "I suppose you earned it. You think she'll tell me much?"

"I don't know. She did say her dad raped and murdered a girl in his truck's sleeper when she was just six. She thought it was normal. He's her hero. Her weak spot."

"Good to know." He glanced over his shoulder at his SUV. "You know what's interesting?"

Exhaustion threatened to take over. I blinked and focused on Lennox. "What?"

"You shot Mary in the left arm because she held the gun with it."

"Right."

He studied his manicured nails. "The medical examiner believes Lionel Kent was shot by someone right-handed. From the looks of it, that's not Mary's better hand."

Anxiety fluttered through me, but I couldn't quite make the connection. "Her father must have been right-handed."

"I don't know about that," Lennox said. "But he must have had a rush of energy."

Now everything snapped together, his unspoken accusation making my stomach sour. "It happens." Honestly, I didn't want to know the truth. In the last hours, something had shifted within me, as if my internal wick that burned for justice had been extinguished.

"You want to go with me to interview her?" Lennox let the subject drop.

"Thanks, but no. I want to get some rest and then get back to Philadelphia. And I think my days as a private investigator are over."

Lennox raised his eyebrow. "The National Center for Missing and Exploited Children?"

I started to ask how he knew, but then I realized. "Todd told you. I'm thinking about it. I'm not sure yet. But I need to do something different."

"If you decide to pursue it, let me know. I'll put in a good word."

I didn't know what to say, so I nodded. "I'll let you know."

He held out his hand. "Thanks for your help."

I shook it, feeling completely out of place. "Thanks for trusting me tonight."

"I didn't have much choice." He grinned. "I was afraid she'd end up dead."

"But you never worried about me?"

Lennox laughed, squinting against the rising sun. "Girl, I was never worried about your safety. The only person who can take you down is you. And that's something you'll have to decide for yourself." He squeezed my shoulder. "I'll see you around. Or maybe not. As long as no more Preachers turn up, I think you'll be just fine."

I watched him drive away, sitting motionless. He'd basically given me a free pass to start over. I wasn't going to get another one. Somehow, I needed to find the strength to take it.

FORTY-ONE

TWO WEEKS LATER

"You're leaving." Chris stared at me from the comfortable confines of his couch. His shoulder was still bandaged, his skin still yellowed with bruises. He'd been home from the hospital for a week, and I hadn't been able to muster the courage to go see him.

"The National Center for Missing and Exploited Children offered me a position as a case analyst," I said. "I'll be working with law enforcement to provide them the information they need to track down child sex offenders."

He looked at me with haunted eyes. "In D.C."

"That's right."

Agent Lennox had come through with his recommendation. I'd taken the offer without any preamble because I'd promised Kelly I would. For now, her faith in me would have to be enough to push me forward.

"What about us?" Chris said.

I tried to make my smile gentle. "There is no us. We're friends, I guess. Despite the way you went about it, I think I understand. But I need some space. And I need to start fresh."

"You think that's possible?" His dark laugh erupted from the pit of his belly. "That you can just forget who you are?"

"I don't know. But I have to try. And so should you."

Mary wasn't talking, as we'd expected. She'd gone into a fury when Lennox brought up her father, rambling on about what a great man he was. But she never broke. So far, Lennox hadn't gotten the information he needed for the families. But he wasn't giving up.

"I don't know how to do that," Chris said.

"No one really does. I think you just have to put one foot in front of the other and take it day by day." I moved for the door, but he pushed himself off the couch, his hand closing around my arm.

"What did you mean by space?"

This was the part I'd dreaded. I felt like a jerk, but I also knew I'd fulfilled my end of the bargain. I'd done right by Chris. "I mean I won't be seeing you for a while. I need to put your mother and everything that happened between you and me in the past, and I can't do that if we're still communicating." His expression sagged into heartbreak. "I'll check in with you from time to time, see how you're doing. I hope you keep up with the counseling with your aunt and uncle. That's your best hope."

"But you understand me," he said throatily. A chill ran through me. His mother had said the very same thing. "I need you."

I pulled away. "You need to understand yourself first. Both of us do. And we have to do that separately." I reached the door, surprised by how much I just wanted to get away from him and everything he represented. "Take care of yourself."

The left side of his mouth twisted up into a sad smile. "You too. I hope that one day you can accept who you are and be proud of it. Wouldn't it be better if you could just show it to the world?"

I shivered, the memory of Mary's voice staining my thoughts. "Thanks. I'll let you know when I'm settled in D.C."

"Please do." I left then, needing to get away from the suffocating sadness rolling off Chris. I'd like to say I felt lighter as I left his building, as if the act represented cutting the ties to my old life. But I wasn't that naïve. Those ties would always drag behind me. Every day would be a struggle to leave them alone. But I'd promised Kelly—and myself—that I would try.

My hand drifted to my coat pocket, where I'd stuffed the package that had arrived just before I left for Chris's. Surely it was some sort of joke, a needle from Beth Reid, who could have heard about the spoons from Deputy Frost.

The wind lapped at my face, but the bitterness of winter had eased over the last week. Spring circled the city, changing the very density of the air and lifting everyone's mood. I couldn't enjoy the sweetness right now. My mind was too focused on the small set of silver measuring spoons that had been delivered to my apartment this morning.

They were sterling silver, heavy and gleaming, with a delicate scroll pattern in each spoon. A crimson ribbon held them together.

A lousy joke on the reporter's part. Mary used wooden spoons. And these were just lovely, too small to be any sort of weapon.

That didn't stop the dagger of anxiety in my side. The spoons were probably antiques. They might be evidence. I should call Todd or even Lennox. But that meant I'd be sucked back into my old story, and all I wanted to do was move forward.

A flash of color caught my eye. Blooming purple monkshood preened in the window of the corner flower shop. Too bad they were poisonous to cats. My place needed brightening up in the worst way. Orchids, maybe. Mousecop would be safe with those.

I turned the package over in my hands and thought about new starts and old wounds. About how sometimes we can't possibly know the darkness inside of people, no matter how much we care about them or how much we think we know. How the chains of the past weigh down the future, if we let them.

I took a deep breath, tossing the silver spoons in the trash-can, and entered the flower shop.

A LETTER FROM STACY

Dear reader,

Thank you so much for reading *The Girl in the Cabin*! I had a lot of fun researching and writing the entire Lucy Kendall series despite the dark overtones. If you read and enjoyed the book and want to get updates on the next release in the series, just sign up at the following link. Your email address will never be shared, and you can unsubscribe at any time.

www.bookouture.com/stacy-green

As always, the best part of writing is the reaction from readers. If you loved Lucy and Chris as much as I do, I would love it if you could leave a short review. Getting feedback from readers is amazing and helps encourage new readers to try my books for the very first time.

Thank you so much for reading,

Stacy Green

KEEP IN TOUCH WITH STACY

www.stacygreenauthor.com

facebook.com/StacyGreenAuthor

twitter.com/StacyGreen26

instagram.com/authorstacygreen

Made in the USA
Las Vegas, NV
15 February 2025

18178479R00173